A Noise from the Woodshed
short stories

by Mary Dorcey

Published in 1989 by ONLYWOMEN PRESS, Ltd.,
Radical Feminist and Lesbian publishers
38 Mount Pleasant, London WC1X 0AP.

'A Country Dance' was first published in *Girls Next Door: lesbian feminist stories*, edited by Jen Bradshaw and Mary Hemming, The Women's Press, London, 1985. 'Sweet, Practised Endings' was first published in *The Pied Piper: lesbian feminist fiction*, edited by Anna Livia and Lilian Mohin, Onlywomen Press, 1989. 'The Husband' will be published in *Wildish Things: An Anthology of New Irish Women's Writing*, edited by Ailbhe Smyth, Attic Press, Dublin, 1989.

Cover illustration Sarah Ball.

Printed and bound in Denmark by Nørhaven.
Typeset by Columns, Reading, Berkshire, UK.

British Library Cataloguing in Publication Data
Dorcey, Mary, 1950–
  A noise from the woodshed.
  I. Title
  823'.914 [F]

ISBN 0-906500-30-2

Mary Dorcey was born and brought up in County Dublin, Ireland. She has lived in England, France, the U.S.A., and Japan. Her first collection of poetry, *Kindling*, was published in 1982 by Onlywomen Press. Since then her stories and poems have appeared in numerous journals and anthologies in Britain, the U.S.A., and Ireland, including: *New Angles* (Oxford University Press), *Bread and Roses* (Virago), *In The Pink* (The Women's Press), *Beautiful Barbarians* (Onlywomen Press), *Ain't I a Woman* (Virago), *Naming The Waves* (Virago), *Mad and Bad Faeries* (Attic Press), *Feminism in Ireland* (Pergamon Press) and *Girl's Next Door* (The Women's Press). She is one of the writers interviewed in *Into the Mainstream: How feminism has changed women's writing* (Pandora).

Mary currently divides her time between Dublin and the West coast and has recently completed a new collection of poetry.

For Carole

My thanks to Gray who gave me an electric typewriter; and to Dorothy who lent me her house.

CONTENTS

A Noise from the Woodshed   1

A Sense of Humour   23

A Country Dance   44

The Husband   64

Miss Callaghan's Day Out   81

Flowers for Easter   107

Introducing Nessa   130

Sweet, Practised Endings   160

Nights Underground   181

A Noise from the Woodshed

You were walking along through the river – that is to say along the path that was flooded – a wild orange torrent of water, cascading. You had forgotten once again to wear galoshes – who in god's name ever remembers to wear galoshes these days? Certainly not women of your advanced thought and sophistication, not to say outlandish ways and habits. So there you were – are, but this is fiction and must remain consigned to the regions of certainty – stumbling on the stepping stones, submerged and slithering, up to your knees in trouble and water with cold feet again, when she came along. Like a warrior in white armour, did she come, gallant and fearless though double-breasted, come like an answer to prayer; a maiden's prayer – yours – though no maiden, and sweeping down from her white charger sweep you up and bear you across the river to sanctuary? Or did she come like a woman; unheralded, unassuming, a woman struggling to keep a footing, to make a living, to make a loving?

Yes, that was it, she came like a woman, with a woman's courage into your life, into the torrent and helped; with all the simple things – all the small everyday, do all over again things – like making the breakfast, doing the shopping, scrubbing the bath, remembering to turn on the blanket, washing up when

1

you're too tired, and never being too tired; loving to love or be loved in any order and who's counting?; listening, oh yes, hours, weeks, years of listening and talking, knowing when to stop and give you a kick in the ass more literal than metaphorical; being the one you can ask if you look alright before going out to face them, being the one who asks you if she looks alright – and no need to ask – yes gorgeous, facing or not, in or out – being the one you can be all these things with, this or that, you now, she later, in any order and who's counting? Women do these things countless times, so fast and so often any one would lose count. It was men who started the whole business of counting: numbers and keeping a ledger. And how was it for you? Can you for one second imagine one woman asking another and how was it for you? Where has he been for the last three hours?

Anyway, she came along like a woman when you were standing there up to your neck in life and because she was wearing wellingtons (though she had never so much as heard of Baden Powell, much less his motto), and had kept her legs dry she said, climb up, I'll give you a picky-back. And you did, and she did, and she ferried you over the rushing brackish water, keeping her footing on the shifting sands, and high up on her back you kept your head and well above water, and when you·gained the bank she set you down the way a woman does, not waiting for thanks, not noticing that she's done you a favour and that just for the moment she was better prepared than you. And all the way across the smell of her hair was in your nose – the earth warm, straw warm, jasmine sweet scent of her hair – and the curls of it tickling your cheek, and you were laughing like you were your own child being carried, and whipping her flanks as you used to when these rides were a regular occurrence, but you were promising yourself, feeling the lovely muscles of her flanks between your thighs, that the moment she set you down you were going to get very serious. And two grown women getting serious, looking into each other's eyes seriously; seeing one another entire, absolute and not as some stop-gap,

2

mediator, sympathiser, counsellor in the doings of men, that look; that long, tasting, touching look is one of the most serious and the best things going. And who can keep it going without laughing? And that's another of the best things – that laughing that women are always doing: not the belly laugh, the guffaw, the snicker, the cracking a joke – no, this laughter in the joy of harmony, of doing something well together, at the same time, at the absurdity of managing the physical world, (women being left mostly in charge of it), such as folding a sheet, or holding the ladder while the other climbs up, digging a bed for an apple tree, pulling socks onto a small child's feet that will not stop wriggling, covered in sand and itchy between the toes, composing a concerto before tea, dictating a letter to the press, rehearsing their maiden (that word again) speech, pushing the shopping trolley in the super-market, playing bingo – that laughter you hear everywhere between women friends, sisters, mothers, daughters, lovers, doing some simple thing together – going with the thing instead of trying to get the better of it, and laughing at the absurdity of its going its own way. Well you promised yourself that when you got to the other side of the water, you would get very serious.

You were back in the house five days before either of you noticed the noise from the woodshed. The rain had been coming down like cats and dogs, and the dogs and cats had been coming down like rain, pit-patting, pat-pitting all over the house with wet ears and cold noses into rooms and out again; the gutters were leaking, emptying their cargo of drenched summer leaves, splashing onto the clothes blowing on the line: skirts and frocks and jeans and shirts and socks and hats that must have belonged to more than one person, you thought, and did. We should take the clothes in, she said. Yes, you said, biting her thigh, and the books were lying all around unread on the shelves, and the hens were squawking unfed in the yard, and the beaches, tossed by the sea, uncleaned, and the potatoes sprouting sprouts, unplanted, chaos ripening all about you, lost in wonder. It was small wonder you had not noticed the noise from the woodshed. Listen, she said, that noise! And you raised yourself for the first time in days, and listened. Was it a bird or a cat or the wind singing in the willows; willows weeping in a grove of tears below your feet?

But wait – what is this? Where have you taken us now? You are losing the run of the thing entirely, racing on regardless without description or report. You were last heard of crossing the river, ferried on the broad plane of her back, her flanks warm between your thighs, and promising yourself that the moment you reached the bank you would get serious. And you did, oh you did. You got as serious as two women can get without laughing. And you were not laughing then as you fell to your knees in the wild bright poppies, fell to your backs, to your shoulders, to your breasts, to your face, fell to your senses in the long green growing grass, her wellingtons still wet and muddy from the river and no time to remove them, and who cares, they were not in the way entirely, or not to begin with, attention being concentrated right then not on feet but on hands and mouths (but when you at last discovered her feet, you were glad of boots that had kept this last delight to last, and your feet naked and loved from the first, toe by toe). And there you were, fully serious, lying low on the low lying bank of the river, the orange water thrashing in its bed, its stones upturned, its ripples foaming. And isn't this just what you would expect from two women messing about in the country unchaperoned, unbridled by labour or conscience, fording streams, scaling mountains, running sylph-like through woods and green pastures, women of a certain persuasion with nothing better to do? And there was nothing better to do all the live-long day, lived long and hot and cool in the breeze of the river, in the length of the grasses, from the first stepping out of the gushing water to the very last – and what was last? – laughter or crying, hollering, rolling about in sun and wild poppies, half drowning in mouth to mouth resuscitation?

And when you stood up, you dressed for the world, following historical precedent in this much; you drew

4

on your assemblage of garments: shirts and skirt, jeans
and blouse, belts and socks, bracelets and rings and
one pair of wellingtons. And she said, why don't you
come home, for she had one and you being temporarily between homes, wandering vagrant and curious,
and seeing the shell that you carried like a world on
your back; seeing how well it would fit with hers, she
being temporarily fully equipped with the trappings of
fittings and fixtures called home. Why don't you come
back for something to eat, she said, and speaking of
something to eat, she kissed your bruised, bitten neck,
and the midges circled waiting their turn, and she said
at your nape, why don't you come back. Home then
you went and no need to ask, for as long as you
needed it, or each other, as it always was, and you
needed each other so long and so fast that you halted
your journey three or four times, falling down to the
earth that lay all around to receive you, birds startled
from their nests to air, frogs croaking, dogs howling
until, finally tired and exalted, you reached the house
in the forest with the red tiled roof, the wide
windows, the painted chairs, the open hearth. And
then it was hunger, sudden, imperious and into the
kitchen to sate it. And you made everything you could
imagine and ate everything you made, she making one
course and you the next, luckily liking exactly the
same things to put in your mouths, and the same
things to do to them first as you had earlier on the
bank of the river. And then the western sun was
coming through the window, pink and amber and
there was the washing up to be washed up you said,
but first, she said, let me show you the loft. And the
loft was Cleo's loft because she had started it, thinking
she needed more space; a space of her own after some
time and then, after more time, on the very morning,
in fact, they were to begin work on the roof, she
thought she needed more space still, and the next day
she set off for Africa, or India, or Australia to find it,
the slates still stacked in the yard and no knowing
when she might be back to get on with it, being a
claustrophobic, Cleo, as well as dark skinned and
beautiful, though it had taken Africa and Australia for

5

her to know it – her claustrophobia that is – and now she was wandering the peace camps of Europe searching for peace. And having suffered in the same way yourself – claustrophobia that is – and known others similarly affected, you asked no further, but said what a fine loft it was; and it was four walls, timber floor and high arching rafters growing out from the side of the house like a tree, more of a tree house than a loft, with the birds coming in and the sky coming in and the sighing of boughs. Weeping willows, she said, weeping their unruly tears in a grove below your feet. And you said, look out there, looking out where a window might have been if there had been a window. What's that? There, where the chimneys rise smoking and the television aerials wave and the walls stretch long and concrete and she said oh, that; that's one of the power stations for the nuclear family, and the streaks of coloured cloth, she said, were the tents of the women who had set up camp in a circle around it, making a peace camp with their bodies and lives, it being as good a place as any to make a peace camp and no need to go to England or Australia. And she told you some of the other things that were going on: unearthing imperialism, saving the whale and the beaches, reclaiming the fields and the night, cleaning the rivers and disturbing the minds, redistributing the capital, housing the homeless, whispering the forbidden addresses for women in distress, making refuges for the refugees: victims of the happy homes. There was as much to do here as anywhere, and as many to do it, and you could do it too, and why not – help with the writing and washing the clothes, painting the canvasses and milking the Nubian goats, feeding the hens and finishing the unfinished symphony, not to mention the loft, raising vegetables and hell, living off the fat of the land and each other's. And you saw then, and why not before? a brass bed in the corner, under the eaves – if there had been eaves; a wide and welcoming bed with white linen sheets turned back as a mother might have turned them back – and a woven yellow blanket: corn yellow, butter yellow, covering it. And there, where

6

the roof was just started, on the morning that Cleo left, was a very good place to lie down, she said, with the stars coming in through the rafters and the rain raining somewhere else for a change. And what about the washing up, you asked, looking at the debris on the painted tables and the washing up can wait to be washed up, she said, and it did, that evening, and it waited and waited and, even the next morning, it waited until it was almost evening again and hardly worth starting it then, and anyway you had still three clean glasses to go and a bottle of Chateauneuf du Pape by the bed – even popes having their uses. And everything waited: the phone to be answered, the books to be opened, the letters to be written, the whales to be saved, the plants to be planted, and the cats wailing in the shrubbery, and the sky coming in through the rafters, and the butterflies coming in, and the moon coming in, and even a bat coming in, and the scent of nightscented stock scenting the air.

But this cannot be normal surely? This impromptu lying about in strange places, this loss of purpose and perpendicular, this reckless wastage of time and crockery, this surrender of sense to the senses, this wallowing in all flat surfaces: carpets and floorboards and baths and riverbanks and beds of pine needles – oh yes, even up there in the woods – nowhere spared; the groaning of boughs over your flesh – no it cannot be all like this, surely?

Well it isn't at all, all like this, you might tell them, if you could put yourself in the mood long enough to tell them. There is so much else going on and failing to go on. There is work and the lack of it, money and the getting of it, love and the losing of it. There is all this death and dying, this destruction and hunger and torment. There are so many sick and sorrowful, misused and abandoned: their screams in your eyes and ears. There are hospitals, prisons and waiting rooms – waiting for the sick and sorrowful, the misled and forgotten. There are soldiers and surgeons and scientists waiting to cure to death, waiting to kill for peace. There are men on the street just waiting for someone like you and men at home with the doors

7

locked who have found you already. There are nuclear weapons, ideological weapons and conventional weapons, fire, flood, and famine, waiting to keep the right people safe from the wrong people. There are beatings and rapings, torture and lies. Oh what lies – the lies of the family happy and loving, the lies of the father kind and forgiving, lies about mothers, the good and the wicked, lies about children lawful and not, there are lies about needing a gun and lies about needing a man – the one thing they have in common is needing one to protect you from the rest of them – there are lies about strong governments and caring states, lies about instinct, nature and choice, lies about progress getting on, a better deal, lies about self-defence, humane killing and the national good. There are lies about law and its orders, judges and judged, decency, civilisation and standards. There are lies about what everyone is prepared to do if anyone takes away from him the things that keep him doing the things that he's accustomed to doing. There are lies about true religions, original sin and the saving of souls. There are lies about why we are here, and where we are going, and about who will be there to greet us, and that lie holds together all the other lies, for it is a wise and forgiving father who will be there on arrival day, and we have all known protective loving fathers, and no one who has heard is not shaken with the fear of it. Father forgive you for you know not what you do – father – who art – which art (depending on brand identification) in heaven making our hell.

There is all this going on around and inside us. We all have mothers and sisters and daughters, sick and dying, lonely and grieving. We are all mothers and daughters, sisters and friends and there is no closing the eyes to it, no parachute drop, no emergency exit. And sometimes it's all too much, the struggle uphill and far beyond sight, so many dropping by the wayside, hopeless, wasted. There are the ones who won't help, the ones who can't help and the ones who got too tired trying. There are the ones who have seen it all and can't be bothered. There is always the turning on each other like kittens in a weighted sack on the way to the river. Expecting more from each other than from anyone else and giving less. There is all that blood and betrayal, that collaboration and silence. The fear in the marrow bone born and bred.

So that day, when she came along, it was almost too late for you. When she swept you up in the nick of time, and carried you over the waters, and laid you down in long grasses, and committed love with you, and staggered home drunken and laughing, shouting for joy and just for the sake of it, and did not stagger out again for days, being so busy, preoccupied with bodily surfaces and passages, and all that talking to be gone through – that day was no commonplace day – rest assured. If it were, even you out there in the wilderness would have heard by now. That day was one of the special days, of triumph and discovery, of breaking through, opening the door from the given into the dreamed of: the possible world in the making, and you made it in the making, the making of anger and questions and loving, and laughter up there loftily in the loft, swaying in arms and trees, babes in arms, love a bye baby, the cradle will fall, and down will come tyranny, silence and all. That was out of the ordinary, the building of days to follow that have been envisioned and half remembered. She came along just in time, weary and world steeped as you were; too tired to go on almost, never mind forward or outward, not to mention help with the hens, finish the symphony, save the beach and the whale, redistribute the profits, build refuges for the victims of the basic unit of society battered in their happy homes. You were battered yourself, more metaphorical than literal, but no less painful for that. She had come like a woman, a saviour in a white hatchback and saved you from doubt, tired eyes and wet feet, set fire to your loins and carried you off, coming as you had for so many in the past, come as so many have come for you and each other; women wandering highways and byways, saving the whales and the clinics, coming upon each other and lending a helping hand, or foot or breast or mouth or whatever seems most useful at the time, snatching each other from boredom and flood in

9

mountains and lakes and housing estates, from lies and inertia, from getting on and keeping up, from bearing up and saving face.

And lying up there in the loft preoccupied with skin and bone and the in-between, you eventually got round to talking about all this, your tongues at last free to talk, the willows winding below, the sky flying in through the rafters, the goats bleating at the gate, you thought of all the others like this: the days and the women having them – these days plucked from the jaws of Fairy Liquid, bouncing babies and germ free drains; more and more women having them – these days of langour and insurrection, armed to the teeth and undressed to kill, riding about backstreets and country lanes rescuing each other from race, class and creed. And not only in mountains and lakesides, oh no she said, long before pastoral bliss, it was breaking out in the cities, spreading through offices, factories and shops, bus queues and bank queues and dole queues, elevators and escalators, health centres, drug centres, back streets and boulevards (would you pass me the bread and the garlic butter, I'm hungry again, you said), washeterias and coffee houses, court houses and parliament houses, boathouses and halfway houses, houses of ill repute and public houses (oh yes certainly public houses, she said, swilling her vintage wine), public houses and women's houses out by the river, down by the docks, damp ceilings, paraffin heaters and half-lit, rickety stairs that women scaled night after night to talk about their women's problems, sitting in a ring about their women's bodies and their departures from the norm: the suffering, treacherous, uncertain organs you were raised to abhor. But all this talk of problems and organs and their departing from the norm, in sterility, fertility, thrush and vaginismus, of tumours benign and malign, pap smears and press smears, speculums and speculation, breast exams, pre-natal and post natal exams, of tensions real and imagined; pre-menstrual and post menstrual, of menarche and its inevitable menopause, of estrogen rising and progesterone falling, of flushes and hot flashes, of pills and despair, of having the right attitude or the

10

wrong, (oh mother in heaven yes, you said) of appendectomy, tonsilectomy, mastectomy, hysterectomy and even lobotomy, of getting hysterical or keeping cool – all this talk of physical freight and lumber, of hereditary, environmental or just plain mental, all this talk made some women wonder must there not be more to it than this, and there was, and no wonder, when they got down to it, instead of putting up with it, and looking down and going down and getting into it, they got it going (ah yes, I remember it well, she said), and once gotten going this getting it together was hard to stop, this departing from the norm and who's trying, because it was fun and fine and feeling good, and it brought on days, weeks of self-indulgence and knowing pleasure, wallowing in blissful know-how, revelling in abandon, shared secrets and shames and delight and work and wanting and terror and protest and cooking and cleaning and getting the children to bed, and starting all over again and phoning a friend and saying so it isn't just me, it's the same for you and why did nobody tell us before?

Before, yes, hasn't all this happened before, one of you asks, hasn't it always been this way, women getting on with it, working together, cooking, cleaning, talking, listening and putting the babies to bed, doing these things all over the place expected and unnoticed? Oh yes, one of you says, it's all been going on before, going on for millennia before, except that it wasn't going on for themselves. No it certainly, most definitely, wasn't. It was all self-sacrifice and the good of the race. Women racing each other for the sake of the race, the species especially needing a woman's hand and the hands rocking the cradles and not cradling the rocks. Yes it was all going on, creation and labour and no rest on the seventh day. And being interrupted when they got it going well, and being abused when they came up with something better. It was women doing it all and getting no credit, women not allowed near it and still getting the blame, women doing it all, and then all over again, but having no power to halt or to change it. It was all effort and toil,

11

silence and service and singing the children to sleep and no wallowing and no abandon.

Whereas now, she said. Whereas now, you said, you can scarcely trust a woman to fetch water from the well or drive the children to extra-curricular activities, without having her run into one of these vagrant warrior types with two breasts and a white hatchback just looking for someone to rescue and lose themselves all over again. These women wandering about, unbridled, unbroken, footloose, tongue loose, hand and fancy free as birds or fish or some undiscovered species. The thing is catching, infectious, and fever hospitals overcrowded already. It would be frightening if it weren't funny. Indeed it would, she said, and you quietly uncorked the last bottle of Chateauneuf du Pape.

So it was one of those days, it might have been the third or the fourth or some other day entirely but one of those days anyway. You were up on a ladder fixing a leaking gutter, and she was at the bottom holding the middle rung to keep it steady, and passing you up hammers and nails and putty and saws and books and photographs and anything else you might need, and she was explaining to you her problems as a painter – an artistic painter, let it be known, and you were listening, and saying, every now and again, such useful, empathetic things about wall painting and ceiling painting and floor painting and things undreamed of by Michelangelo and in between times, as she handed up the hammer and the putty and the photographs of the one before and the one before her, of her aunt and her sister and one of her brothers – the better one – she was telling you about her mother, about the problem she was making for herself, by leaving her unphoned for as long as it was taking to tell you about the problem, and what with going up and down rungs for inspiration and consolation, and slices of Bavarian cheesecake – her sister's recipe, for bites and embraces, it was surprising how much of the gutter got fixed. And then the cat came along, or two or three: an uncle, a grandniece and a half sister, and they walked along the roof, two paws on the slates, the other two in the gutter, which is the only way a cat knows to walk along a sloping roof, unless at the very crest of it which, on this occasion what with hammer and nails and ladders and photographs, was far beyond reach. Get down, Uncle Ivor, she said, or Bluebell or Poppy or whoever it was, and it might have been any one of a number too awful to contemplate (so you didn't) not to mention the damn dog. It's as well we're not painting it, she said, and it was, because on other occasions when she had been, one or other, two or four (cats) not to mention the damn dog – and you didn't – had ambled along and done their cat thing and the paw trail led over and in, up stairs and down to your lady's chamber in blotches of scarlet and mediterranean blue. And when the goats devoured the ivy and the hens laid eggs in the chimney, you laughed and went on working, and the phone rang unanswered and the letters lay unposted and you forgot them and old quarrels – for already you had had them – old quarrels when she behaved like her father, whose behaviour she hated, or you behaved like your mother, a thing you feared was slowly creeping up on you infecting small gestures and phrases. Not that your mother's hereditary taint was the worst taint you could imagine. Oh no very much indeed, no. After all, you might have resembled your brother, the wrong brother. Or you rehashed or revived older quarrels of other lovers and times, who had left their stain like cat paws in the wet paint of an earlier heart.

Indeed it was as well you were only fixing the gutters, because on other days, lovers and mothers aside, when you were making the dinner, or adding a bit to the symphony, saving the whale, or lazy beds dug for potatoes (and no beds have ever been lazier, what with the sun shining that way on the bare skin of her back, and the spade being heavier in your hands than any spade before it, and the wood warm and piercing your hands with little splinters of desire – oh desire among the lazy beds getting lazier) and potatoes you know, contrary to common opinion, being the most fragile of vegetables, easily bruised or spoilt, and she said, yes you've told me before, very often before, and you had, of course, because a good potato is hard to find, even in a country where thousands died for the want of them, and you feel for potatoes and cherish their delicacy: flowery and open and butter melting thick and yellow in their whiteness. And you were putting in these potatoes, hanging out the sheets or some such, and she was reading to you passages from a notorious and much slandered feminist philosopher whose words were many and startling and interwoven and made your head spin (spinning being just one of her favourite words and a much sought after trade, had you known it), which was all fine and well, this weaving, except that it did not get the washing done. And then you dropped a sheet in the mud, and had to drag it inside and start all over again with the cats climbing in the sink to chase the suds, and the hens flying in the window, and why hadn't you by this time got a washing machine, other women have, and if you want that kind of life why don't you go back to the suburbs where you came from, and if only you had held the sheet in the first place, and who is it who always complains about not finding time for feminist philosophers, yes but not when we're hanging up sheets in a north east wind. It was beds we were digging, beds you fool, have you forgotten beds for fragile potatoes easily bruised, ah, easily bruised yes, and in the sun too, don't you remember what you said about sun on the back? Ah yes, beds it was, you're right, lazy beds and laying out the lazy beds and digging in the spuds, and with that you left the suds overflowing the sink and followed the cat trail of scarlet and mediterranean blue upstairs to the loft that was Cleo's until she needed more space. Given any excuse, this is what happens which explains the gutters leaking, the sheets unwashed, the mothers unwritten to, the whales unsaved, the cats running riot, the feminist philosophers unread – and if we don't support them she said, who will, I mean actually go out and buy the goddamn books, not just get them on loan from friends?

And it was one of those days and it led to one of those nights and more of those mornings.

14

And that was long before you noticed the noise from the woodshed. A startling and disturbing noise that might have been many things or one. Do you hear that noise, she asked, looking up from the list of power stations for the nuclear family you were compiling at the kitchen table. And you looked up, and you did hear, and you both wondered if it had just begun or if it might have been going on for days, perhaps since you came, being so busy with lists and laundry and things in between, you might well not have noticed anything going on. There had been other noises before, of course, she said, mostly of an animal or vegetable origin: the time she found the bird, for instance, bald and featherless, that might have been a newborn blown from its nest, or an adult struck by disease, and she fed it mashed catfood in case it was a newborn which should have been eating regurgitated worms; then there was the vagrant goose escaped from a poultry farm where it failed to lay its golden egg; and the blue whale, or dogfish, or was it a seal, someone had brought up from the beach for saving; and the fox you caught raiding the garbage you had forgotten to leave out: bags and bags of black plastic refuse, foul rotting rubbish that had been on the way to the dump the morning Cleo decided she had had enough of the loft and took off on her Yamaha for somewhere more spacious. This Cleo, you were tempted to say, sounds a hard act to follow, more literal than metaphoric. Yes, she said, as if you had said it, which after all you very well might have – impossible to follow, even when you knew where she was going, but she had beautiful eyes, an amazing way with whales, and no woman could write a better symphony, another week and we'd have had it finished. In that case, you said, we had better get the rubber gloves, anxious to put the day on a more solid footing, you thought (more metaphoric than literal – your mind growing helplessly lateral, it should have thought boots – and would shortly), in case it's the garbage again or a goose or a dog or a seal making free with it. But the gloves, when you found them, were punctured – and who was it who was forever borrowing them for the garden so that when you came to do the washing they let in jets of scalding soapy water – and it couldn't all be blamed on the cats, inquisitive and temperamental as they were (not to mention the dog) – do you hear them on the roof this instant? And you did, and she said, don't bother with that now, it's the other noise we have to deal with. Out you went then, armed only with two odd rubber gloves, a sweeping brush and one pair of wellingtons, and thank goodness once more for the discovery of rubber, for you might soon be up to your knees in decaying refuse, as she had been before, alone, lonely and lovelorn: knowing where to look but having promised not to; a chase or a search of any kind being the one thing a claustrophobic could not take. As you knew, having known something of claustrophobia yourself. Out you went.

When you got to the woodshed you paused, stopped in your tracks, because the noise had stopped and you didn't know where it had gone. You would have paused anyway, not being sure what you might find, and putting off the evil hour of angry geese or dead foxes. And then she opened the door, because you couldn't go on standing there forever, and it was what you had come for after all, and in the light from the door you saw a big red sleeping bag laid out on the straw, and in the next moment you saw the two heads at the top of it, one dark and one fair, and then the heads came up fully, and you saw the shoulders and one breast of two women, one black, one white though brown skinned, young, of unidentifiable class and culture, these things being impossible to define from bare skin and bone. Oh it's you, she said, which meant nothing to you. Yes, they said, it's us – they said it together, as if they were used to saying things together. We heard the noise, she said. Yes, that was us, they said. We should have known, she said, I mean recognised it, knowing you were coming back. And of course you should have too and now that she said it you did – recognise the sound. It wasn't, after all, for the want of hearing it. But then other people are different, especially if you haven't even heard them speaking or weeping or singing, and anyone can make

16

a mistake about these things, and you had. But now you knew. And from their voices talking now you also knew they were from the continent of North America. And she told you she had met them before and invited them to stay anytime. She had seen them in the hardware store or was it the haberdashers? and spotted them. There are always women being spotted this way and other women going around spotting – it is one of the things you have come to expect. How did you know, they had said to her. Oh I don't know, I just spotted you somehow. After that they had come to stay, Janette and Janelle from the U.S.A., and they wanted to sleep in the open in their big red sleeping bag under the stars, and, well, she said, there's always the woodshed if it rains. She remembered that now. They were on an asylum visit from the city where they worked in a women's refuge for battered women and raped women and women who had been molested as children and children who had been molested before they ever got to be women. And they needed a holiday from it – a vacation, as they said, though not speaking together, speaking separately now that they had grown used to the light and your faces. And there were four breasts now above the sleeping bag, full fleshed and dark skinned, and three arms, the last arm belonging to the woman with short red hair under the sleeping bag still. And they had slept out under the sky for three nights, needing the night and the stars and no noise but their own, or a bird's or an animal's or a leaf's or a stone's, or whatever it is that makes all the racket in the country when everyone says – how quiet it is – how do you stand the silence?

And after three days of this they had gone off or on, the way visitors do, especially women from the United States of America who have come to see Europe, or find their sanity, or escape it, after five years working with molested and battered women to whom they listen and listen and say very little, trying hard not to say all the things they want to, for this is non-directive counselling and it is listening without directing, which is almost impossible with all this pain that is so familiar and known in your bones. And so they listen

17

and learn, learn more than they ever wanted to learn,
and keep silent until the time somebody says – listen
you need a break – five years is too long for anyone to
listen without a break. And so they stop listening for a
while, and go off to find Europe, and find the
haberdashers, or was it the grocers? which is where
she spotted them, and invited them home to sleep in
the woodshed, or out under the stars, at least until the
rain came, which was five days ago, but she hadn't
noticed, being so caught up with your life since
crossing the river. Well, she said, we're glad it's you
and not a badger or rat or fox, or some other hapless
creature, and this is certainly no day for the garbage.
Certainly not, they said, it's a day for the river (for
they had crossed it too, the same one, or another, but
they certainly had crossed a river). Indeed it is – why
don't you come? Well we're kind of okay here, they
said, speaking together. Okay so, she said, and there's
always the loft if the rain gets cold – it's not quite
finished of course, we were just getting round to the
roof the day Cleo left. Fine, they said, we're real good
with roofs and, being women from the North American continent, they probably were, being real good
with all making and fixing and getting acts together
and quite undiscourageable, which was something to
say in this climate of rain and rivers and cats walking
through the gutters so that you could not get at the
roof to mend it even when you started. And another
thing, she said, in that case, no doubt thinking of the
windows. And you could see that there was enough to
keep them going for weeks, and they had weeks to
keep going, they said, and no better place to spend
them, and there was always the loft. They said they
would remember if the rain got cold and then the
three arms joined the other arm under the red sleeping
bag, and you closed the door and walked back up the
path. And you said, thank the mother it wasn't the
garbage, this is no day for going to the dump. No, she
said, it's a day for going anywhere else, almost
anywhere else; shall we go and leave the gutter and
the hens and the list of power stations for the nuclear
family and the letters to your mother and the feminist

18

philosophers. This is no day for philosophy. But, you said, if we interpret philosophy as meaning love of wisdom, or life, this is just the day it is for, and why not dump it all and go and philosophise by the river? Ah, the river. And, anyhow, you said, now that there were Janelle and Janette from the United States making it in the woodshed, and when they got tired or thirsty or hungry or too hot or cold, they were bound to come out — sometime anyway — more or less, and then they could help with the symphony and the goats — and don't go through all that again please, she said, and you did not but definitely, when it came to feminist philosophy, it was mostly written by women from the American continent, she had to agree and if they would not read it, who would? and that was bound to be some sort of help. Too many bounds, she said, in this conversation, almost as bad as ifs and buts, but she saw your point and agreed with you. And that was a weight off your mind which was tired of weights and bounds and wanted to go boundless, the weight off your feet by the river, any river.

Alright, she said, but first, she said, we should go into town and buy some stuff to finish the loft: some wood and nails and hammers and saws and, anyway, you never knew who you might meet in the hardware store, it being some time since she had been in being so preoccupied with your life outside it. Alright, you said, but remember, no spotting, whoever you spot, the loft and the woodshed being temporarily spoken for.

And on the way you collected a bottle of wine and your flute and she took her knapsack and fiddle. It was a day for the old tunes, walking arm in arm down the road till you came to a stream, sitting down together, love, and who knows, you might even hear the nightingale sing. Or at least a blackcap, its melodious song commonly mistaken, or a whitethroat or stonechat. And into the car you got, putting out the hens and some hydrangea plants waiting to be planted, or they might have been rhododendron, or even azalea, that should have been waiting in the woodshed but could not be now. And as the morning was hot, the sun hot on the windscreen, on your cheek, on your neck, on your arms, as you drove, and dazzling her eyes so that she put on her shades, as she called them, that made her sultry and unknown and glamorous, which she was anyway, and the only woman you knew with such an extraordinary collection of household trappings, not to mention garden and farmhouse. And you said, I think this turn on the left is the fastest road to the river, and it might have been, and it was not only the heat of the sun on your neck that was making you sweat: a lovely light sweet earthy sweat unlike horses or ladies, the latter who only glow. And you were glowing too, though no lady. And she knew the way to the river even better than you, and no wonder, having carried how many others across it, you did not ask, though of course you had asked before, and even considered counting, but now the number escaped you, if you had ever established it, and in no time at all you saw the water winding dark and wide and orange, frothing creamy white at its edges and around the snarl of black polished wood hazel, or yew or sycamore, which had fallen across it, forming a dam so that it was deeper and darker on the other side, deep enough for swimming or bathing as ladies would say. And will we, she said, and took off her clothes (being no lady) which were not many; fewer than the first day when the weather was cooler. And you said, this is where it all began, or some of it, the best part of it, do you remember? There's no hurry, she said, no hurry at all, we have all we need; the wood and the hammer and food enough for four, and we can start on the loft tomorrow, or the next day, or whenever the rain gets cold. And you lay down on the bank, the grass tickling your face, and she said, do you remember, and how could you not, with so little to distract you, and so much the same, only better now that there had been talk and quarrels and reconciliation and forgetting and fixing things that should have been fixed long ago, now that she knew you looked just like your mother and not at all like your father, and now that she knew you had your sister's voice, and you knew the names of the ones before, and had read old letters and had looked at the photographs, and now that the symphony was almost finished, and a start made on the book, and the Nubian goats milked. It was better; substance and texture, shading and tone being added to what had seemed beyond improvement but was not because now it was better even than before. Do you remember, she said, the first day and you did, you loved remembering the feel of her flanks as she carried you over, her strong back under your thighs and you urging her on, smelling the jasmine smell of her hair and promising yourself to get serious – oh so serious. And have you talked yet about women getting serious and all that it leads to? – looking into each other's eyes and taking one another seriously, seeing one another whole and entire not as stop gaps, mediators, sympathisers, that long lasting, tasting, touching look that is one of the best things going, and if it happens to be at the side of a river when birds are starting up in the fields surprised by you – larks, you think they are, who spin in the sky with such glorious larkful spinning, up in the air like that and a cuckoo – yes a cuckoo calls that cuckoo way from across the heather, a place so distant you can hardly imagine and yet so clear – so heartstillingly, sound breakingly clear, it comes that call, and who will not answer? Falling into the grass then, the wild red poppies, the cowslips, the speedwell speeding blue all round, waiting all around, the long supple green tassled grass: falling into it two women tired from the business of making a living, a loving, making each day a new living, tired from the business of standing up to be counted – and oh they are counting – never stop – and who started all that business anyway? – tired of counting, two women fall into the cowslips and the lark rises and the gutters wait for another day and philosophy waits and the potatoes lie lazy for another day.

And it was another of those days. And more and more women are having them – days that is – snatched from drought and the torrents of life. More and more women riding about footloose, tongue loose and fancy free, crossing the river when they come to it: the deep, rushing tide, keeping their heads and well above water and gaining the bank; they lie down where the grass lies green and growing in wait all round, lie down where the yellow iris waves in wait, the wild poppies blow and, a cuckoo – yes, it was unmistakably from over the heather – a cuckoo, calls.

A Sense of Humour

She sat at the kitchen table and stared out the window
to the backyard, where the rain splashed down on the
dull metal of the Guinness kegs and spilled into the
used beer bottles stacked open mouthed in plastic
crates. She was waiting for her father to be finished his
breakfast. Without looking up from his newspaper that
stood propped against the milk carton, he pushed his
cup towards her: 'Is there any more in the pot?' he
asked, and she filled his cup to the brim, carelessly so
that the tea sloshed over into the saucer. It seemed to
her that she would always be waiting – waiting for
summer or for winter; when the days would be short
or fine, waiting for the children to come home from
school, waiting for them to grow up, waiting for her
parents to grow old; waiting for freedom, for the day
when there would be no one left to make her feel
guilty.

Her father lifted his tea and she watched him swill
the milky liquid round the mug in a slow circular
movement, as he always did, before sucking it noisily
into his throat. Their neighbour, Maurice Kennedy,
was to be buried that morning and he had a few
minutes to spare before leaving for the church. Her
mother had tried to hurry him over an hour ago
coming through the kitchen on her way out, wearing
her red woollen coat and the patterned scarf Breda

23

had sent from Medjugorge. 'Mind you keep an eye on the clock, John, or you'll be the last in.' She paused at the mirror to settle her hair, patting it nervously with a gloved hand, setting loose a waft of scent that drifted back across the room: the *Madame Rochas* that she kept for holidays, weddings and funerals.

'Will you look after things so, Kate?' She glanced quickly about the room, her gaze resting for a moment on the children's toys scattered over the floor: a colouring book, paintbrushes and crayons, a one legged doll sprawled against the table rung. Kate did not turn or answer her mother. She did not want to see the remote, pained expression that came into her face whenever her attention was drawn to the children.

'Robbie Spillane is in the bar this long time,' her mother called back as she pulled the door shut behind her.

It was Robbie she had hoped Kate would marry; Jim Spillane's son who farmed a hundred acres or more, Robbie who was single yet, though he could have any girl in the parish for the asking. But Kate had chosen someone else – she had married Liam Lynch who worked in Keynes garage in the town, and so was it anyone's fault but her own that things had worked out as they had?

'Well, I'd best be off if I'm to get there at all,' her father stood up heavily, pushing his chair out from the table, lifting his jacket slowly from the back of it. Would Liam come to this, she wondered, in another twenty years – the pale, bloodshot eyes, the tremor in the speech. Her father did everything cautiously these days; with deliberate effort. Standing by the door in his Sunday suit he looked cramped and foolish; keeping his head lowered, not wanting to be noticed; the raw skin of his wrists, his great hands jutting awkwardly from the smooth serge cuffs.

She began to clear his dishes from the table, carrying them one by one to the sink. She was glad when she heard the latch fall behind him. It was an ease to be alone, out of reach of people's voices, of her mother's gaze. Though she did not know why she should still care what her mother thought or said. She

24

told herself that her mother was an old woman, set in her ways – a woman who had always known hardship and had learned only to bear it without complaint. But from childhood she had been controlled by her mother's face; by her eyes that turned away from you with an expression of injury and surprise that made you feel, whatever it was you had done, it was something else she had wanted. You could not argue with it. To understand you could only watch and listen very closely; listening especially to the things she would not say and to the small unimportant affairs that she made much of. She had never cared for Liam, though she would not say so. And perhaps it was for that reason Kate had gone out with him in the first place, goaded by her look of silent disappointment.

'Mammy, Deirdre has taken my paints.'

Her youngest daughter, Maireid, was standing in the doorway, her pale cheeks mottled by tears. She pulled a strand of her corn coloured hair to her wet mouth:

'Robbie told her to give it back to me, but she won't.'

Robbie. Kate had forgotten him. He would be inside waiting still. She did not want to see him, not this morning. She had not the energy for making herself pleasant. She had hoped to get the laundry done while her parents were out. That way she would have a little time to herself in the afternoon. She dried her hands on the back door towel:

'Didn't I tell you not to leave your toys all over the room, Maireid,' she said, 'you know how it annoys your granny.' She walked out of the kitchen and through the small back sitting room that led to the bar. Maireid came skipping along after her, her shoes slipping on the polished linoleum.

The saloon bar was a long narrow room; a concrete extension built onto the main house ten years ago when there was still profit in the bar trade. Her mother had expected great things from it. She had wanted to attract tourists and the young men who had made money from salmon fishing and from work on the building sites in England. But that was in the boom time of the early seventies. Things had changed. It was only the old men who came now – the old and those who had no work. The young had emigrated for good and the visitors, such as they were, preferred the new resort hotel at the strand. But empty or crowded Kate hated the place. She hated the smell that always hung in the air of stale cigarette smoke and the odour from damp clothes. She hated the bare, beige coloured walls and the light that shone from two fluorescent bars on the ceiling. She disliked most of all their customers; the men who came every day whether they had money in their pockets or not. The idle and the shiftless who sat at the formica covered tables or leaned against the bar drinking until they were stupid with it and could no longer remember why it was they were here and not in their own homes. Customers who knew well that her father had never been heard to refuse anyone a drink. A decent man, as they all said of him.

Robbie sat at the bar drinking a pint of stout. He was a black haired, heavy set man with lazy, good-humoured eyes.

'How are you Kate, you didn't go to the funeral so?'

Kate went behind the counter and lifted down a couple of glasses.

'No,' she said, 'Maireid is coming down with a dose of flu. I thought it was best to keep her home. And did you hear Deirdre fell off the bike yesterday on her way from school.'

Robbie took a mouthful of stout and gave a low snort of laughter that made his shoulders shake:

'Is that so – by God it seems you're lucky to have them in one piece.'

He always laughed in this way as though her troubles were a comfort to him, making her feel for a moment that there was not so much wrong with the world. She set another glass under the tap for him. Maybe her mother had been right after all. Maybe she should have married him. A farmer's wife she would have been. She could have kept hens and a few goats. She would have liked that well enough. She could have had a little money of her own. She looked at his mild blue eyes and tried to imagine them distorted by anger. She could not. But then who would believe it of Liam? Even her mother who never approved of him

26

would not accept the picture she painted. Two sides to every story, was all she would say. Kate looked at his big, square hands closed around the belly of his glass. Was there anything you could tell from a face? Who knew what a man was like at his own fireside?

'There's a session at Grogan's tonight Kate, it should be good crack.'

She took a box of peanuts from the floor and pulled open the cardboard lid. Let him go to Grogan's she thought. There was nothing stopping him. It had nothing to do with her anyway. She glanced over at the girls who were playing under a blanket beside the Kosangas heater, squirming about under cover, tickling each other's feet, giggling with pleasure. How easy it was for children to make up; they moved from grief to joy as quickly as clouds blown from the sun. No time but the present was real to them. Maireid was four and Deirdre six. It would be another ten years before Kate would be free to do as she pleased. Robbie set a five pound note on the counter:

'Will you have one with me, Kate?'

'No thanks, Robbie, not now.'

The peanut packets were attached in rows of four to a sheet of cardboard. She took one from the box and stuck it with a drawing pin to the wall beside the till. What was the point of it, she thought, of his coming here day after day staring at her with his big soft eyes as though there was an understanding between them? What understanding could there be? He might smile as much as he liked – it changed nothing. She was a married woman and would be for the rest of her life if she were never to set eyes on Liam again. She took the note Robbie had given her and putting it into the till slammed the door shut.

'Maireid – Deirdre,' she called, 'will you go inside and clear up the kitchen before Granny gets home.' Seeing their startled faces as they pushed the blankets from their heads, she felt contrite and softened her tone:

'Robbie will you look after yourself,' she said, 'I'll be inside if you want me.'

In the kitchen she began sorting the clothes for the

washing machine. She lifted them from the yellow plastic laundry basket and divided them according to fabric and colour, setting them in bundles at her feet. With so many things needing to be done separately it hardly seemed worth using the machine. She carried a pair of blue jeans to the sink and held them under the cold tap to rinse out a blood stain. She watched the foaming soap run red and trickle over her hands into the basin. Fifteen years of this behind her and maybe another fifteen to go. Where did her body find the energy for this ceaseless activity? Month after month purging and renewing itself, cell by cell. And for what? What use had she now for the whole process? It made her irritable to think of it. She piled the clothes roughly into the machine, sheets and towels first. She would have to do two runs at the least. She poured in the detergent and pushed the starter button. Once in action the steady whoosh and whirl of the water spun back and forth soothed her. She sat on a chair and stared vacantly at the white froth bubbling behind the curved glass door.

'It was a great send off, Kate, the whole parish turned out.' Her mother had come home ahead of her father. She was standing at the stove drinking a cup of tea, her coat on still and her scarf loose around her collar. She looked almost like a city woman, Kate thought, done up like that; ten years younger, her cheeks flushed with excitement, little gusts of perfume rising still from her neck and tightly permed hair.

'Even Tim O'Connor – I haven't laid eyes on him for years.'

Tim O'Connor was an elderly bachelor who lived alone by Rinnmor. Kate remembered how as children they used to tease him. They would climb the wall into his yard and chase the hens, clapping their hands so that the creatures flew squawking against the wire of the coop. It was not the fowl they were after but himself. It amused them to set up such a din that he would come running from the house, half dressed sometimes, to see what the matter was. When he caught sight of them he would hurry back inside, bolting the door behind him. He had a mortal fear of children, no one knew why. His mother was long since dead and he was one of the many ageing men who lived on remote farms, going without human company for so long that they lost the power of speech altogether or took to wandering the roads talking aloud.

'He looked like a scarecrow with that old black coat on him,' her mother laughed, 'but sure God help him, there's not a bit of harm in him.'

That was what they always said. Even those known to be violent were spoken of in this way, indulgently, as a little simple but meaning no harm. Their existence in the community seemed a reassurance almost; as if their loneliness and dissolution provided a visible proof that God had intended no man to live unmated.

'Was Tim there – that's a wonder alright,' Kate said and smiled, making an effort to share her mother's mood. It was rare enough to see her in high spirits. She passed a packet of biscuits across the table to her and looked at the rough, swollen fingers that reached out to take it. She had once been a tall, goodlooking woman, with dark brown hair falling almost to her waist. Kate could see her still carrying one of the little ones to bed – Breda or Michael – lifting them high in her arms so that their heads brushed the ceiling. 'Catch a baby – catch a baby,' they would squeal with delight. Now everything about her seemed to have shrunk; her skin, her bones, her hair that was cut short and had grown white, her eyes that had dulled and faded. There was a knowing pride in her smile as she crumbled a biscuit to dip in her tea:

'Did I tell you I had a letter from Breda this morning?'

So, it was not only the excitement of the day out that had her in good humour. She had heard from Breda.

'How is she?' Kate asked. Breda, her youngest sister, had done well for herself. She had left home two years ago and worked now as a trained nurse in London renting her own flat in Kentish Town. The good news would mean that she had mentioned again the young doctor she had been seeing. Her mother had gone over for a visit in the summer and since then she had not ceased singing Breda's praises: the stylish life she led, her fashionable clothes and well paid job. To hear her talk you would think it was a credit to herself that Breda had made such a success. Kate listened and marvelled that she could forget so easily.

'I'd say she'll have great news for us shortly,' her mother said now, casting a rapid glance about the room as though fearful of being overheard.

Kate stood up and fetched the kettle from the stove. She refilled the pot with boiling water and poured a fresh cup for herself. She remembered all too well what her mother chose to forget. Breda had left home on New Year's Day. She had brought one suitcase and enough money to tide her over for the first week. She had had her hair set the day before and had borrowed the belted grey raincoat that Kate had bought for her honeymoon. They had seen her off at the boat.

'It's only a visit,' she had called down from the rail of the deck. 'I'll be home in the spring.' But they had all known that she would not be. And her mother, Kate thought, suspected more than that; suspected what Breda refused to confide to any of them. She had made no comment. The least said the soonest mended was her policy in all trouble, great or small. What went unspoken, for her, did not exist, and she had not laboured all these years to build about her children a life she thought fitting, to have them rupture it at a stroke. No, Breda must find her own solution, and whatever she chose, it must rouse no trace of scandal. All this was conveyed clearly without a word exchanged.

Kate looked at the rain dribbling down the window. It would continue like this for days now. She would get none of the clothes dry. She remembered that night; Breda's anxious eye and forced smile, waving her white scarf from the deck until long past harbour and she wondered why it was she herself had offered so little in the way of help. She was, after all, the eldest and already a married woman. But she had been cut off from Breda by her own worries, and caught in the net of silence that was cast over all their lives. She looked at her mother who was sitting opposite her now on the far side of the table, her legs crossed, her hands joined in her lap, the line of pink lipstick broadening the line of her clenched lips. Reality, she thought, was made up of the things men did, what could be spoken of in public without lowering the voice. And the rest – all that concerned women only was veiled; a secret, so that even sisters lied to each other.

'Will you let me at the stove for a few minutes, Kate, 'till I put on your father's dinner.' Her mother did not stir from her chair but she lifted her eyes to the china clock on the wall above the range. The hands stood at twenty to one. Kate heard the dogs set up a wild bark of greeting and she recognised her father's footsteps in the yard.

'Sit where you are – I'll do it, Mam.'

She went to the fridge and took out a packet of frozen chips. She cut open the wrapper and turned the stiff blonde straws of potato onto a dinner plate. Then she lifted the frying pan down from the press. Her father came through the door carrying a newspaper under his arm.

'There was a fierce crowd above in O'Rourkes,' he said as though to explain his delay. 'John Pat was losing the run of himself altogether.' He took off his cap and loosened the buttons of his jacket before sitting down in the armchair that was kept free for him. He turned the pages of his paper, banging them roughly into place with the back of his hand. When he had it folded into a neat square he reached into his pocket for his reading glasses.

'Will you want beans with your chips Mam?'

'Heat them for your father I suppose but don't bother for me. A drop of soup is all I want.'

A drop of soup – don't bother for me! If she had not her father to see to, Kate thought, her mother would not bother to cook a meal again. She would live on bread and tea.

31

'Did you see Breda's letter?' her mother fixed her eyes on the back page of the paper. She spoke lightly; casting the words vaguely into the air but Kate felt the barb in them. If her father's attention was to be caught at all it had to be done before he reached the racing results.

'Give it over to me so,' he said, lowering the paper impatiently, 'while I have on my glasses.'

Her mother took a small blue envelope from her bag and passed it across to him.

'Well?' she asked at last, when he had finished reading and sat holding the letter in his hand.

'Well what?'

'Her news of course, what else?'

'What news?'

'Isn't it as plain as day that she intends marrying Martin?'

'Maybe so,' he replied, 'I saw no mention of engagement plans.'

'Maybe so, maybe so – is that all you've to say? You wouldn't notice the sun itself, John Dillon, unless it fell out of the sky and hit you. Give it back to me if that's all you can manage on the subject.' She leaned over and snatched the letter from his grasp. He did it intentionally, she knew, to torment her. For years he had gone on in this manner, resisting her in every-thing. Nothing she did or said could make him show a moment's attention to the affairs of his family. 'Your children,' he called them. It was his revenge, of course, for coming between him and his pleasures. She had fought him in the past, bitterly; pleaded with him to spend one evening at home at his own fireside. And this was how she was rewarded. He had given up drink and life with it. She was left with the ghost of a man who could do nothing, only read his paper and brood over the hearth.

'Kate,' she turned with a look of angry appeal to her daughter. But Kate refused to be drawn in. She set her father's plate on the table, a knife and fork beside it.

'Your soup is in the pot, Mam, it's nearly cooked.' She would go upstairs; the beds had still to be made.

As she climbed the back steps she heard the silence

settle behind her, heavy and corrosive. Without her as witness there was no point for either of them in continuing.

She opened the door of the bedroom that she shared with Maireid and Deirdre. The light was dim because of the rain, and the small north facing window had misted over. She made up each of the three beds in turn, tucking the covers in tightly. She tidied away the clothes the girls had left strewn about the floor and crawled on her hands and knees under Maireid's bed to retrieve the hot water bottle. When she was finished, she sat down for a moment to catch her breath. Her gaze was drawn to a tangle of blue crayon marks at the bottom of the wall. A wave of depression came over her. Did other people live like this, she wondered, in such disorder and purposelessness? Could a life be made up of no more than this – of making meals and clearing up after them, of washing and ironing, of watching the television, of eating and of going to sleep? Maybe she had her life. Maybe there was only one real event in anyone's, and she had had hers – marriage and the birth of her children. Was that it? She remembered her wedding day – the hope and excitement of that morning eight years ago. Spring; the twenty-fifth of April, a blue sky when she woke, the sun shining, the laughter and fuss of her sisters as they had helped her to dress in this room. She remembered the drive to the church, the primroses growing all along the roadside and the lambs in the fields running back from the car. Her mother had said that she was too young but how could anyone, she had thought, be too young for happiness?

She looked at her face in the mirror of the dressing table. Her pale hair fell limply about her shoulders. She looked at the little furrow that had come between her brows and the two deep lines running on either side of her mouth. She used to wonder as a child how it was some women let their face grow hard and bitter. She had thought it would be an easy thing to prevent. She made herself smile, but the line stayed fixed on her forehead. She gathered up her hair and held it in a loose knot behind her neck. She had been goodlooking once. The beauty of the family, they said. She could look alright still if she could have a little happiness, a bit of laughter and fun. Perhaps she should go out with Robbie, why not after all, she thought? Where was the harm in it? He was not bad, Robbie, it was not as though he was like Liam, anyone could see that. He had a kind face and gentle ways. He would be good to her, spoil her, make her smile again. Why should she care what they said? She had been patient long enough and got no thanks for it. They said she was lucky because she had food on the table and a roof over her head. Because she had children who kept her busy running after them from morning to night, they thought she had no time to be lonely. But the feeling you had for your children only kept alive the appetite for love without satisfying it.

She went to the wardrobe that stood by the window and took from it two woollen jerseys. They were her best – a blue lambswool with a deep vee neck and the other cherry red with small white buttons on the shoulder. Looking in the mirror, she held each to her face in turn, holding the sleeve to her outstretched arm. She liked the red best but maybe it was a bit harsh for her complexion. She swept her hair up again and tried the blue. Yes, it brought out the colour of her eyes – she would wear it and her red skirt with it. She would go to Grogan's with Robbie. And maybe afterwards they could go on to the Strand Hotel. It was lovely there. They had pink shaded lamps on the wall and a candle on every table. There would be music and dancing. It was years since she had danced. She began to do a little step about the room, holding out her arms as if dancing with a partner. She sang – 'Some enchanted evening, you may meet a stranger, you may see him smiling across a crowded room . . .' and she laughed aloud. Then she heard the slam of the back door below. It must be nearly two-o-clock. She would go down and make something to eat.

34

The kitchen was empty. Her father had finished his meal and gone out to the fields. The dishes were stacked neatly in the draining tray. Her mother must be inside in the bar. She would have a while to herself. She could listen to the radio in peace. She listened to the programme they had for women at this time most days, if her mother was not in the room, and if the girls were quiet. It made her feel better somehow to hear other women talking about their problems – things she had not had to face herself. Women from all over the country came on to it; ordinary women, housewives and mothers like herself. But it was the girl who introduced it that Kate liked. There was such sympathy and understanding in her voice, it seemed as though she were talking just to Kate. She switched on the transistor radio that stood on the shelf over the sink.

'The great thing, of course, is communication,' a woman with a northern accent said, someone Kate had heard before – a social worker or journalist.

'It really is essential to sit down and talk things through.'

They always went on like this, people on radio and writing in magazines – about dialogue and the importance of trust. She tried to picture anyone she knew making time to sit down and discuss their feelings. She could not. The weather and the price of cows, who had died and who had married, that was what you talked about in the country. No one ever mentioned feelings. Maybe it was too dangerous in a place where the same families lived heaped on one another like cattle in a barn, generation after generation. If she had been able to talk to Liam would it have made a difference? Could anyone have found words capable of stemming the tide of bitterness that was in him?

'Kate, have you seen the floorcloth, I want it for a minute?' Kate heard her mother's footsteps coming along the corridor, her slippers making the soft shuffling sound of a spade through wet sand. She did not want her to come in. It would only irritate her to find Kate listening to the programme. She would say nothing, but she would come into the room and potter about making noise while she cleared up; rattling the cutlery in the sink, opening and closing the fridge door. She did not like to hear women discussing their personal lives in public. 'Are they never done complaining?' she had asked once when she heard a woman on the television telling about a rape case. There was only one person a woman should turn to in time of trouble and that was the priest. When Kate had come home first her mother had asked her to go and see Father Cusack. 'Would you not have a word with him,' she had said, 'he has experience of these things.' You could confide in a priest because he had heard it all before and because he had no one belonging to him to whom he could repeat it.

'I don't know where I left the cloth – I only left it down a minute ago.'

Kate tilted back her chair, inclining her head towards the radio so that she could hear it still above her mother's voice.

'It depends on whether the local G.P. is sympathetic or not, unfortunately,' the northern woman was saying, 'it's very difficult still for rural women and those in small communities.' Rural women – they meant people like herself. It was strange to think that she fitted into some accepted category. There were so many different labels these days – city women, suburban women, single women, working women, professional women. It seemed that everyone had a name, could be slotted in under some special heading. Why was it, then, that she felt she belonged nowhere, that she felt completely adrift in the world?

'Kate, did you not hear me? I said we needed another case of coke in from the yard.' She made no reply but she got up from her chair. There would be no peace now until she turned off the radio. She would go into the bar and listen to it there.

She carried a crate of minerals from the yard through the side door of the bar. Maireid and Deirdre having finished their lunch were sitting by the Kosangas playing with jars of water and some flowers they had brought in from the fields. Robbie was at the corner table with Mossy Sheehan and Tom Walshe dealing cards. They had six pints lined up beside them. They were shouting and laughing, banging the cards down on the rickety three legged table. The smoke from their cigarettes filled the room, hanging in clouds beneath the low ceiling. Kate wiped little streams of beer from the counter with a sponge cloth and dried a few whiskey glasses. Neither the men nor the children noticed her presence. She switched on the radio; an old fashioned one with a netted front they used to call the wireless.

'It's something you can't explain to anyone till it happens to themselves,' it was a different woman now, from Dublin she thought, speaking slowly and deliberately, 'you live in fear day and night. There's no one you can talk to. The first time it happened was Christmas Eve. The thing I remember was Mary, the youngest, standing at the top of the stairs screaming. He did not even seem to see her. He just went on hitting me across the face with his open hand.' Kate set down the glass she was polishing. She was afraid she might break it. Her hands were shaking. The voice came on from the radio, haltingly, as though it were a great effort to get out the words. It was dull and monotone; like a child repeating a lesson, only no child's voice could hold such hopelessness.

'After that, it happened again. Always after the pub. Shouting and yelling, beating me about the head and chest. One time my face was so bruised and swollen I could not leave the house for days. I did not mind for myself. I could have put up with it, it was only when he started on the children I had to do something.'

Each word came at Kate with the force of a blow. All her nerves tightened, her senses contracting as she tried not to hear, not to see. And yet she stood fixed, listening as the words came on relentlessly, driving against a barrier in her; the barrier she had erected so as not to feel, not to remember. But she recognised the language as if it had been cut from her own flesh.

37

'Once I tried to escape. He caught me and threw me down the stairs. I had a broken arm that time.'

She stood with the dishcloth in her hand, trembling. Ten years confronted her in this stranger's grief. She burned with shame as if it were her own life revealed to the world in these harsh broken phrases. She reached to the shelf and turned the radio off.

'Kate.'

Robbie was leaning against the bar staring into her face. She had no idea how long he had been there.

'I'll be with you in a minute – I have to see to the girls,' she said, forcing herself to speak calmly and then walked quickly out through the bar door though the children were still playing on the floor. She sat down in the hall on a chair beside the phone. Her breath came in short painful gasps. She bent her head towards her knees and covered her face. She tried not to think – to make her mind a blank. She could not bear to have it all come over her again today. She had been happy. She was to go out tonight. She would wear her new jersey. She would dance. The children were inside playing, she could hear their voices. Her mother was working in the kitchen. She was in her own home now, safe, she told herself. No one could harm her, there would be no shouting, no violence. No one would ever raise a hand to her again. Liam could not come here. It could never be like that again; like the first time. Like the first night he had struck her, so drunk he could hardly walk across the bedroom floor. Struck her with all his force, opening her lip. She had got away from him – locked herself in the bathroom with a chair against the door, sat on the cold tiles until it was morning. It could not be like that again. Like the time she had forgiven him – all those times; made up with him because she could not bear to see only the violence. She had told no one. It was their shame – only theirs. The hurt was buried inside her and only he could comfort it. In the end she did not even try to escape. She knew she deserved it. He would not beat her and abuse her unless she did; unless she was all the things he called her. The pain was final then. She knew that she was stupid, vicious, ugly; everything he named her and when she slept with him again it made her the whore he said she was. But only he could absolve her because only he knew how base she was. That knowledge was what had kept her with him so long.

'Mammy.'

Maireid had come and put her arm around her, pushing her head along her cheek. Her hair where it parted in the middle had the sweet sharp smell of apples.

'What's wrong, Mam?'

'Nothing love,' she kissed Maireid's hair drying her eyes in it and held her close to her breast. Nothing would ever harm her again, she wanted to promise that. Maireid pulled open her clenched fingers. There was a fifty pence piece inside her palm. She had picked it up from the counter as she had left the bar. The woman had given a number to call – she had heard it just before she switched off the radio. Seven o six something – a Dublin number. She could ask the operator or ring the station. She could call that woman and tell her there was an escape. She could call her just to talk to her. They said that helped.

'Mam, come back in, Robbie wants you.'

It was Deirdre standing at the other end of the hall. Kate stood up and, taking Maireid's hand, walked back along the corridor.

Robbie was at the counter still. She smiled at him.

'Kate, fill another for me,' he pushed his glass towards her, 'and have one yourself.'

'Thanks – I'll have a Harp so.'

She took two glasses from the shelf and put one under the Guinness tap and one under the Harp. She filled the Guinness first. She watched the brown foaming liquid crawl up the curved side. Robbie was talking still, telling her something that made him laugh. Between each sentence he threw back his head and roared with laughter. The stout was settling in the glass, the froth slipping down again changing to dark black.

'Just imagine it Kate – wouldn't it make you die laughing?'

39

She looked up at him. His wide fleshy shoulders were shaking, his eyes were squeezed tight but although he was laughing they had lost their good humour.

'What's so funny Robbie?' she said making an effort, putting a smile on her lips, wanting to see the joke.

'Amn't I just after telling you girl – where have you been at all? Tom O'Brien, that's what's funny.'

'What about him?'

'What I said of course. Look will I go over it again from the start – slowly?'

'Go on.'

'Well, I told you about him before. Didn't I tell you about him bringing the gear home from London? The stuff he gets in Soho and places like that – the red light district, you know,' he winked at her and took the first swallow of his pint. 'Well, as I was saying, the last time he decided to bring home a bit extra. He had the videos as usual and a few other gadgets. But this time seemingly he decided to buy a blow-up as well.'

'A what?' Kate stared at him.

'A dummy – you know – an inflatable woman; one you blow up, like the boats.' He laughed again and wiped the stout from his moustache, 'well, like I told you, he had this great idea for her, for a bit of crack and to make a few bob out of her. He had her down in the cowhouse and he was charging the lads a fiver a go. Jesus Kate, she had tits on her the size of melons, only massive, I'm not joking you. He had the lads lining up. Anyhow there they all were yesterday; Mick Hogan, Peader and Jim Murray down in the shed, having it off – taking turns, you know, when who should come in – who should come in, in the middle of it; not a word of a lie, flinging open the door so that they were nearly knocked from their standing, only the mother. Julia O'Brien herself. Well bejasus Kate, when she saw what they were at she let a shriek out of her like a scalded cat. Poor Mick – I never saw a lad taken so short. He couldn't get the trousers on fast enough. I tell you Kate, he lost almost more than his turn that day.' His broad face was contorted, he held his hands across the flesh of his belly as it shook with laughter.

'Did you ever hear such crack – wouldn't you give your right arm to have seen it?'

Kate stared at him; at his quivering body, at the tears running down his cheeks. She saw what he meant now. She saw it all, the whole picture rising clear before her. She saw Mick Hogan, in the old black sweater he never left off, she saw Peader Walsh's thin, lugubrious face, she could see them gathered in the cowhouse at the back of O'Brien's yard, leaning against the wooden stalls, smoking. She saw them laughing, as Robbie was laughing now, their faces red and swollen, as they pushed against the rubber body. She saw their hands grasping at the breasts until the flesh squeaked under them. She saw the blank face of the doll, without eyes or mouth; a thing to be used, to be pushed and mauled, their pleasure beaten from her. A woman's face, dumb and blind as hers had been, a body passive and unresisting as her own.

'Jesus, Kate, you're not laughing, girl – have you no sense of humour at all?'

She did not see her hand lift the pint glass from the counter, she did not feel herself thrust it forward. She did not know what she had done or that she had done anything at all until she saw the yellow foam streaming down Robbie's forehead, the dark stout running into his eyes and down his cheeks that were still spread with laughter.

'Fucking Jeezus,' she heard the roar that came out of his wide mouth, but she did not see the men behind him lift their heads from their stupor over the cards and stare at her in bewilderment and horror. She did not see that her daughter came running after her, crying out to her as she herself ran from the bar.

'Kate – what is it? Kate?'

She saw her mother standing by the sink barring her way to the door. She saw the small shrivelled eyes, the look of sorrow and accusation they carried in them always. The look that had grown into her own face, that had tied Kate to her, to her husband, to this kitchen, to the smoke and tumult, the raucous laughter of the bar where they drank before going back to their wives.

'Kate – for the love of God . . .' she said, but Kate pushed past her, her hands grasping the thin bone of her mother's shoulders.

'Let me alone – let me out of here,' she said or shouted as she pushed by her and away from the door, the door that opened to the fields. She ran then through the darkness, through the drenched, thick grass, out across the land until she stood alone in the silence of the spread night.

She looked up and saw the sky, with its thousand glittering points of light. She opened her mouth wide and drew down great lungfuls of the sweet, cool air. She breathed it in until the shivering in her body was stilled, until she was calm again. With the corner of her apron she wiped away the spatters of beer that she felt suddenly wet on her face and hands. She looked at the stars. She looked at the distance between them, measuring the time and space that divided them; the space and time their light must traverse to reach her eyes. She felt herself slipping outwards into the lit, clear, sheltering darkness. She closed her eyes, her face uplifted, as though to bathe in it. And the stars stood still, shining though she could not see them, precise and brilliant, each one defying time and space to reach her. A wave of exultation rose in her, a burst of consciousness so swift and sudden that she almost jumped from the ground where she stood and heard herself in the same instant cry aloud for joy. She opened her eyes and gazed about her, marvelling. What a little thing had held her captive – what a small, insignificant, scarcely visible thing had kept her prisoner! She had believed in place. She had believed in circumstance, she had allowed herself to be bound by the trappings of situation: this sky, these patched, stony fields she could hardly now discern, a circle of hills, a house, a voice, a face, a pair of hands. The trivia of place – furniture, that could be found anywhere. She stood still, every nerve in her body attending. She heard the sea roaring at the cliff. The sea that edged each night closer to the land she stood on. The wind ripped at her, froze her cheeks so that she could scarcely part her stiffened lips to smile. For she was smiling; her head thrown back, her eyes wide open. She heard the sound of a car passing below her on the blackened road. A car travelling to Dublin. There were always cars passing on the road, every day, every night, driving away out of this place to another. Going from here to somewhere else.

A Country Dance

On the arm of your chair, your hand for a moment is still; the skin smooth and brown against the faded, red velvet. I touch it lightly with mine. 'Maybe what she needs is more time,' I say.

The air is dense with cigarette smoke, my eyes are tired. You stare past me and begin again to fidget with a silver bracelet on your wrist. I make my tone persuasive: 'Time to regain her identity, a sense of independence, and . . .'

The words are swept from me in a sudden upswell of sound as last orders are called. The climax of the night, and so much left unsaid, undone. Every man in the room is on his feet, shoving for place at the bar, the voices bluff, seductive, as they work for one last round.

'Here, John, two large ones . . .'

'Pat, good man, four more pints . . .'

You ignore them, your gaze holding mine, your attention caught once more by the hope of her name.

'What did you say about independence?'

'I said you need it, need to cultivate it,' something perverse in me all at once, wanting to disappoint you. Your eyes drop, slide to the fireplace where the coal burns with a dim red glow.

'Ah, I thought it was Maeve you meant.'

And what matters after all which way I put it? In

these stories aren't all the characters interchangeable? The lights are turned up full now, the evening over. And you as much in the dark as when we started. If I had used less tact; if I had said straight out what everyone thinks, would it have made a difference? I twist the stub of my last cigarette into the glass ashtray. No, whatever I say you will hear what you choose. Your misery safely walled beyond the reach of logic, however much you may plead with me to advise, console. If you were not fully certain of this, would you have asked me here tonight?

'Time, ladies and gents, please – have you no homes to go to?' The barman turns, the great wash of his belly, supported just clear of the crotch, tilts towards us. He swipes a greasy cloth across the tabletop, forcing us to lift our drinks: 'Come on now, girls.'

I take another sip of my whiskey and replace the glass emphatically on the cardboard coaster. You clasp your pint to your chest, swilling the dregs in languid circles.

'I don't think I can bear it much longer.'

I look at you, your dark eyes have grown sullen with pain, under the clear skin of your cheek a nerve twitches. Years ago, I would have believed you. Believed your hurt unlooked for – believed even in your will to escape it. Now, too many nights like this one have altered me. Too many nights spent in comforting others, watching while each word of sympathy is hoarded as a grain of salt to nourish the wound. On the blackness of the window I watch beads of rain glance brilliant as diamonds, each one falling distinct, separate, then merging – drawn together in swift streams to the ground. Why try to impose reason? Let you have your grand passion, the first taste of self-torment – never so sweet or keen again.

'Look, will you have another drink?' I say in a last attempt to cheer you, 'they might give us one yet.'

Instantly your face brightens. 'Thanks, but you've bought enough,' you say, and add lightly as if you'd just thought of it, 'Did you see someone has left a pint over there – will I get it?'

Without waiting for a reply, you slide your narrow

hips in their scarlet jeans between our table and the bar. You reach for the pint of Harp and a half-finished cocktail. The barman swings round. 'Have you got twenty Marlboros?' you ask to distract him. While he roots on a shelf above the till, you slip the drinks over to me and turn back with a smile. Seeing it, placated, he tosses the cigarettes in the air, beating you to the catch. 'What has such a nice looking girl alone at this hour?' he asks, his voice oiled, insistent. You stand and say nothing. Your smile ransom enough. 'Go home to your bed,' he says, and throws the pack along the wet counter.

'Jesus, the things you have to do around here for a drink.' You fling yourself down on the seat beside me, close so that our knees and shoulders touch.

'You don't have to,' I say.

'Is that right?' you answer and raise one skeptical eyebrow. You pick up the cocktail glass and hold it to your nose. 'Is it gin or what?'

'I don't know and I certainly don't want it.'

Fishing a slice of stale lemon from the clouded liquid, you knock it back and reach for the Harp.

'Easy on,' I say, 'you'll be pissed at this rate.'

You take no notice, your head thrown back, drinking with total concentration. I watch Pat, the young barboy, guide customers to the door. A big woman, her pink dress stretched tight across her thighs, is hanging on his arm. She tells him what a fine looking lad he is, and laughs something caressively in his ear.

'Ah, wouldn't I love to, Molly, but what would Peter have to say?' Slapping her flanks with the flat of his hand, he winks across at me, and slams the door behind her. Outside, in the carpark, someone is singing in a drunken baritone: 'Strangers in the night, exchanging glances, wondering in the night . . .'

'At this stage of the evening,' I say, 'everyone is wondering.'

'About what?' you ask. You run your fingers idly through your long hair, puzzled but incurious.

'Nothing,' I reply. 'A silly joke – just the crowd outside singing.'

You have noticed no singing, much less the words that accompany it. Your gaze is fixed resolutely on the uncleared tables – you have spotted one more in the corner. It's obvious now that you have no intention of going home sober, but we cannot sit here all night and I do not want Paddy to catch you lifting leftovers.

'Well, if you want to stay on,' I say smiling at you, as though it were the very thing I wanted myself, 'why don't we finish what we have in comfort, next door?' I look towards the hallway and an unmarked wooden door on the far side. You are on your feet at once, gathering our glasses, not caring where we go so long as there is a drink at the end of it.

A thin Persian carpet covers the floor of the residents' lounge. On the dim papered walls hang red, satin shaded lamps with frayed gold fringing, and three framed prints – hunting scenes – men and animals confused in the dark oils. A few of the regulars have drawn armchairs up to the fire. Pipe tobacco and the scent of cloves from their hot whiskeys hang together in the air. A man is kneeling over the coal bucket, struggling to open the tongs. He has the red face and shrunken thighs of the habitual toper. 'What the bloody fuck is wrong with this yoke anyway?' he says.

'Here, let me,' leaving him the tongs, you lift the bucket and empty half its contents into the grate. You rattle the poker through the bars, shifting the live coals from front to back. Dust crackles. After a moment, shoots of yellow flame break from the new untouched black.

'Nothing like a good fire,' the man announces, rubbing together his blue-veined hands, 'I always like to build up a good fucking fire.'

His eyes follow the line of your flank, taut and curved as you bend to the hearth. His tongue slides over his bottom lip. 'Always like to build up a good fire,' he repeats as though it were something witty.

He looks towards me; suddenly conscious of my presence and gives a deferential nod. 'Excuse the language,' he calls over. He has placed me then as protector, older sister. And why not after all? Is it not the role I have adopted since that first day I met you in Grafton Street, walking blinded by tears, after one of your quarrels? Did I not even then, that first moment laying eyes on you, want to protect you, from Maeve – from yourself – from that reckless vulnerability of yours, that touched some hidden nerve in me? But it was not protection you wanted, it was empathy. You wanted me to look on, with everyone else, impassive, while you tormented yourself struggling to retain a love that had already slipped into obligation. Though you would not see it – you would see nothing but your own desire. Night after night, following her, watching; your wide, innocent eyes stiff with pain, while she ignored you or flirted with someone else. Waiting because at the end of the evening she might turn, and on an impulse of guilt ask you to go home with her.

'The last one, I think, do you want it?' You hand me an almost full pint of Guinness – brown, sluggish, the froth gone from it. I accept with a wry smile, why not – nothing worse than being empty-handed among drunks, and you clearly will not be hurried.

'Are they residents?' you ask with vague curiosity, looking towards the threesome on the opposite side of the fire.

'No, just regulars,' I say, and none more regular than Peg Maguire. Peg who is here every night with one man or another, drinking herself into amiability. A woman with three children who might be widowed or separated – no one asks. With her blonde hair piled above her head, lipstick a little smudged at the corners, her white coat drawn tight about her as though she were just on the point of departure, Peg – shrewd, jaunty – always careful to maintain the outward show. 'But you know country hotels: once the front door is shut you could stay forever.' I should not have said that, of course, it encourages you. You will have to stay over with me now, I suppose, you are long past driving.

I take a deep draught of the bitter stout, letting it slip quickly down my throat, and to keep this first lightness of mood, I ask you about the college. You are bored, dismissive. Second year is worse than first, you tell me – the life drawing is hopeless, you have only one male model and he wears a g-string; afraid of getting it on in front of women. 'Anyway, I haven't been there for a week – too stoned,' you add as if that exonerated you. Tossing your head back to sweep the hair from your face. For which of us, I wonder, do you present this elaborate disdain.

'You'll come to a sorry end,' I warn you. 'All this dope and sex at nineteen destroys the appetite.' I have made you smile, a slow, lilting smile, that draws your lips from white, perfect teeth.

'Is that what happened to you?' you ask.

'Perhaps it is. I would say I have decayed into wisdom. A forty-hour week and a regular lover – no unfulfilled lust masquerading as romance.'

'Don't tell me you are not romantic about Jan,' you look at me intently, your eyes at once teasing and solemn, 'when anyone can see you're mad about her.'

'That's one way of putting it, I suppose. At least the feeling is mutual so there is no aggravation.'

'And what about Liz?' you ask. 'Was it not very hard on her?'

'Oh, Liz had other interests,' I say. 'There was no heartache there.'

I have shocked you. You want fervour and longing, not this glib detachment. Should I tell you I am posing, or am I? Is there anything I cherish more than my independence? You lean forward, the cigarette at your mouth, gripped between thumb and forefinger, urging some story of need or rejection.

'You know, it is possible for people to care for each other without tearing their souls out,' I hear my voice, deliberately unemotional. 'All this strife and yearning is a myth invented to take our minds off the mess around us. Happiness distracts no one.' And what is it that impels me to disillusion you? Is it only that this intensity of yours so clearly hurts no one but yourself? With impatience you fan the trail of blue smoke from your face and cut me short.

'Ah, you are always so cynical. You would think thirty is middle age the way you go on. Anyway it's different for you. You have your work – something you really care about. It's all different.'

And so, maybe it is. What answer could I give you that would not be twisting the knife?

You stare into the fire, blazing now. The flames bouncing up the chimney throw great splashes of light about the room. Dance on the red brown of your hair. You have finished your cigarette. Your hands in your lap are curiously still – palms upturned. My own lean, fidgeting. I look about the room, at the rubber plant in the corner, the gilt-framed mirror above the mantel-piece – from it my eyes stare back at me, to my surprise still bright and sharp; a gleaming blue. I notice the faint tracing of lines at the corners. First signs. Give up the fags for good next week – get a few early nights. I look towards you. Your lips are at the rim of your glass, sipping at it, stretching it out. Do you dread going home so much?

'You can stay over with me, you know. Anna is in town – you can have her bed. Maybe you would come jogging in the morning – do you good.'

Roused for a moment, you regard me slowly, from shoulders to thigh, appraising me. 'Aw, I'm not in your shape,' you say. 'I wouldn't last more than a mile.'

'Well, you can walk while I run,' I answer, but your gaze has slipped back to the fire, watching the leap of the flames as if they held some private message. We sit in silence, lulled by the heat and alcohol until I break it to ask – 'What are you thinking?' Foolish question, as though you would tell me. But you do, holding my eyes to yours, you answer slowly: 'I was wondering if I might ring Maeve – she could be . . .'

'At this hour? You are incorrigible.' I do not try to hide my irritation. 'I thought you said you were going to keep away for a week . . .'

You begin to smile again. For a moment I wonder if you are playing with me. Then your face shuts, suddenly, as though a light had been switched off. 'You are right, of course. I'd forgotten.'

And why should I strain to follow these moods? If it were not that you look so forlorn, huddled in your chair, like an animal shut out in the rain.

'You are inconsolable, aren't you?' I say, hoping to tease you out of it. 'Tell me, have you not, even for five minutes, been attracted to another woman?'

You turn away abruptly, as though I had struck you, and ask over-loudly; 'Do you think we can get something to take away?'

'Is it a drink you want?' one of Peg's friends calls over. He has been listening to us for some time, his gaze flickering between us like a snake's tongue. 'I'll get you a drink,' he offers.

'It's all right thanks,' I say quickly.

'No, no, I insist. Name your poison, girls.' His speech is slurred. Conscious of it he repeats each sentence. 'Pat will give us a bottle – no trouble.' He hauls himself up from his chair, clutching the mantelpiece. Peg grabs at his arm.

'Pat has gone off hours ago – don't bother yourself.'

'No bother. Got to get these lassies a drink. Can't send them home thirsty,' he rolls a watering eye at us.

'And what would you know about thirst – you've never been dry long enough to have one.' Peg is an old friend and wants no trouble with me. 'Sit down, Frank and don't be annoying the girls.'

'Who's annoying anyone, Peg Maguire – certainly not you – not if you were the last bloody woman on earth.'

We have set them bickering between themselves now. Time to go. But you are edgy, persistent. 'Is there really no chance of another drink?' you ask Peg. She lowers her voice and gives you a conspiratorial look.

'What is it you want – would a six-pack do? If you come with us to the Mountain View, I'll get you something there. They've a disco with late closing.'

'The very thing,' Frank roars. 'A disco tit. Let's all go. Two such lovely young women need . . .' he staggers to his feet once more and begins to sing, 'I could have danced all night – I could have danced all night and still have begged for more. I could have spread my wings,' he wheels his arms in a jagged circle almost knocking Peg's glass, 'and done a thousand things, I'd never done . . .'

'Will you for God's sake hold on to yourself,' Peg

snaps furiously, and pushes him forward.

'Are you right then, girls,' she nods towards us. 'I'll give you the lift down and you can walk back. It's only ten minutes.'

Well, that has done it. There will be no stopping you now. We will not get home, 'till you are soused. And why should I try to deter you? Have I anything better to offer? All the tired virtues. Useless. I should be exasperated by you, dragging me all over the country as if a pint of stout were the holy grail. But something about you halts me. As you move to the door, something exaggerated in you – the turn of your shoulders, your head thrown back as though pulling from harness. Defiance and vulnerability in every line. Something more than youth. Something more than me as I was before I learnt – and who was it who finally taught me? – the hard-won pleasures of realism and self-sufficiency. Yet if I had the power to bestow them on you, this very instant, would I want to?

In the unlit carpark we find Peg's Fiat and pile in – Frank pulling me towards his knee: 'If you were the only girl in the world and I was the only boy.' Rain slashes at the windscreen, one wiper stuck halfway across it. Peg seems to drive by ear. Wet fir trees arching over us make a black tunnel of the road. The road to God knows where. I recognise none of it, letting myself be carried forward – lapsing into the heedless collective will. All needs converging in the simple drive for one more drink. 'Nothing else would matter in the world today . . .' Frank's whiskey breath encircles us. We reach tall, silver gates, pass them, and sluice through rain-filled craters in the drive, the wind snapping at our wheels. A furious night – clouds blown as fast as leaves across the sky. Lights ahead – the tall Georgian house bright in welcome. Braking almost on the front steps, Peg jumps out, leaving the door wide: 'I'll put in a word for you.' We follow, our faces lowered from the rain. In the hallway with the bouncer, her blonde head bent to his ear, she is confidential, explaining that we want only a takeaway – no admission. Solemn as a mother entrusting her daughters. Then she turns back to the car and her boys waiting outside. She throws a wicked grin at me over her shoulder – why? – 'Enjoy yourselves girls,' and she is off.

Out of the night – into a frenzy of light and sound. We push through the black swing doors. Red and purple light, great shafts of it, beat against the walls and floor. The music hammers through my chest, shivering my arms. A man and woman locked together, move in a tight circle at the centre of the room. In the corner, beside a giant speaker, two girls on stiletto heels dance an old-fashioned jive. We push through the wall of shoulders at the bar, country boys shy of dancing. 'Two large bottles of stout,' I order. The barman reaches for pint glasses and shoves them under the draught tap. 'Bottles – to take away,' I call across to him. But it is useless, he has already moved to the far end of the counter to measure out whiskey.

'We will just have to drink them here,' you say, putting your mouth close to my ear so that I feel the warmth of your breath. So be it – at least we are in from the rain for a while.

We choose a corner table, as far from the speakers as possible, but still I have to shout to make you hear me.

'It's easier if you whisper,' you say, bringing your lips to my ear once more, in demonstration.

'You are used to these places, I suppose.' It is years since I have sat like this. Though so little has altered. The lights and music more violent maybe, the rest unchanging. Nobody really wants to be here, it seems. Young women dressed for romance display them-selves – bringing their own glamour. The men stand banded in council, shoulders raised as a barrier, until they have drunk enough. The faces are bored or angry. Each one resenting his need, grudging submission to this ritual fever.

You finish half your pint at one go and offer the glass to me. I down the remainder and together we start on the next, laughing. A rotating light on the ceiling spins a rainbow of colours; blue, red, gold, each thrust devouring the last. Smoke hangs in heavy green clouds about us. As though it were the fumes of

53

marijuana, I breathe it deep into my lungs and feel suddenly a burst of dizzy gaiety . . . the absurdity of it all – that we should be here. And back to me come memories of years ago – adolescence, when it might have been the scene of passion, or was it even then absurd? The pace slows and three couples move to the centre of the floor. 'I don't want to talk about it – how you broke my heart.' The voice of Rod Stewart rasps through the speakers in an old song. But a favourite of yours. We have danced to it once before – in the early hours at Clare's party two weeks ago, when Maeve had left without you. You stand beside me now and in pantomime stretch your hand. 'Will you dance with me?' You walk ahead on to the floor. Under the spotlight your white shirt is luminous – your eyes seem black. You rest your hands on your hips, at the centre of the room, waiting.

'If you stay here just a little bit longer – if you stay here – won't you listen to my heart . . .' We step into each other's arms. Our cheeks touch. I smell the scent of your shirt – the darkness of your hair. Your limbs are easy, assured against mine. Your hands familiar, hold me just below the waist. We turn the floor, elaborately slow, in one movement, as though continuing something interrupted. The music lapping thigh and shoulder. 'The stars in the sky don't mean nothing to you – they're a mirror.' Round we swing, round; closer in each widening circle. Lost to our private rhythm. The foolish words beating time in my blood.

I open my eyes. The music has stopped. Behind you I see a man standing; his eyes riveted to our bodies, his jaw dropped wide as though it had been punched. In his maddened stare I see reflected what I have refused to recognise through all these weeks. Comfort, sympathy, a protective sister – who have I been deceiving? I see it now in his eyes. Familiar at once in its stark simplicity. Making one movement of past and future. I yield myself to it; humbled, self-mocking. Quick as a struck match.

As if I had spoken aloud, with a light pressure of my hand, you return to consciousness and walk from the floor.

I follow, my skin suddenly cold. I want as quickly as possible to be gone from the spotlight. I have remembered where we are: a Friday night country dance, surrounded by drunken males who have never before seen two women dance in each other's arms. All about the room they are standing still, watching. As we cross the empty space to our table no one moves. I notice for the first time Brid Keane from the post office: she is leaning against the wall, arms folded, her face contorted in a look of such disgust, it seems for a moment that she must be putting it on.

'Let's get out of here – as soon as you've finished your drink,' I whisper.

'What – do you want another drink?' Your voice rises high above the music that has begun again. I stare at you in amazement – is it possible that you haven't noticed, that you don't yet know what we've done? Can you be so naïve or so drunk that you haven't realised whose territory we are on?

And then someone moves from the table behind and pushes into the seat opposite us. Squat, red-faced, his hair oiled across his forehead. He props an elbow on the table, and juts his head forward, struggling to focus his eyes. His pink nylon shirt is open, a white tie knotted about the neck.

'Fucking lesbians,' he says at last, 'Are you bent or what?' The breath gusting into my face is sour with whiskey. We look towards the dancers writhing under a strobe light and ignore him.

'Did you not hear me?' he asks, shoving his face so close to me, I see the sweat glisten on his upper lip. 'I said are you bent – queers?' He drives his elbow against mine so that the stout spills over my glass.

A familiar anger rips through me, making my legs tremble. I press my nails into the palm of my hand and say nothing. I will not satisfy him so easily.

'What were you saying about the music?' I throw you a smile.

'I asked you a question,' he says. 'Will you give me a bloody answer.' He runs the words together as though speed were his only hope of completing them.

'I said it's lousy,' you reply, 'about ten years out of date.'

He looks from me to you and back again with baffled irritation and his voice grows querulous. He asks: 'Look, would one of you lesbians give me a dance.'

A friend has joined him now, leaning over the back of your chair, a grin on his lips sly and lascivious.

'Will you not answer me?' the first one shouts, 'or are you fucking deaf?'

Drawing my shoulders up, I turn and for the first time look directly into his eyes. 'No,' I say with warning deliberation, 'we are not deaf, yes, we are lesbians and no, we will not give you a dance.'

He stares at us stupefied, then falls back into his seat, breath hissing from his chest as though a lung had burst. 'Jesus, fucking, Christ.'

You give a whoop of laughter, your eyes wide with delight. It seems you find him hugely amusing. Then you're on your feet and across the room in search of the toilet or God knows another drink.

I have my back turned to him when I feel the pink-sleeved arm nudging mine again. 'Hey, blondie – you've gorgeous hair,' he says, giving an ugly snigger. 'Did anyone ever tell you that?' It is a moment before I recognise the smell of singed hair. I reach my hand to the back of my head and a cigarette burns my fingertips. With a cry of pain, I grab hold of the oily lock across his forehead and wrench hard enough to pull it from the roots. He stretches his arm to catch hold of mine but I tear with all my force. 'You fucking cunt!' he screams.

Suddenly someone catches hold of us from behind and pulls us roughly apart. It's the bouncer – a big red-haired man in a grey suit. When he sees my face he steps back aghast. He had plainly not expected a woman.

'I don't know what you two want,' his voice is cold, contemptuous, 'but whatever it is you can settle it between you – outside.' He drops the hand on my shoulder, wheels round and walks back to his post at the door. At the sight of him my opponent is instantly subdued. He shrinks back into his seat as though he had been whipped, then slowly collapses on to the table, head in his arms.

You return carrying another drink. I wait until you are sitting down to whisper: 'We have to get out of here, Cathy – they're half savage. That one just tried to set fire to my hair.'

'The little creep!' you exclaim, your eyes sparking with indignation. 'Oh, he's easily handled – but the rest of them, look.'

At the bar a group of six or seven are standing in a circle drinking. Big farm boys in tweed jackets – older than the others and more sober. Their gaze has not left us, I know, since we walked off the dance floor, yet they have made no move. This very calm is what frightens me. In their tense vigilance, I feel an aggression infinitely more threatening than the bluster of the two next us. Hunters letting the hounds play before closing in?

'I think they might be planning something,' I say, and, as if in response to some prearranged signal, one of them breaks from the group and slowly makes his way to our table.

His pale, thin face stares into mine, he makes a deep bow and stretches out his hand. 'Would one of you ladies care to dance?'

I shake my head wearily. 'No, thanks.'

He gives a scornful shrug of the shoulders and walks back to his companions. A moment later another one sets out. When he reaches us, he drops to one knee before you and for the benefit of those watching, loudly repeats the request. When you refuse him he retreats with the same show of disdain.

'They can keep this going all night,' I say, 'building the pressure. With their mad egotism anything is better than being ignored.' And I know also what I do not say, that we have to put up with it. They have us cornered. Under all the theatrics lies the clear threat that if we dare to leave, they can follow, and once outside, alone in the dark, they will have no need for these elaborate games.

'What can we do?' you ask, twisting a strand of hair about your finger, your eyes attentive at last.

'I'll go off for a few minutes. Maybe if we separate, if

they lose sight of us, they might get distracted.'

Five minutes later, pushing my way through the crowd to our table, I find you chatting with the one in the pink shirt and his mate, smoking and sharing their beer like old drinking pals. How can you be so unconcerned? I feel a sudden furious irritation. But you look up at me and smile warningly. 'Humour them,' I read in the movement of your lips. And you may be right. They have turned penitent now, ingratiating: 'We never meant to insult you, honest, love. We only wanted to be friendly.' His head lolling back and forth, he stabs a finger to his chest: 'I'm Mick, and this is me mate Gerry.'

All right then, let us try patience. At least while we are seen talking to these two the others will hold off.

'You know, blondie, I think you're something really special,' with the deadly earnest of the drunk, Mick addresses me. 'I noticed you the second you walked in. I said to Gerry – didn't I Gerry? Blondie, would you not give it a try with me? I know you're into women – your mate explained – and that's all right with me – honest – that's cool, you know what I mean? But you never know 'till you try, do you? Might change your life. Give us a chance, love.' He careens on through his monologue, long past noticing whether I answer or not. On the opposite side I hear Gerry, working on you with heavy flattery, admiring your eyes (glistening now – with drink or anger – dark as berries), praising the deep red of your lips – parted at the rim of your glass. And you are laughing into his face and drinking his beer. Your throat thrown back as you swallow, strong and naked.

Mick has collapsed, his head on the table drooping against my arm. 'Just one night,' he mutters into my sleeve, 'that's all I'm asking – just one night. Do yourself a favour.' His words seep through my brain, echoing weirdly, like water dripping in a cave. Drumming in monotonous background to the movements of your hands and face. Half turned from me, I do not hear what you answer Gerry, but I catch your tone; languorous, abstracted, I watch you draw in the spilt froth on the table. Your eyes lowered, the lashes black along your cheek, one finger traces the line of a half moon. Behind you I see the same group watching from the bar; patient, predatory. My blood pounds – fear and longing compete in my veins.

And then all at once, the music stops. Everyone stands to attention, silent. The disc-jockey is making an announcement: the offer of a bottle of whiskey, a raffle, the buying of tickets – gripping them as the music and dance never could. This is our moment, with Gerry moving to the bar to buy cigarettes and Mick almost asleep, slumped backwards, his mouth dropped open. I grasp your hand beneath the table, squeezing it so that you may feel the urgency and no one else, and look towards the green exit sign. We are across the floor, stealthy and cautious as prisoners stepping between the lights of an armed camp. At the door at last, 'Fucking whoores – you needn't trouble yourselves to come back,' the bouncer restraining fury in the slam of the swing doors behind us.

And we are out.

Out in the wet darkness. The wind beating escape at our backs. I catch your hand. 'Run and don't stop.' Our feet scatter the black puddles, soaking our shins. The fir trees flapping at our sides beckon, opening our path to the gates. So much further now. The moon will not help – hidden from us by sheets of cloud – withholding its light. We run blind, my heart knocking at my ribs; following the track only by the sting of gravel through my thin soles. 'Come on – faster.' The gates spring towards us out of nowhere – caught in a yellow shaft of brightness. A car rounds the bend behind us, the water flung hissing from its tyres. We dodge under the trees, the drenched boughs smacking my cheek. The headlights are on us, devouring the path up to and beyond the open gates. The window rolled down, I hear the drunken chanting – like the baying of hounds: 'We're here because we're queer because we're here because we're . . .' 'Great fucking crack, lads . . .' Gone. Past us. Pitched forward in the delirium of the chase – seeing nothing to left or right. A trail of cigarette smoke in the air.

'All right – we can go on now,' you say, laughing –

drawing me out from cover. 'Do you think it was them?'

'Yes, or worse. We had better be gone before the next lot.'

We run on again, through the wide gates to the main road. The alcohol is washing through me now, spinning my head. My heart is beating faster than ever, though the fear has left me. You are beginning to tire. 'We are almost there,' I urge you, marvelling that you can still stand, let alone run. The rain darts in the gutter, the leaves slithering under our feet. Jumping a pool I slip towards you. Your arm outflung steadies me. You're laughing again – the long looping kind you do not want to stop. 'You're worse than I am,' you say.

The moon all at once throws open the night before us, scattering in sequins on the tarred road, silver on the hanging trees. I see the house massed and still in its light.

'We are home,' I say.

You slow your pace and let go of my hand. Your eyes under the white gleam of the moon are darker than ever – secretive.

'Are you laughing at me?' I ask, to capture your attention.

'I'm not – really,' you answer, surprised.

I lift the latch of the gate, softly so as to wake no one. How am I to keep this? To keep us from slipping back into the everyday: the lighted, walled indoors – all the managed, separating things. And what is it I fear to lose? Any more than my desire – dreaming yours. Any more than a drunken joy in escape?

The cat comes through a gap in the hedge, whipping my shins with her tail. I lift her to me and she gives a low, rough cry.

'She's been waiting for you,' you tell me.

I turn the key in the kitchen door. You step inside and stand by the window, the moonlight falling like a pool of water about your feet. I gaze at your shoes for no reason; at the pale, wet leather, muddied now.

'Well, that looked bad for a moment,' I say, putting my arm round you, not knowing whether it is you or myself I am consoling. 'Were you not frightened at all?'

'Oh yes, I was,' you answer, leaning into me, pulling me close. 'Yes.'

And so, I have been right. So much more than comfort. I slide my lips down your cheek, still hesitant, measuring your answer. And you lift your open mouth to meet mine. I have imagined nothing, then. Everything. All this long night has been a preparation – an appeal. You untie the belt of my raincoat. I feel your hands, still cold from the night rain, along my sides: 'I'm freezing. Are you?'

'Yes.'

'Are there beds anywhere in this house?'

'We might find one.'

You laugh. I take your hand and silently, as though fearful of waking someone, we cross the hall together and climb the wooden staircase.

The room is dark but for a shaft of moonlight which falls across the double bed, with its silver and wine red quilt, that waits at the centre of the floor. I light a candle by the window. You sit on the cane chair and unlace your sneakers, slowly, knot by knot. Then stand and drop your clothes – red jeans and white shirt – in a ring about them. I turn back the sheets and step towards you. Downstairs the phone sounds, cracking the darkness like a floodlight. It rings and rings and will not stop. 'I had better answer it,' I say and move to the door.

'Who was it?' When I return, you are sitting propped against the pillow, easy as though you spent every night here. I cannot tell you that it was Jan, feeling amorous, wanting to chat, imagining me alone.

'Jan . . .' I begin, but you do not wait to hear. Reaching your hand behind my head you pull my mouth towards you. I feel, but do not hear the words you speak against my lips.

The rain drives at the window, shivering the curtains. The wind blown up from the sea sings in the stretched cables. Your body strains to mine, each movement at once a repetition and discovery. Your mouth, greedy and sweet, sucks the breath from my lungs. I draw back from your face, your long dark hair

and look in your eyes: you are laughing again – a
flame at the still black centre. Your tongue seals my
eyelids shut. Your hands, travelling over me, startle
the skin as if they would draw it like a cover from
muscle and bone. We move – bound in one breath –
muscle, skin and bone. I kiss you from forehead to
thigh. Kiss the fine secret skin beneath your breast, the
hard curve of your belly.

The wind moans through the slates of the roof. The
house shifts. Beneath us the sea crashes on the stones
of the shore. Your voice comes clear above them
beating against mine, high above the wind and rain.
Spilling from the still centre – wave after wave. And
then, a sudden break; a moment's straining back as
though the sea were to check for one instant –
resisting – before its final drop to land. But the sea
does not.

You lie quiet above me. I taste the salt of tears on
my tongue.

'Are you crying? What is it?'

'No, I'm not,' you answer gently, your head turned
from me. Maybe so. I close my arms about you,
stroking the silk of your back, finding no words. But it
does not matter. Already you have moved beyond me
into sleep. I lie still. Clouds have covered the moon,
blackening the window of sky. I cannot see your face.
Your body is heavy on mine, your breath on my cheek.
I soothe myself with its rhythm. The rain has ceased. I
hear once more the small night sounds of the house:
the creak of wood in floorboards and rafters, the purr
of the refrigerator. Then suddenly there comes a loud
crash – the noise of cup or plate breaking on the
kitchen's tiled floor. My breath stops – you do not stir.
I hear the squeal of a window swung on its hinge. A
dull thud. Footsteps?

Before my eyes a face rises: mottled cheeks, beads of
sweat along the lip. A wild fear possesses me that he
or his friends have followed us, come here to this
house in search of us. I slide gently from under you. I
creep to the door and stand listening for a moment,
breath held, before opening it. Silence . . . Nothing but
the hum of the 'fridge. And then . . . a soft, triumphal

62

cry. Of course – the cat. How well I know that call. Elsie has caught a rat or bird and brought it home through the window. In the morning there will be a trail of blood and feathers on the carpet. Time enough to deal with it tomorrow.

I go back to bed. Lifting the sheet I press near to your warmth, my belly fitting exactly in the well of your back. I breathe the strange, new scent of you. A shudder goes through my limbs. I reach my hand and gently gather the weight of your breast. I feel the pulsing through the fine veins beneath the surface. You stir, sighing, and press your thighs against mine. You murmur something from sleep – a word, or name. Someone's name.

My arms slacken. I taste your tears, again, on my lips. In the morning what will we say to each other? Drunk as you were it will be easy to forget, to pretend the whole thing an accident. No need then to prepare an attitude – for Maeve (when she calls, as she will, as before, thanking me for taking care of you), for Jan – for ourselves. The night is fading at the window. The bare branch of the sycamore knocks on the wall behind us. Words echo in my mind, the words of the song we danced to, foolish, mocking: 'The stars in the sky mean nothing to you – they are a mirror.' And to me? What was it I said this evening about romantic illusion? I reach out my hand for the candlestick on the table. As I lift it, the flame flares golden. My movement has woken you. You regard me, for an instant, startled. How childish you look, your forehead smooth, your eyes washed clear. Was it only your hurt that set a cord between us – that lent you the outline of maturity? 'I thought I heard a noise downstairs,' you say.

'Yes, but it was nothing,' I kiss your eyes shut. 'Only the cat with a bird,' I answer as you move into sleep, your cheek at my shoulder. 'Nothing.'

Far out to sea, a gull cries against the coming of light. For a little longer night holds us beyond the grasp of speech. I lean and blow the candle out.

The Husband

They made love then once more because she was leaving him. Sunlight came through the tall, Georgian window. It shone on the blue walls, the yellow paintwork, warming her pale, blonde hair, the white curve of her closed eyelids. He gripped her hands, their fingers interlocked, his feet braced against the wooden footboard. He would have liked to break her from the mould of her body; from its set, delicate lines. His mouth at her shoulder, his eyes were hidden, and he was glad to have his back turned on the room; from the bare dressing table stripped of her belongings, and the suitcase open beside the wardrobe.

Outside other people were going to mass. He heard a bell toll in the distance. A man's voice drifted up: 'I'll see you at O'Brien's later', then the slam of a car door and the clatter of a woman's spiked heels hurrying on the pavement. All the usual sounds of Sunday morning rising distinct and separate for the first time in the silence between them. She lay beneath him passive, magnanimous, as though she were granting him a favour, out of pity or gratitude because she had seen that he was not, after all, going to make it difficult for her at the end. He moved inside her body, conscious only of the sudden escape of his breath, no longer caring what she felt, what motive possessed her. He was tired of thinking, tired of the labour of anticipating her thoughts and concealing his own.

He knew that she was looking past him, over his shoulder towards the window, to the sunlight and noise of the street. He touched a strand of her hair where it lay along the pillow. She did not turn. A tremor passed through his limbs. He felt the sweat grow cold on his back. He rolled off her and lay still, staring at the ceiling where small flakes of whitewash peeled from the moulded corners. The sun had discovered a spider's web above the door; like a square of grey lace, its diamond pattern swayed in a draught from the stairs. He wondered how it had survived the winter and why it was he had not noticed it before. Exhaustion seeped through his flesh bringing a sensation of calm. Now that it was over at last he was glad, now that there was nothing more to be done. He had tried everything and failed. He had lived ten years in the space of one; altered himself by the hour to suit her and she had told him it made no difference, that it was useless, whatever he did, because it had nothing to do with him personally, with individual failing. He could not accept that, could not resign himself to being a mere cog in someone else's political theory. He had done all that he knew to persuade, to understand her. He had been by turns argumentative, patient, skeptical, conciliatory. The night when, finally, she had told him it was over he had wept in her arms, pleaded with her, vulnerable as any woman, and she had remained indifferent, patronising even, seeing only the male he could not cease to be. They said they wanted emotion, honesty, self-exposure but when they got it, they despised you for it. Once, and once only, he had allowed the rage in him to break free; let loose the cold fury that had been festering in his gut since the start of it. She had come home late on Lisa's birthday, and when she told him where she had been, blatantly, flaunting it, he had struck her across the face, harder than he had intended so that a fleck of blood showed on her lip. She had wiped it off with the back of her hand, staring at him, a look of shock and covert satisfaction in her eyes. He knew then in his shame and regret that he had given her the excuse she had been waiting for.

He looked at her now, at the hard pale arch of her cheekbone. He waited for her to say something, but she kept silent and he could not let himself speak the only words that were in his mind. She would see them as weakness. Instead, he heard himself say her name, 'Martina,' not wanting to, but finding it form on his lips from force of habit: a sound – a collection of syllables that had once held absolute meaning, and now meant nothing or too much, composed as it was of so many conflicting memories.

She reached a hand past his face to the breakfast cup that stood on the bedside table. A dark, puckered skin had formed on the coffee's surface but she drank it anyway. 'What?' she said without looking at him. He felt that she was preparing her next move, searching for a phrase or gesture that would carry her painlessly out of his bed and from their flat. But when she did speak again there was no attempt at prevarication or tact. 'I need to shower,' she said bluntly, 'can you let me out?' She swung her legs over the side of the bed, pushing back the patterned sheet, and stood up. He watched her walk across the room away from him. A small mark like a circle of chalk dust gleamed on the muscle of her thigh – his seed dried on her skin. The scent and taste of him would be all through her. She would wash meticulously every inch of her body to remove it. He heard her close the bathroom door behind her and, a moment later, the hiss and splatter of water breaking on the shower curtain. Only a few weeks ago she would have run a bath for them both and he would have carried Lisa in to sit between their knees. Yesterday afternoon he had brought Lisa over to her mother's house. Martina had said she thought it was best if Lisa stayed there for a couple of weeks until they could come to some arrangement. Some arrangement! For Lisa! He knew then how crazed she was. Of course, it was an act – a pretence of consideration and fairmindedness, wanting it to appear that she might even debate the merits of leaving their daughter with him. But he knew what she planned, all too well.

He had a vision of himself calling over to Leinster

Road on a Saturday afternoon, standing on the front step ringing the bell. She would come to the door and hold it open, staring at him blankly as if he were a stranger while Lisa ran to greet him. Would Helen be there too with that smug, tight, little smile on her mouth? Would they bring him in to the kitchen and make tea and small talk while Lisa got ready, or would they have found some excuse to have her out for the day? He knew every possible permutation, he had seem them all a dozen times on television and seventies' movies, but he never thought he might be expected to live out these banalities himself. His snort of laughter startled him. He could not remember when he had last laughed aloud. But who would not at the idea that the mother of his child could imagine this cosy Hollywood scenario might become reality? When she had first mentioned it, dropping it casually as a vague suggestion, he had forced himself to hold back the derision that rose to his tongue. He would say nothing. Why should he? Let her learn the hard way. They would all say it for him soon enough: his parents, her mother. The instant they discovered the truth, who and what she had left him for, they would snatch Lisa from her as ruthlessly as they would from quicksand. They would not be shackled by any qualms of conscience. They would have none of his need to show fine feeling. It was extraordinary that she did not seem to realise this herself; unthinkable that she might, and not allow it to influence her.

She came back into the room, her legs bare beneath a shaggy red sweater. The sweater he had bought her for Christmas. Her nipples protruded like two small stones from under the loose wool. She opened the wardrobe and took out a pair of blue jeans and a grey corduroy skirt. He saw that she was on the point of asking him which he preferred. She stood in the unconsciously childish pose she assumed whenever she had a decision to make, however trivial: her feet apart, her head tilted to one side. He lay on his back watching her, his hands interlaced between the pillow and his head. He could feel the blood pulsing behind his ears but he kept his face impassive. She was studying her image in the mirror, eyes wide with anxious vanity. At last she dropped the jeans into the open case and began to pull on the skirt. Why – was that what Helen would have chosen? What kind of look did she go for? Elegant, sexy, casual? But then they were not into looks – oh no, it was all on a higher, spiritual plane. Or was it? What did she admire in her anyway? Was it the same qualities as he, or something quite different, something hidden from him? Was she turned on by some reflection of herself or by some opposite trait, something lacking in her own character? He could not begin to guess. He knew so little about this woman Martina was abandoning him for. He had left it too late to pay her any real attention. He had been struck by her the first night, he had to admit, meeting her in O'Brian's after that conference. He liked her body; the long legs and broad shoulders and something attractive in the sultry line of her mouth. A woman he might have wanted himself in other circumstances. If he had not been told immediately that she was a lesbian. Not that he would have guessed it – at least not at first glance. She was too goodlooking for that. But it did not take long to see the coldness in her, the chip on the shoulder, the arrogant, belligerent way she stood at the bar and asked him what he wanted to drink. But then she had every reason for disdain, had she not? She must have known already that his wife was in love with her. It had taken him a year to reach the same conclusion.

She sat on the bed to pull on her stockings, one leg crossed over the other. He heard her breathing – quick little breaths through her mouth. She was nervous then. He stared at the round bone of her ankle as she drew the red mesh over it. He followed her hands as they moved up the length of her calf. Her body was so intimately known to him he felt he might have cast the flesh on her bones with his own fingers. He saw the stretch marks above her hip. She had lost weight this winter. She looked well, but he preferred her as she used to be – voluptuous: the plump roundness of her belly and arms. He thought of all the days and nights of pleasure that they had had together. She certainly could not complain that he had not appreciated her. He would always be grateful for what he had discovered with her. He would forget none of it. But would she! Oh no. She pretended to have forgotten already. She talked now as though she had been playing an elaborate game all these years – going through ritual actions to please him. When he refused to let her away with that kind of nonsense, the deliberate erasure of their past, and forced her to acknowledge the depth of passion there had been between them, she said, yes, she did not deny that they had had good times in bed but it had very little to do with him. He had laughed in her face. And who was it to do with then? Who else could take credit for it? She did not dare to answer, but even as he asked the question he knew the sort of thing she would come out with. One of Helen's profundities – that straight women use men as instruments, that they make love to themselves through a man's eyes, stimulate themselves with his desire and flattery, but that it is their own sensuality they get off on. He knew every version of their theories by now.

'Would you like some more coffee?' she asked him when she had finished dressing. She was never so hurried that she could go without coffee. He shook his head and she walked out of the room pulling a leather belt through the loops of her skirt. He listened to her light footsteps on the stairs. After a moment he heard her lift the mugs from their hooks on the wall. He heard her fill the percolator with water, place it on the gas stove and, after a while, its rising heart beat as the coffee bubbled through the metal filter. He hung onto each sound, rooting himself in the routine of it, wanting to hide in the pictures they evoked. So long as he could hear her moving about in the kitchen below him, busy with all her familiar actions, it seemed that nothing much could be wrong.

Not that he believed that she would really go through with it. Not all the way. Once it dawned on her finally that indulging this whim would mean giving up Lisa, she would have to come to her senses. Yes, she would be back soon enough with her tail between her legs. He had only to wait. But he would not let her see that he knew this. It would only put her back up – bring out all her woman's pride and obstinacy. He must tread carefully. Follow silently along this crazy pavement she had laid, step by step, until she reached the precipice. And when she was forced back, he would be there, waiting.

If only he had been more cautious from the beginning. If only he had taken it seriously, recognised the danger in time, it would never have reached this stage. But how could he have? How could any normal man have seen it as any more than a joke? He had felt no jealousy at all at the start. She had known it and been incensed. She had accused him of typical male complacency. She had expected scenes, that was evident, wanted them, had tried to goad him into them. But for weeks he had refused to react with anything more threatening than good-humoured sarcasm. He remembered the night she first confessed that Helen and she had become lovers: the anxious, guilty face, expecting God knows what extremes of wrath, and yet underneath it there had been a look of quiet triumph. He had had to keep himself from laughing. He was taken by surprise, undoubtedly, though he should not have been with the way they had been going on – never out of each other's company, the all-night talks and the heroine worship. But frankly he would not have thought Martina was up to it. Oh, she might flirt with the idea of turning on a woman but to commit herself was another thing. She was too fundamentally healthy, and too fond of the admiration of men. Besides, knowing how passionate she was, he could not believe she would settle for the caresses of a woman.

Gradually his amusement had given way to curiosity, a pleasurable stirring of erotic interest. Two women in bed together after all – there was something undeniably exciting in the idea. He had tried to get her to share it with him, to make it something they could both enjoy but, out of embarrassment, or some misplaced sense of loyalty, she had refused. He said to tease her, to draw her out a little, that he would not

70

have picked Helen for the whip and Jack boots type. What did he mean by that, she had demanded menacingly. And when he explained that as, obviously, she herself could not be cast as the butch, Helen was the only remaining candidate, she had flown at him, castigating his prejudice and condescension. Clearly it was not a topic amenable to humour! She told him that all that role playing was a creation of men's fantasies. Dominance and submission were models the women had consigned to the rubbish heap. It was all equality and mutual respect in this brave new world. So where did the excitement, the romance, come in, he wanted to ask. If they had dispensed with all the traditional props what was left? But he knew better than to say anything. They were so stiff with analysis and theory the lot of them it was impossible to get a straightforward answer. Sometimes he had even wondered if they were really lesbians at all. Apart from the fact that they looked perfectly normal, there seemed something overdone about it. It seemed like a public posture, an attitude struck to provoke men – out of spite or envy. Certainly they flaunted the whole business unnecessarily, getting into fights in the street or in pubs because they insisted on their right to self-expression and that the rest of the world should adapt to them. He had even seen one of them at a conference sporting a badge on her lapel that read, 'How dare you presume I'm heterosexual.' Why on earth should anyone presume otherwise unless she was proud of resembling a male impersonator?

And so every time he had attempted to discuss it rationally they had ended by quarrelling. She condemned him of every macho fault in the book and sulked for hours, but afterwards they made it all up in bed. As long as she responded in the old manner, he knew he had not much to worry about. He had even fancied that it might improve their sex life – add a touch of the unknown. He had watched closely to see if any new needs or tastes might creep into her lovemaking.

It was not until the night she had come home in tears that he was forced to re-think his position.

She had arrived in, half drunk at midnight after one of their interminable meetings, and raced straight up to bed without so much as greeting him or going in to kiss Lisa goodnight. He had followed her up, and when he tried to get in beside her to comfort her, she had become hysterical, screamed at him to leave her alone, to keep his hands away from her. It was hours before he managed to calm her down and get the whole story out of her. It seemed that Helen had told her that evening in the pub that she wanted to end the relationship. He was astonished. He had always taken it for granted that Martina would be the first to tire. He was even insulted on her behalf. He soothed and placated her, stroking her hair and murmuring soft words the way he would with Lisa. He told her not to be a fool, that she was far too beautiful to be cast aside by Helen, that she must be the best thing that had ever happened to her. She was sobbing uncontrollably, but she stopped long enough to abuse him when he said that. At last she had fallen asleep in his arms, but for the first time he had stayed awake after her. He had to admit that her hysteria had got to him. He could see then it had become some kind of obsession. Up to then he had imagined it was basically a schoolgirl crush, the sort of thing most girls worked out in their teens. But women were so sentimental. He remembered a student of his saying years ago that men had friendships, women had affairs. He knew exactly what he meant. You had only to watch them, perfectly average housewives sitting in cafés or restaurants together, gazing into each other's eyes in a way that would have embarrassed the most besotted man, the confiding tones they used, the smiles of flattery and sympathy flitting between them, the intimate gestures, touching each other's hand, the little pats and caresses, exasperating waiters while they fought over the right to treat one another.

He had imagined that lesbian lovemaking would have some of this piquant quality. He saw it as gently caressive — tender and solicitous. He began to have fantasies about Martina and Helen together. He allowed himself delicious images of their tentative, childish

72

sensuality. When he and Martina were fucking he had often fantasised lately that Helen was there too, both women exciting each other and then turning to him at the ultimate moment, competing for him. He had thought it was just a matter of time before something of the sort came about. It had not once occurred to him in all that while that they would continue to exclude him, to cut him out mentally and physically, to insist on their self-sufficiency and absorption. Not even that night lying sleepless beside her while she snored, as she always did after too many pints. It did not register with him finally until the afternoon he came home unexpectedly from work and heard them together.

There was no illusion after that, no innocence or humour. He knew it for what it was. Weeks passed before he could rid his mind of the horror of it; it haunted his sleep and fuelled his days with a seething, putrid anger. He saw that he had been seduced, mocked, cheated, systematically, coldbloodedly by assumptions she had worked carefully to foster; defrauded and betrayed. He had stood at the bottom of the stairs – his stairs – in his own house and listened to them. He could hear it from the hall. He listened transfixed, a heaving in his stomach, until the din from the room above rose to a wail. He had covered his ears. Tender and solicitous had he said? More like cats in heat! As he went out of the house, slamming the door after him, he thought he heard them laughing. Bitches – bloody, fucking bitches! He had made it as far as the pub and ordered whiskey. He sat drinking it, glass after glass, grasping the bowl so hard he might have snapped it in two. He was astounded by the force of rage unleashed in him. He would have liked to put his hands around her bare throat and squeeze it until he'd wrung that noise out of it.

Somehow he had managed to get a grip of himself. He had had enough sense to drink himself stupid, too stupid to do anything about it that night. He had slept on the floor in the sitting room and when he woke at noon she had already left for the day. He was glad. He was not going to humiliate himself by fighting for her over a woman. He was still convinced that it was a temporary delirium, an infection that, left to run its course, would sweat itself out. He had only to wait, to play it cool, to think and to watch until the fever broke.

She came back into the room carrying two mugs of coffee. She set one down beside him giving a little nervous smile. She had forgotten he had said he did not want any.

'Are you getting up?' she asked as she took her dressing gown from the back of the door, 'there's some bread in the oven – will you remember to take it out?'

Jesus! How typical of her to bake bread the morning she was leaving. The dough had been left as usual, of course, to rise overnight and she could not bring herself to waste it. Typical of her sublime insensitivity! He had always been baffled by this trait in her, this attention, in no matter what crisis, to the everyday details of life and this compulsion to make little gestures of practical concern. Was it another trick of hers to forestall criticism? Or did she really have some power to rise above her own and other people's emotions? But most likely it was just straightforward, old fashioned guilt.

'Fuck the bread,' he said and instantly regretted it. She would be in all the more hurry now to leave. She went to the wardrobe and began to lift down her clothes, laying them in the suitcase. He watched her hands as they expertly folded blouses, jerseys, jeans, studying every movement so that he would be able to recapture it precisely when she was gone. It was impossible to believe that he would not be able to watch her like this the next day and the day after. That was what hurt the most. The thought that he would lose the sight of her, just that. That he would no longer look on while she dressed or undressed, prepared a meal, read a book or played with Lisa. Every movement of her body familiar to him, so graceful, so completely feminine. He felt that if he could be allowed to watch her through glass, without speaking, like a child gazing through a shop window, he could have been content. He would not dare express it,

74

needless to say. She would have sneered at him. Objectification she would call it. 'A woman's body is all that ever matters to any one of you, isn't it?' And he would not argue because the thing he really prized would be even less flattering to her – her vulnerability, her need to confide, to ask his advice in every small moment of self-doubt, to share all her secret fears. God how they had talked! Hours of it. At least she could never claim that he had not listened. And in the end he had learned to need it almost as much as she did. To chat in the inconsequential way she had, curled together in bed, sitting over a glass of wine till the small hours, drawing out all the trivia of personal existence: the dark, hidden things that bonded you forever to the one person who would hear them from you. Was that a ploy too? a conscious one? or merely female instinct? to tie him to her by a gradual process of self-exposure so that he could not disentangle himself, even now when he had to, because there was no longer any private place left in him, nowhere to hide from her glance, nowhere that she could not seek out and name the hurt in him. This was what had prompted her, an hour earlier, on waking, to make love with him: this instinct for vulnerability that drew her, like a bee to honey, unerringly to need and pain: this feminine lust to console; so that she had made one last generous offering – handing over her body as she might a towel to someone bleeding. And he had taken it, idiot that he was; accepted gratefully – little fawning lap-dog that she had made of him.

She was sitting at the dressing table brushing her hair with slow, attentive strokes, drawing the brush each time from the crown of her head to the tips of her hair where it lay along her shoulder. Was she deliberately making no show of haste, pretending to be doing everything as normal? It seemed to him there must be something he could say; something an outsider would think of immediately. He searched his mind, but nothing came to him but the one question that had persisted in him for days: 'Why are you doing this? I don't understand why you're doing this.' She opened a bottle of cologne and dabbed it lightly on her wrists and neck. She always took particular care preparing herself to meet Helen. Helen, who herself wore some heavy French scent that clung to everything she touched, that was carried home in Martina's hair and clothing after every one of their sessions. But that was perfectly acceptable and politically correct. Adorning themselves for each other – make-up, perfume, eyebrow plucking, exchanging clothes – all these feminine tricks took on new meaning because neither of them was a man. Helen did not need to flatter, she did not need to patronise or idolise, she did not need to conquer or submit, and her desire would never be exploitative because she was a woman dealing with a woman! Neither of them had institutionalised power behind them. This was the logic he had been taught all that winter. They told one another these faery stories sitting round at their meetings. Everything that had ever gone wrong for any one of them, once discussed in their consciousness-raising groups, could be chalked up as a consequence of male domination. And while they sat about indoctrinating each other with this schoolgirl pap, sounding off on radio and television, composing joint letters to the press, he had stayed at home three nights a week to mind Lisa, clean the house, cook meals, and read his way through the bundles of books she brought home: sentimental novels and half-baked political theses that she had insisted he must look at if he was to claim any understanding at all. And at the finish of it, when he had exhausted himself to satisfy her caprices, she said that he had lost his spontaneity, that their relationship had become stilted, sterile and self-conscious. With Helen, needless to say, all was otherwise – effortless and instinctive. God, he could not wait for their little idyll to meet the adult world, the world of electricity bills, dirty dishes and child minding, and see how far their new roles got them! But he had one pleasure in store before then, a consolation prize he had been saving himself. As soon as she was safely out of the house, he would make a bonfire of them – burn every one – every goddamn book with the word woman on its cover!

She fastened the brown leather suitcase, leaving open the lock on the right hand that had broken the summer two years ago when they had come back from Morocco laden down with blankets and caftans. She carried it across the room, trying to lift it clear of the floor, but it was too heavy for her and dragged along the boards. She went out the door and he heard it knocking on each step as she walked down the stairs. He listened. She was doing something in the kitchen but he could not tell what. There followed a protracted silence. It hit him suddenly that she might try to get out of the flat, leave him and go without saying anything at all. He jumped out of bed, grabbed his trousers from the chair and pulled them on, his fingers so clumsy with haste he caught his hair in the zip. Fuck her! When he rooted under the bed for his shoes, she heard and called up: 'Don't bother getting dressed, I'll take the bus.' She did not think he was going to get the car out and drive her over there surely? He took a shirt from the floor and pulled it on over his head as he took the stairs to the kitchen two at a time. She was standing by the stove holding a cup of coffee. This endless coffee drinking of hers, cups all over the house, little white rings marked on every stick of furniture. At least he would not have that to put up with any longer.

'There's some in the pot if you want it,' she said. He could see the percolator was almost full, the smell of it would be all over the flat now, and the smell of the bloody bread in the oven, for hours after she was gone.

'Didn't you make any tea?'

'No,' she said and gave one of her sidelong, maddening looks of apology as though it was some major oversight, 'but there's water in the kettle.'

'Thanks,' he said, 'I won't bother.'

He was leaning his buttocks against the table, his feet planted wide apart, his hands in his pockets. He looked relaxed and in control at least. He was good at that – years of being on stage before a class of students. He wondered if Helen would come to meet her at the bus stop, or was she going to have to lug the suitcase alone all the way up Leinster Road? He wondered how they would greet each other. With triumph or nervousness? Might there be a sense of anti-climax about it now that she had finally committed herself after so much stalling? Would she tell Helen that she had made love with him before leaving? Would she be ashamed of it and say nothing? But probably Helen would take it for granted as an insignificant gesture to male pride, the necessary price of freedom. And suddenly he wished that he had not been so restrained with her, so much the considerate, respectful friend she had trained him to be. He wished that he had taken his last opportunity and used her body as any other man would have – driven the pleasure out of it until she had screamed as he had heard her that day, in his bed, with her woman lover. He should have forced her to remember him as something more than the tiresome child she thought she had to pacify.

She went to the sink and began to rinse the breakfast things under the tap.

'Leave them,' he said, 'I'll do them,' the words coming out of him too quickly. He was losing his cool. She put the cup down and dried her hands on the tea towel. He struggled to think of something to say. He would have to find something. His mind seethed with ridiculous nervous comments. He tried to pick out a phrase that would sound normal and yet succeed in gaining her attention, in arresting this current of meaningless actions that was sweeping between them. And surely there must be something she wanted to say to him? She was not going to walk out and leave him as if she was off to the pictures? She took her raincoat from the bannister and put it on, but did not fasten it. The belt trailed on one side. She lifted up the suitcase and carried it into the hallway. He followed her. When she opened the door, he saw that it was raining. A gust of wind caught her hair, blowing it into her eyes. He wanted to say, 'Fasten your coat – you're going to get cold.' But he did not and he heard himself ask instead:

'Where can I ring you?' he had not intended that, he knew the answer. He had the phone number by heart.

She held open the door with one hand and set down the case. She stared down at his shoes and then past him along the length of the hallway. Two days ago he had started to sand and stain the floorboards. She looked as if she was estimating how much work remained to be done.

'Don't ring this weekend. We're going away for a while.'

He felt a flash of white heat pass in front of his brain and a popping sound like a light bulb exploding. He felt dizzy and his eyes for a moment seemed to cloud over. Then he realised what had happened. A flood of blind terror had swept through him, unmanning him, because she had said something totally unexpected – something he had not planned for. He repeated the words carefully hoping she would deny them, make sense of them.

'You're going away for a while?'

'Yes.'

'Where to for Godsake?' he almost shrieked.

'Down the country for a bit – to friends.'

He stared at her blankly, his lips trembling, and then the words came out that he had been holding back all morning:

'For how long? When will you be back?'

He could have asked it at any time, he had been on the verge of it a dozen times and had managed to repress it because he had to keep to his resolve not to let her see that he knew what all this was about – a drama, a show of defiance and autonomy. He could not let her guess that he knew full well she would be back. Somewhere in her heart she must recognise that no one would ever care for her as much as he did. No one could appreciate her more, or make more allowances for her. She could not throw away ten years of his life for this – to score a political point – for a theory – for a woman! But he had not said it, all morning. It was too ridiculous – it dignified the thing even to mention it. And now she had tricked him into it, cheated him.

'When will you be back?' he had asked.

'I'll be away for a week, I suppose. You can ring the

flat on Monday.'

The rain was blowing into her face, her lips were white. She leaned forward. He felt her hand on his sleeve. He felt the pressure of her ring through the cloth of his shirt. She kissed him on the forehead. Her lips were soft, her breath warm on his skin. He hated her then. He hated her body, her woman's flesh that was still caressive and yielding when the heart inside it was shut like a trap against him.

'Goodbye,' she said. She lifted the case and closed the door after her.

He went back into the kitchen. But not to the window. He did not want to see her walking down the road. He did not want to see her legs in their scarlet stockings, and the raincoat blown back from her skirt. He did not want to see her dragging the stupid case, to see it banging against her knees as she carried it along the street. So he stood in the kitchen that smelled of coffee and bread baking. He stood over the warmth of the stove, his head lowered, his hands clenched in his pockets, his eyes shut.

She would be back anyhow – in a week's time. She had admitted that now. 'In a week,' she had said, 'ring me on Monday.' He would not think about it until then. He would not let himself react to any more of these theatrics. It was absurd, the whole business. She had gone to the country, she was visiting friends. He would not worry about her. He would not think about her at all, until she came back.

Miss Callaghan's Day Out

The hawthorn is in flower once more, one week later than last year; its blossom heavy as snow on the black branch. They whisper that I have lost all sense of time. They are mistaken. It warns me: its thorned fingers reaching to my window, it taps the hours and the seasons. Light slips white and sharp from its spread branches. Opening the curtains, Sister Josephine says: 'Look Miss Callaghan, at all the golden daffs, aren't they gorgeous?' But my mother never cared for daffodils.

'Oh my dark Rosaleen do not cry do not weep, the priests are on the ocean green, they march along the deep.' My father told us stories and recited poetry in the long evenings, the armchair drawn up to the fire. I lie in my bed, the pink candlewick spread pulled to my cheek and do not weep. He took me on his knee, his breath sang in my ear with the special scent it had always. 'This is the way the ladies ride over hedges and ditches and into the sea.' I held tight to the chain of his watch and saw my face dance in its silver palm. I had long, dark hair and blue eyes, like violets. His treasure, he called me – mo stóir. But Rosaleen was Ireland and I knew that.

'We are not quite ourself, this morning, are we Miss Callaghan?' Sister Josephine said, taking my tray. But today we are more ourselves than ever. We left our breakfast unfinished only because the tea was cold and the egg, when we cut off its head, thin and milky. Let them wonder. Let them tease out the riddle themselves. I have been working all winter – ever since Nuala said what she did, I have been racking my brain. I have said the words over each night in the sheath of my iron bed; telling them to my beads until I have them almost by heart. I am ready at last. The final stones turning.

'Aren't you the great one altogether,' they say, opening cards, shuffling flowers. It is Mrs. Heffernan's birthday. All morning they have been drooling over her as with a newborn child – holding the spoon to her mouth, wiping egg from her chin. 'Aren't you the proud girleen?' as if it were something clever to be ninety-two years old. My father died at fifty-three, though he had not a grey hair in his head. 'The finest man in the county Kilkenny. God rest his soul.'

'Rest. We must rest ourself Miss Callaghan or we will not be well enough for our walk this afternoon.' I have been resting for years and am not well yet. I told them so, but Sister Josephine answered: 'For oft, when on my couch I lie in vacant or in pensive mood, they flash upon that inward eye that is the bliss of solitude. We must know that one, Miss Callaghan.' But I do not want to. The bliss of solitude. They taught it to us at the convent; reciting line after line, sitting row upon row, knees together, back straight, eyes fixed on the Sacred Heart that bled on the green wall for our sins. Mother Madeline's fingers twitched in the air as if pulled by strings, her starched veil, pushed upward, left a crimson seam on her forehead. Like a wasp her voice droned; showing no favour to prayers, poems or multiplication tables. She was a Sister of Charity and her heart was given to God.

'Along the lake, beneath the trees.' Our rooms are strewn with yellow petals; stiff green stalks in every vase. They are growing wild as daisies in the garden. My father would not have asked me to repeat the lines. A thin, English verse. Mangan was his poet and violets the flowers he loved best. Yet it was not violets that he gave to my mother, coming home on the first

82

tram, waking the house with his singing. When he knocked at her door he stood still on the threshold, his voice muffled, and his arms, when they held out the tall sheaf of blossoms, trembled. But she never cared for daffodils, then or afterward. Taking Nuala by the hand, she strode from the room, pushed past him at the doorway: 'Take yourself and your flower garden out of my house.' The petals spilled from his grasp, falling torn and yellow on his jacket and black polished boots. He did not stoop to pick them up.

'She has lost all sense of time, you know,' they congratulate each other, their lips smiling sadly. But they are misinformed. Each day I remember something more, drawn up from the well, hand over hand as my father taught me. Soon I shall have it all – I shall see the face and hear the words. I shall know why and whom. They come to me with their tricks, demanding: 'Miss Callaghan, surely you remember when?' But I have grown cautious and give no more than name, rank and serial number. They have no notion of what I keep stored. I mark time by the garden; the coming and going of leaves, the starlings and the swallows, the buttercups and the wallflowers, the moon and the hawthorn. It has snowed seven times since they brought me here. My father said put your money on anything with a seven in it; giving me sixpence to place on Prince Peerless, number twenty-one. We were at the Galway races where the riders and horses were a glittering rainbow spun on the green turf. The snow came as we drove home, falling on the earth and grass, covering roofs and telegraph wires, closing everything from sight, making everything equal. My father said, 'Don't tell your mother,' meaning the sixpence lost on Prince Peerless and I never did, then or later.

'We cannot go out today – the path is treacherous – we might fall and hurt ourself, Miss C', they said this winter when the snow fell. They say it every winter. We are not allowed to fall. We must grip our walkers with both hands and tread softly, slipper after slipper. But someone gets permission to sortie, always, for very soon the whiteness is pitted with ugly orange wounds – boots and shoes that cannot keep still. The

holes fill with rain; fray at their edges, the thaw sets
in, the silence stripped back like a rug.

'Thanks be to God, we can exercise now – we were
getting a wee bit stiff.' And so we shamble forth and
the world resumes its shape; the grey chimney stacks,
the cables swinging black above our heads, the noise
and scuttlings of life.

'Miss Callaghan, your sister Mrs Courtney to see
you.' It began when I remembered her name. How well
they hid it from me. Each time she came they would
lead me aside to whisper: 'Miss Callaghan, your sister,
Mrs Courtney to see you.' But I have never known any
Courtneys. I recognised her from the way she touched
her fingers to her hair as she drew near. She must
always be seen at her best. Her hair is white, though
wound about her head as before, her hands are fat and
ribbed with blue veins. When we were children they
made us play together. She had white skin and yellow
hair. We played in the fields and in Mannion's
orchard. We climbed the eucalyptus tree that grew by
the gate, its leaves falling like whips of hair tossed and
tangled. Our frocks were of white muslin with wide
lace collars. If we caught them on the brambles or
going over the wall, it was I who had to mend them,
being the clever one with my hands. I was the elder
sister and must keep tight hold of her hand coming
and going to school. She called me teacher's pet and
Miss Lady Oh and my mother loved her best.

'Do you not remember the house in Galway, Bette –
Flaherty's field, the eucalyptus – how we used to fire
the nuts at old Peter; the smell of cat it left on our
hands. Mammy used to be livid!'

And she was with me always and ever after because
I had let go Nuala's hand. I remembered. I tried for a
long time to shape the words, but my tongue was too
thick and slipped against my teeth. She asked if I
remembered, but she did not wait for my reply
because it frightens her when my jaw slacks and
spittle comes on my lips. But it had all returned to me
then – the day, the place and her name. I remembered
coming home, the grass squelching in Flaherty's field,
how the stream had swollen with rain and spilled

84

from its banks. Nuala dropped my hand and rushed forward calling: 'Look at me – look at me, I'm a fish leaping,' and she jumped from stone to stone, scattering yellow pearls of spray. But the water sucked at her feet and she toppled down, her shoes slipping off the smooth green rock. Blood came out of her knee and trickled through the dark stocking. I wiped it with my handkerchief and tore off a strip to bind the wound. We set off, her arm across my shoulders. It was nearly night when we reached home; purple clouds hanging from the sky and trees. When my mother asked what had happened, Nuala turned her eyes from me. She said that crossing Flaherty's field I had let go of her hand. My mother bathed and dressed the wound and gave her porter cake to eat because she said she had fallen on the hard stones and hurt herself. But Nuala had white skin and yellow hair and was her favourite always.

'She's tired now – her concentration isn't good, you see.' But it was, because I had remembered. I tried to let them know but my jaws stuck. I had remembered my mother's voice; how she called Nuala her little lamb and raised her hand high to bring it down on mine, my palm flinching, the pain reaching to my shoulder. Nuala was her name and must be still – I have never known any Courtneys. I tried to tell them but they did not wait. They said, 'She's worn herself out, God love her,' and gripped my arms, one at each side and led me to my bed, my head swinging back and forth against the green walls. When she kissed me goodbye, kissing my cheek, I tried to say her name but tears blocked the way in my throat. 'Oh she's very fond of you, Mrs Courtney,' they smiled, but I knew that she was Nuala. I had remembered her name and I had remembered my mother.

'She's hardly conscious – it won't be long now.' But it was. I lay in my bed. The leaves fell off the beech tree and the wallflowers withered. No one came to visit me, not even Larry, old faithful as they call him ever since that first time when I put on my violet dress and tied up my hair and he took me to the Theatre Royal. They brought me oranges and black grapes and held the spoon to my mouth. Father Lavin knelt on the floor, a purple sash across his shoulders and pressed warm oil to my brow with the flat of his thumb. My right arm lay on the candlewick bedspread beside me. They put it out in the morning and back beneath the covers at nightime. If thy right hand offend thee cut it off, but they did not need to because it lay perfectly still beside me and bothered no one. They warmed milk for me to drink and brought me coconut creams. I told them that Mother Gabriel had given me biscuits after the May procession, and they said oh Miss Callaghan, always the great one for stories – don't be bothering yourself going over things now. But it was no bother.

I heard our feet shuffling the gravel like the sighing of wind through the fir trees. We walked to the grotto of Mary Immaculate. In our arms we carried great bunches of flowers gathered in the laundry field when the grass was still wet with dew. Our voices broke the air with the sound of bells ringing: 'Oh lily of the valley, oh mystic rose, what tree or flower is half so sweet as thee?' We knelt at her feet and prayed until the pebbles cut into our knees. We made a special intention for the virtue of purity. Lilies are for purity, and snowdrops. They were not lilies that we lay before her feet but daffodils – a host of golden daffodils. As we marched back to the convent gate we sang: 'The bells of the Angelus call us to pray, in sweet tones announcing the Sacred Ave, Ave, Ave, Ave Maria.' We were children of Mary, the blue mantles that we would wear in our graves we wore that day, they billowed in the wind like sails, cracking. They told us not to turn our eyes to sea where the waves rolled on the water as if struggling to free themselves. But I looked. It was then that I fell down; white froth coming on my lips. Someone said that I had caught cold picking flowers in the wet grass before breakfast, but Anne Murray said that my father had died on the first Friday in May. They carried me to the abbey and gave me hot milk to drink and coconut creams. Mother Gabriel said that God calls the good first. Why, then, had he called my father and no one else? I told Nurse

Kenny but she said; holding the spoon to my lips: 'Drink up now like a good girl and don't be worrying your head with old stories.'

'Look at me, look at me – I'm dancing!' Mrs Tierney calls out, skipping along the corridors, door after door, 'look at me, look at me,' disturbing my curtains this morning before I was half dressed. Her feet go tap-tip like water dripping in a sink, tip-tap on the waxed brown floors. She skips to show off her shoes and socks; that is why she is here, because she is a show-off, a notice box. In her hair she has tied a pink bow, she wears ankle socks and scarlet slippers.

'Look what they brought me yesterday,' she says, kicking up her satin slippers. Sister John the Baptist, the escaped nun, says: 'Christ in every eye that sees me, Christ in every ear that hears me,' and stamps her foot. Every ear hears her, she makes sure of that. Vincent Shanley told me in the Wicklow Arms that I had a slender foot and well-turned ankle, but no one ever brings me slippers. Hop Scotch Tierney calls them pumps and says she is training for the corps de ballet; arching her neck for the dying swan. But I said 'All corps and no ballet. Mrs Tierney you are seventy-seven years of age – too old for the limelight,' and I glared at her, making a gnashing sound with my teeth so that she hopped out of my path. When I was no more than half way up the passage, I heard the noise of her skipping again behind me. That is what I have to put up with here – noise and conceit. Ballerinas and Mother Superiors! I would not so much as have offered them the time of day in Galway. My father said, 'Show me your friends and I'll tell you who you are.' But after Vincent Shanley I brought no one to my mother's house.

'I see you have a packed lunch, Miss C. Are you going on a picnic?' Old Nolan caught me pouring tea into my flask at breakfast time. Curiosity killed the cat. I have told none of them yet. I have bided my time, counting the buds on the hawthorn, waiting for the very last one to open before making my final preparations. Nolan is a braggart and not to be relied upon. She turns the conversation to outings and picnics at every opportunity because she has a son who takes her to Greystones for tea on Sunday afternoons. I answered Mrs Nolan that I had no taste for picnics but that my daughter would be calling shortly to take me to the seaside. That was a lie but she was not to know. She opened her locker and took from it her relic of Saint Martin de Paoris and began to rub the scaly skin of her arms and hands.

'Craw thumpers and frustrated spinsters,' my mother said, 'in thy sweet mercy grant to me to suffer and to die for thee. Who could mean it? Hypocrites!' And she refused to make the stations of the cross even in Lent. I visit the chapel every morning and pray to Jesus hanging from his nailed palms to make me pure as his Holy Mother. Mrs Nolan says where would we be without our children. Not here I say. I have no child and never will. My mother thought it unsuitable. Blushing like a schoolgirl. 'It's well one of us has sense,' she said when I told her about Frank Dempsey. Most unsuitable; she knew his family – Free Staters, all of them.

'What a lovely dress, Miss C. – blue for your eyes. You look fresh as a bride this morning.' Nurse Kenny helped me on with my court shoes, holding the horn to my heel as they used to in Clery's. It was in Clery's that I bought the wedding hat; pink with a wide brim and white satin ribbon. The church was on Hadding-ton road; not our own parish, but more appropriate to festivity, and Una obtained a dispensation. The water in the canal raced under the weir and blew back yellow beads of foam. I waited for my mother to pass some remark on my hat, but she was holding the Redmonds in conversation and gazing at Una, who was leaving her forever. We drank champagne that bubbled over wide lipped glasses.

'Drink to me only with thine eyes, and I won't ask for wine,' Vincent sang, and lifted his glass to Una. The women gathered round and kissed her then, and the men whispered in each other's ears and laughed out loud. When they had all gone back to their own houses and children, and Larry and Una had driven off in a shining black car with tin cans tied rattling behind them, Mammy and I were alone in the sitting room. We sat by the fire for tea, she said it was not worth spreading the cloth.

'Aren't you the spoilt girl to be going out for a jaunt.' I told the little one, Nurse Mullen, so that she would not inquire why I needed my best, that my sister was calling at twelve sharp. She buttoned up my grey coat and brought my hat with the violet trimming. When she lifted my bag she said: 'What has it so heavy – is it the crown jewels we're making off with or what?' It is not crown jewels – they took away my necklace and my bracelets when they brought me in. 'The silver might tarnish, Miss C.' It is only the flask that Una gave me for Christmas and six sandwiches wrapped in tin foil. Each evening this week I have put something aside from my tea – ham, cheese or tomato, and stored them in my locker. Now I have quite sufficient for my needs. I will buy fresh provisions at the station in Calais. My father sat beside me on the train leaving Galway and drank from a golden hip flask, the fields rolled from the window as waves beaten back from the shore. He said it was as well for a gentleman to be independent. Nurse Mullen held my elbow as we walked along the corridor, our shoes shuffling together between the high green walls. She said, 'Don't leave us for too long Miss C.' and settled me in, near reception, with my bag in my lap. I watch at the window for Larry on the first Sunday of every month. When the red bonnet of his car turns in through the golden gates I walk to the front steps to meet him. Once we drove to the Powerscourt Demesne in County Wicklow. The waterfall flowed down the cliff, black and foaming as poured stout. It roared in our heads so that we did not speak. He wrapped a green and blue squared blanket round my knees and we watched the water slipping between orange stones faster than the wind could catch it. When it turned under the wooden bridge it was lost from our sight. I asked him to tell me why they had taken away the photograph that Nuala brought. He rolled up the window and opened a box of Dairy Milk chocolates. He said it was, perhaps, for safekeeping.

'What beautiful eyes, Miss C. She's smiling at you,' they said. They were wrong. She was looking over her shoulder with her receiving a gentleman smile, looking at someone standing behind me. She had on her crocheted shawl with the Tara broach, and she sat on the banks of the Seine, 'The canal Miss C., the Royal Canal,' with Lily Kavanagh, and her eyes had the soft green look the water must have where it flows under the bridges. My father said we would stroll on the boulevards and drink champagne from wide-brimmed glasses. There are twenty-one bridges over the river and eight streets join in the rays of a star. Put your money on anything with a seven in it, and he always did, my mother said. They would not let me see the photograph that Nuala brought but she smiled, placing the silver frame between the Oil of Ulay and the mandarin oranges: 'Sure, where's the harm? Isn't it all over and done with long ago?'

'There's the girl now, we must not mind an old picture.' I was unsettled for weeks after that. I lay in bed with my right arm beside me. No one came. The leaves fell from the trees and the wallflowers turned brown. I watched her smiling, hour after hour from her silver frame smiling at someone behind me. But she did not come to visit. I thought it all out watching her face, her eyes with the green cast the water must have. I grew well and strong as they told me, listening for the tap of the hawthorn and the sight of Nuala walking down the corridor touching her fingers to her hair: 'You must remember Bette, surely?' I did. I grew well and strong. A good girl now, I can wait here by the door and no one pays the least notice. Cool and calm in my Sunday best, when the red bonnet comes through the gates, I am collected.

I have forgotten all my little ways. When they brought me first I had too many. They gripped me between their hands and shook me, they said I did not know my own strength. They took away my bag, my clothes, my jewelry, my watch and my comb, for my own good; for safekeeping. They put me to sleep in a room full of women so that I would not be lonely, with striped curtains round my bed so that I need not be bothered. They gave me a sleeper at bedtime to settle me in, and a red pill in the morning to get me going. We file to the chapel at ten, to the garden at three and to the television lounge at six-o-clock because the devil finds work for idle hands. We weave coloured strings across a frame making baskets and stools for the blind. We count our blessings. We like to keep busy. My mother told me Sally Keogh would not let her mother so much as lift a finger when I brought up the coal and washed the floors and cooked the dinner – and she held her own finger in the air to demonstrate. Here we have nothing to cook or clean; they bring our meals on a trolley and our clothes as we need them. Today I asked Nurse Kenny for my best; my black patent shoes and my hat with the violet ribbon. She helped me to dress: 'Now aren't we smart for our gentleman.' I lift my bag of Spanish leather and make my way to the door and down the stone steps alone. I tell Joe at the desk that I am taking a turn in the garden. 'Old faithful is it today Miss C. – the box of chocolates and the blanket tucked around our knees,' he says and closes one eye. What the eye does not see the heart does not grieve for my mother said but my heart grieved.

'Hail Holy Queen, Mother of Mercy, hail our life, our sweetness and our hope.' I will join my hands about my beads and pay no one the least notice. Not even Hop Scotch Tierney if she passes me kicking up her heels for attention. I do not mind now if she becomes the prima ballerina! They have cut the willow from the orchard wall, I see its sap green and oozing. I heard the wood crack at the last stroke of the axe. 'Isn't that a great improvement now – we have light enough to read the papers.' I must lift my shoes with care so that I do not slip among the fallen boughs. I did not want to read the newspapers but they said it's as well to keep ourselves abreast. My mother kept abreast of everything – of men going to war or coming back, sailors drowned at sea, governments rising and falling, old women burnt in their beds. The voice in the wireless was solemn at breakfast, dinner and tea, but its green eye glittered and winked for all that the heart did not grieve over. I sat by the window where the light was best. I read to her the Irish Press, The Evening Press and, on Sunday mornings, The Sunday Press. When she was too stiff to visit Nan Malone or Josie Skefington, I settled her by the fire, a blanket round her knees, her foot raised on a pouffe. Once she lay in her room for a week, the blinds drawn, the pillows high, letters and photos arrayed around her like trophies. 'She went away from me with one star awake as the swan in the evening moves over the lake.' It was no use asking me to sing, she said, I had inherited none of my father's ability. When Nan Malone came at last to see what the matter was, she turned her eyes from the door. She said that nothing mattered anymore since Una and Nuala had left.

'Jesus, Mary and Joseph, bless us now and at the hour of our agony. Good afternoon, Miss Callaghan.' How dare she bless me! Mother John the Baptist indeed – a scarecrow rigged out for a fancy dress ball. I told Sister Josephine when they brought her in, it's not here she should be. But charity Miss C., she answered, we all have our little ways. She has one too many from the cut of her – her veil over one eye, egg on her chin and her mutterings; hissing ejaculations at anyone that passes. 'My God I love thee, Lord save us we perish.' Five hundred days' indulgence for every one completed. Some people are well in! If you answer her, she stands stock still, claps her hands and calls 'Silence at the back.' Well, she cannot fool me. I give her a wide berth. A spy, no doubt, from the Vatican or worse. They have them everywhere; in the dormitories and the chapel. When I went to confession, during Father Cleary's retreat, I heard distinctly the click of the shutter drawn back on the far side as I began bless me father. Two can play at her game. She need not think she can provoke me any longer. Bowing my head I will call, 'Deliver us, oh Lord, from thine enemies' and pass her by.

My mother did not pray. Not even in Lent. Holy Joes and hypocrites, she said, and any excuse when I left for early mass. It was too late in life to be kneeling on cold benches and piety began at home. Her knees grew out from each other like the branches of an old tree, though my father had likened her to the gazelle. She wore thick ribbed stockings, a woollen scarf at her throat and rubbed her thin hands over the fire. But, 'cold hands, warm heart,' she said, and did not die.

'Hail, Queen of Heaven, the ocean star, guide of our wanderings here below.' I shall rest for a while. It is peaceful here in the dark of the Grotto where the ivy twists about her blue mantle. Her stone white hands are joined about her beads but her lips make no sound. My queen, my mother. She loved gardens always. She loved the willow and the beech, apple blossom and the violets that grew wild in the fields. She never cared for daffodils. The petals fell torn and yellow on his polished boots. I gathered them one by one and pressed them between the pages of the *Golden Treasury*. But he did not read to us again. If I keep my eyes fixed on hers I will not see their marshalled yellowness – they may flutter and dance in any breeze they care to. I shall tread carefully. When John the Baptist has gone from sight I will take the side lane, picking my steps so that they leave no trace. A drag hunt would serve just as well, my father thought, it was only the scent that excited the hounds. He did not like to see the hare caught and torn. When all was said and done he was a gambling man and he liked the odds to be fair. Fair stood the wind for France, France that was ever the ally of Dark Rosaleen. When we were grown up and fine ladies he would take us to Paris to stroll on the boulevards and drink white coffee at pavement cafés. 'Fair stood the wind,' he cried, leaning against the bedroom door. And my mother said, 'Quiet, you'll wake the children.'

'Mother of Christ, Star of the Sea, pray for the wanderer, pray for me.' They said, 'Don't be foolish, Miss Callaghan, you're imagining things. She can never come here.' But I had seen her. Once, before the hawthorn had grown high enough to knock at my window, I saw her walking in the garden, I knew her by the carriage of her head, her smile, and her swift short steps as though off to some secret assignation.

93

But she did not acknowledge me. She had friends in every city: in London, New York, Paris and Boston. They sent cards and letters and presents; they said their doors would always be open. She could charm the birds from the trees, they said. And she wanted them all for herself. The violets grow along the hedges – a purple ribbon stretched to the gates. I will follow their path. Baptist has gone, Mrs Nolan and the Breslin one – my coast is clear. I must step with caution. 'Oh men from the fields come softly within, tread softly, softly, oh men coming in.' I see the Golden Gates ahead and the road beyond them, black between green banks twisting from sight. Slieveen – sly, sly as a fox, she said, always slinking off without her.

I brought her to the Queen's Theatre on Saturdays and to the Green on Sunday mornings. But I invited no one to the house after Frank Dempsey. I made my appointments for Bewleys and settled her by the fire before leaving. And why was it, she asked, in the querulous voice she kept for evening, that we could not entertain as we had done in Nuala's day? The photographs glittered in their silver frames, glittered and winked at each other. I said it was all very fine to talk of entertaining but it was not Nuala who paid the bills. Dockets and bills, she cried, dockets and bills. That was all I had ever been good for: making money and paying bills. And her shoe tapped on the tiles of the hearth and the tassles of her white shawl shook. We were alone that night. Alone in the dark curtained sittingroom, where the silver teapot gleamed in the firelight; gleamed and winked at the photographs in their frames. And there was no sound but the hissing of coal in the flames. So that anyone might have heard the noise that issued from my throat. Anyone might have, but we were quite alone. I fell down because I was tired. Tired of standing knees together, shoulders straight, head high. She dragged at my arm. She said get up this instant – what possessed me – kicking on the floor like a child? But when she saw the white froth on my lips she stopped talking and she let go of my wrist. The yellow flames danced on the wall, the coal spat. They led me down the stairs, one on each

side, their arms about me like bands of steel. I said
Hail Holy Queen, Mother of Mercy, hail our life, our
sweetness and our hope and I counted aloud the steps
of the stairs. There were twenty-one steps. Her eyes
were fixed on the hall mirror where her face loomed;
an old woman's face, blue veins in her cheeks, her lips
drawn back from her gums. She said where is Nuala —
why have they all left me alone?

'Gentle Lady fair as moon, Loreto's guiding star,
shine o'er the path we tread in life, protect us where
we are.' I am at the gate. The bars are closed against
me: the iron cold in my grasp. I must push with all my
force. They swing open at last, moaning; the Golden
Gates arched high above me as did the gates of
Powerscourt Demesne, or was it Mount Jerome where
we went together to visit the graves of her friends. She
had friends in every graveyard. Always visiting, she
loved festivities of every kind. When there was no
longer anyone left to invite her to weddings she went
to their funerals instead. Every morning she read the
names from the Irish Press; every day there was
someone there she knew. She put on her veiled hat of
black feathers and her black patent leather shoes and
set out. When Molly O'Brien died in Paris, they
brought the remains home to Drumcondra. One less
Christmas card to answer, I said, when she buttoned
up her coat and lifted down the hat. Each summer the
O'Briens had asked her to visit. Each summer I offered
to go in her place. What would you do in Paris, she
asked, and time enough for sightseeing when I'm
dead. But she did not die.

'Oh Gentle, Chaste and Spotless Maid, we sinners
make our prayers through thee.' The flowers are
everywhere, petals glistening in the sun, sharp as
glass, cutting my eyes. They were not like this in the
vases in our lockers, there they stood pale and calm.
Now they rock in the wind, back and forth rattling on
their stalks. The fields stretch out from the road, wide
and flat, pockmarked with the yellow of primroses.
But at least no daffodils. In a very little time I will be
in the train, the high backed seat behind me, the
wooden doors slammed shut at either end, dark and

tranquil. I will not bother about the flowers now, there will be more than enough when I arrive. Sheaves of them, bunched and stacked beneath the painted awnings of the street markets; lilies, lupins, peonies, irises, and violets that were my father's favourite. Here the road is rough and winding. The briars lean out over the hedge, black thorns snatching at my cheek. I must not catch my hair or tear my frock. I am tired of mending. Stay on the footpath and keep tight hold of my hand. I drive along this road with Larry on the first Sunday of every month. He calls out the names of everything we pass: flowers, trees and animals. I know them all. I see the caravans ahead. The woman sits on the bank rocking her bundle of blankets. She will call out Fine day thanks be to God can you spare a copper for the child. I have no child, though Nolan says where would we be without them. I must pass on. Softly, softly oh men coming in. Soon the station will be in sight. I will go directly to the ladies' waiting room where a turf fire burns. I will remain there seated until the train collects me at thirty minutes past the hour.

'Miss Callaghan, don't be foolish. Your mother has gone to a far better place.'

'Where?' I asked every day. 'And why does she not come to visit?' But they would not say where. Why is the sky so flat and garish, so thinly spread? I do not remember it this way. I must stay on the footpath and keep tight hold of my hands. The water crouches in its ditch, brown and sluggish. A far better world. I knew what they meant, at last, when Nuala showed me the photograph. I saved the pictures, the stamps and the postcards, I treasured the names: L'Arc de Triomphe, Champs Elysées, L'Etoile, Versailles, Le Madeleine. My father told me we would walk on the boulevards and buy flowers at every street market. She said time enough for sightseeing when I'm dead. But she did not die. She left me behind for safekeeping, left me behind and went in my stead, wearing her tassled shawl and smiling her secret smile of visitings and assignations. I had the photograph. She sat on the banks of the river that had been promised to me where the water flows wide and green under the bridges. My world – not hers. They did not fool me, though they called it the Royal Canal, and took away the photograph. Under the bridges of Paris with you I'll make your dreams come true. Nuala said she would help out, if it were not for the children, and Una said; you know what Larry is; so they left me alone. I brought up the coal and washed the curtains, I made the beds and counted the bills, I read the papers and set the table though she said it was not worth spreading the cloth.

'And this is why I sojourn here, alone and palely loitering.' There is no one on the platform. She is guiding my path. Mother I could weep for mirth. I will sit here on the grass green bench and wait for the carriage to come; shoulders straight, head high. The sun spills onto everything; my hands are cracked and dry in its pallor, it peels the paint from the walls and lights the pools of oil; blue and yellow between the sleepers. My eyelids are heavy in its downpour. If anyone complains I will say a single to Amiens Street station please – that is how we did it. She must have taken this route also; Amiens Street and Kingston harbour. Larry would have carried her bags along the pier and Lily Kavanagh would have kept tight hold of her hand as they crossed the gangplank. The sea would have sucked at the bows of the sailing boats and their masts, shaken in the wind, would ring as communion bells when the priest lifts the chalice high and prays, 'Oh lamb of God who takest away the sins of the world have mercy.' The boats rocked and rang on the water but they were bound hand and foot and could not loose themselves. They took away the photograph so that I would not guess, but Nuala gave it away at last, when she said what she did, that afternoon. I turned every stone. I lay in bed with my right arm beside me, they put it out in the morning and in at night, but I followed the light to the end of the tunnel. She let it slip, Nuala, when I asked her again. She told me, her voice quick and cross: 'Surely you must remember Bette that Mammy has gone to her reward.' And it was then I knew that she had gone to mine.

'Blow, bugle blow, set the wild echoes flying, and

97

answer, echoes, answer, dying, dying, dying.' Mother John the Baptist herself could not offer more aspirations and yet I am watched by bead blue eyes. Eyes that slink at the rim of a scarf. Why are they watching me now? She has drawn on and taken off her gloves three times since sitting down. Preening herself like Nuala. She must always be seen at her best. Or is she signalling to someone? But there are only the two of us here. It is twenty past one, by the station clock, the hands crawl under the dim glass like insects black and thin. When the train arrives I will go to the very last carriage. The wind is growing louder, it tosses the sunlight over the platform, under the door, across the window, leaking into my eyelids. The tracks are soiled and littered with papers, they scuttle between the rails yellowed and dry. On one page they have written in thick, black print: 'Manhunt for Galway Killer'. Why? I remember no murder in Galway. It was not in that city it happened. My father did not like to see the hare caught and torn. He laid poison for the rats when he heard the scrape of their feet above us. When we travelled on the train to Dublin I was not to lean from the windows, nor talk to strangers. Frank Dempsey talked to me. He bought two return tickets to Malahide. He sat close beside me in the carriage and sang, 'The girl that I marry will have to be as sweet and as fair as a nursery, the girl I call my own' and he held my hand in the dark of the tunnels. When I led him up the stairs to the drawing room where the firelight flickered and the coals spat, my mother turned her head. She said never trust a man who wears a bow tie.

That one has taken off her gloves again. She is staring at my feet now – jealousy; green with it like old Nolan. I chose my patent leather and my hat with the violet trimming. Nothing but the best for Paris. Why is the station master whispering? Everywhere the same – whisperings and muttering. They are all jealous because I am going to my reward. They thought they had taken me in completely. They thought I would never remember. For safekeeping, they said, when they took everything from me. Don't

98

be worrying yourself over an old picture, when they hid the photograph but I knew her face by heart.

'Had I the heavens' embroidered cloths, enwrought with golden and silver light.' Why is the sky stretched tight above the houses, blue and thin as though its skin would rip? Perhaps she is a pickpocket. Larry says no one is safe to walk the streets these days. I will not buy my ticket until the instant before boarding. I will not have her looking in my bag. Once seated I will be clear of danger. The doors slammed tight at either end. At Amiens Street I will drink a little tea from my flask. I feel no hunger yet. 'Pommes frites for Madame,' Sister Josephine says when the trolley comes rattling through the wards; 'pommes frites' she says on Friday when they serve out the fried plaice, peas and potato, 'pommes frites' – it's her little joke. At Calais the fishing boats are painted red and blue; swung on the water, the colours leap like startled fish escaping the net. I had the picture, it hung on the wall above the fireplace. But they took it away so that I would not be worried. When the ship reaches port I will travel by express train to Paris. I will sit on the banks of the Seine where the silver skinned poplars grow high. If she comes with her short swift steps, smiling at Lily Kavanagh who never cared for water not even along the banks of the Royal Canal where they strolled on Sundays arm in arm, their voices blown back by the wind over my shoulder – I need not speak. I need do nothing at all but wait, watching the river slip from our sight. She will know what to say.

'The angels answer with their songs, bright choirs in gleaming rows.' I do not like it here, my hands are cold under my gloves. Between the trees, the birds are tossed like scraps of black lace, catching in the branches as they fall. Why are they shrieking? It hurts my ears. The papers scuttle on the sleepers; rats eating through the rafters. She is watching me, her eyes slinking at the edge of her scarf with its yellow foxheads; bead blue eyes that cannot be still, glaring at my rosary. Jealous, all of them because I have nothing but the best; mother of pearl, 'Mother of Mercy, Mother of good council,' I will not be provoked. I will take a turn on the footpath until I hear the whistle of the train. A turn for the worse and a turn for the better. John the Baptist, escaped from the convent, with her veil dipped over one eye – no one dares to detain her – muttering aspirations. I will say one hundred and one and if anyone interrupts, I will clap my hands sharply and call silence at the back. That will keep the hounds at bay. The train will whistle coming through the tunnel mouth, it will alert me in good time. My father squeezed my hand in the dark of the tunnels. A hundred and one steps to the church gate – I see the spire, the bell tower. A hundred and one steps, past the terraced houses, the painted doors, flowers and grasses growing wild behind iron railings. Ninety-nine steps. I will count each one. Walk to the gate and back again. 'I know where I'm going and I know who's going with me.'

The wind is filling my coat, blowing me as a sail faster than my own footsteps can carry me. Footsteps – ringing in my head, ringing on the concrete pavement, the communion bells ringing when the priest lifts the chalice. Whose footsteps ringing faster than my own? Perhaps I should not have worn my patent leather after all. They excite too much attention. The station master stared at them, as though they were not quite the thing. Who is he to judge? You may be sure he has never been to the home of fashion. When I stop, the footsteps continue. Someone else's footsteps, treading in my wake. I will not turn my head, whoever it is. The waves roared and twisted on the shore, pounding themselves on the rocks until they broke into chips and slivers of white bone. I looked back, though we had been bidden not to; I looked, wearing the blue child of Mary mantle we would wear in our graves – I looked back. It was then I fell for the first time; white froth coming on my lips. The waves groaned in pain and crashed to the ground time and time again. I pounded my head against the wall where the firelight glittered and fell down. Fell for the third time. Their white-sleeved arms encircled me like ropes of briar. They led me down the stairs. I counted the steps out loud; there were twenty-one steps, and twenty-one bridges over the Seine. I will cross them all, wearing my hat with the violet trimming, cross them all when I come to them. They will not look under the bridges.

'Oh hark, oh hear, how thin and clear!' A black circle spins above the church spire; spinning black and screaming as it spins. The rooks wheeled above our heads in Flaherty's field. Who are they warning now? I will wait here in the shadow of the wall until they have passed me by. No one can be apprehended in a church. I stand on hallowed ground. I hear them still: clack-click, click-clack, devouring my ears, eating into my head. Mrs Tierney's pumps go, tip-tap, tap-tip, along the corridors, before I am half dressed. Jealousy the root of all evil. Root it out; root and branch. They would all obstruct me. I will not look back. My father said do not turn your head until the tape touches your chest, one backward glance could cost you the race. He was a great athlete in his day and needed his exercise still. She said it was a poor house that could not afford one gentleman and took Nuala with her to open the shop. He died at fifty-three without a grey hair on his head. Mother Madeline told us God calls the best first. But, she said, we all have our vocation and Vincent Shanley would make a fool of me. Marriage was a woman's calling but who called her to Paris? It was my turn. I will wait here, in the soft green grass of the churchyard; the seeds falling on my shoes, until they have passed me by. 'There is a wideness in her mercy like the wideness of the sky.' Here between the tall curved stones, they will not hear me. They rise grey and stiff, back to back, shoulders straight as soldiers on parade. Some lean and stoop as if they might fall between the green blades. My father leaned against the bedroom door when he came home on the first tram, with the special scent his breath had always, but he did not fall.

I will read the names out loud as I used to do, the names laid out in black print. Every stone has its own: 'Charles Farrel beloved father of Mary, Margaret and

Catherine'; 'Sarah Cogan, beloved wife of Joseph, mother of Sheila, Rose and Michael'; 'In memoriam James McBride; brother of Anthony, Arthur, Jane and John'. Every stone has its name — everyone loved by someone. Dust to dust and ashes to ashes. But the stones have kept their names. The Lord giveth and the Lord taketh away. She took everything from me: my home, my life and left in my place. I read the list in the Irish Press every morning, the names laid out between the wedded and newlyborn but there was never a Callaghan. The footsteps have halted. I no longer hear the ringing. The boats rocked and rang on the water. They must be waiting, concealed on the other side. They think they can deceive me. But I have taken off my shoes! Tread softly, softly. He said it was only the scent that attracted the hounds. Our cloaks billowed and cracked in the wind like sails. It was then I fell for the third time.

'In thy sweet mercy grant me to suffer and to die for thee.' 'Hypocrites and craw thumpers', she said, when my father went to first mass before coming home. 'Who did he think he was deceiving?' They cannot fool me. No one can be apprehended in a churchyard. My father told us the story of Thomas à Becket, but he was an English man. A nation of blasphemers. The stone is cold against my cheek. Cold as the waves that broke on the shore into white chips and slivers of froth. I fell at the May procession because the grass was wet and the pebbles cut into our knees. We gathered daffodils from the laundry field before breakfast when they were still dew covered. Yellowness everywhere. Her eyes were yellow when she stared at me — when the poker crashed on her skull. Yellow petals growing in the earth about my feet but these are primroses — a different matter entirely. My hands are cold lodged in their gloves. Cold hands warm heart she said stretching them to the fire. I will walk a few steps and count the stones. There should be twenty-one at least. Trust anything with a seven in it. A turn for the worse a turn for the better, I am turning between stones. 'When I consider how my light is spent, ere half my days, in this dark world and

102

wide.' There were twenty-one steps when they led me down the stairs on the night I fell for the third time; the teapot glittering in the glow of the coal flames.

'Mother most merciful, mother most powerful, mirror of wisdom.' Her eyes were in the mirror, white and staring – an old woman's face. I saw the blood spurting thick and red. Time enough when I'm dead, she said, but she did not die; not that evening nor any other. A name for every grave and everyone loved by someone: Maura Hennessy, Sean Pierce, Harry Collins, Peter Farington, Delia Moore, Gerald Broy, Beatrice Keane, Mary Elisabeth. I know that name! Mary Elisabeth – I remember that. Why have they placed it here? Elisabeth Mary beloved mother of Joan, Donal and Dermot. They have made a mistake with that – it was Nuala she loved best, Una, Colm and Gerard. I have never known any Joans, Donals or Dermots. Why have they written her name on this stone? It was not in the papers. I read the list every day. It was not to *this* place she came to visit her friends, in her black feathered hat, but to Glasnevein or the golden gates of Mount Jerome. Why did Nuala tell me she had gone to my reward if she had not? If she was here all the time with her name carved in stone? Did they seek to deceive me, to send me off on a wild goose chase, to decoy me by boat and train when they had her here all along for safekeeping? But they cannot fool me. I had the photograph and the face in it by heart. Now I have found her name. Mary Elisabeth. They will not hood-wink me. I know where I'm going and I know who's going with me. I know who she was mother of. I hear the footsteps rising. The wind hurling itself through the crooked trees. They cannot touch me. No one is apprehended in a church. I will cling onto her name; my hands gripping her name. They told me to keep tight hold of Nuala's hand. I kept tight hold of the poker. The teapot winked in the yellow firelight. The waves pounded and crashed in my head. Her skin was dry as old newspaper in the flickering light; the Irish Press, the Evening Press, the Sunday Press. I smashed it down, keeping tight hold. My father said he did not care to see the hare caught and torn, the blood spouting from its throat. She fell down, her eyes starting from her paper face. They led me down the stairs. Where is Nuala? she cried – why doesn't she come, why have they all left me alone? Her face was in the hall mirror, her lips stretched back from her yellow teeth. I will keep tight hold of her name. I will not let them take it from me again. 'Remember, oh most loving mother Mary that never was it known that anyone who fled to thy protection, implored thy help or sought thy intercession was left unaided.' They are coming. I hear their breathing. They will drag me down the steps. They are spinning in black circles against the sky; the rooks screamed in Flaherty's field, they are wheeling and catching like black lace in the trees, spinning and screaming as they spin: 'Miss Callaghan, Miss Callaghan, Miss Callaghan,' My name and hers bound together.

'Aren't we the bold girl to run away from home without telling anyone where we were off to Miss C.?'

When they asked me where, I told them Paris, but they said: 'And sure, how could we have gone to Paris in our slippers?' That is how they knew us at the station. 'God works in mysterious ways, Miss C. Weren't we fortunate?'

I clung to my mother's name, the carved letters cold against my cheek. They said: 'Don't let an old stone upset you. What's in a name – isn't the country full of Marys?' I told them I would not leave her, my queen, my mother, now that I had discovered her name and a place where it was written. Sister Josephine's veil was black, it caught the wind as she drew near. Her face was white under the black veil. She reached out her hand; it touched my forehead, cool against my skin. She said: 'Miss Callaghan, you must understand; you will not find her here or anywhere.' I looked at her mouth as the words came out, her white lips trembling: 'And she can never come to visit.' I heard her voice, pale and chill as the hand that touched my forehead: 'Your mother has gone – gone to her reward. Do you understand me now? She has left us – passed over. Your mother is dead, Miss Callaghan, dead, dead, dead.'

It was then the gurgling came from my throat: bright and clear as champagne spilling from the rim of a glass, bubbling up from a well. I heard it ringing in my ears. I put my hand to my mouth, but it would not stop. It rocked me from side to side, rocked me between the leaning stones, my head thrown back, until their white sleeved arms reached out. 'For the love of God, Miss Callaghan, what is there to laugh at?' she asked, as they took me down the steps. Their arms encircled me like bands of steel, but the gurgling still ran from my mouth: flowed like a river and would not cease, flooding from all the years of darkness. 'Mary Elisabeth Callaghan,' I sang, 'gone to her reward' as they led me through the arch of the Golden Gates. 'Mary Elisabeth, gone to her reward, not mine.'

Sister Josephine draws the curtains. The day is begun. The sun spills and splashes over beds, flowers and faces. I clap my hands.

'Oh the Erne shall run red with redundance of blood, the earth shall rock beneath our tread and flames wrap hill and wood, ere you shall fade, ere you shall die, my dark Rosaleen.' When my father stumbled in the corridor, my mother took his hand and led him away to rest in his room. 'Quiet; you'll wake the children.' I lie in my bed, their voices singing in my ears, hands upturned on the candlewick spread, quiet and wide awake.

'Look, look at Miss C., she's sleeping.' They bring me chocolates, grapes and hot milk to drink. John the Baptist comes in: 'Christ in every eye that sees me, Christ in every ear.' Mrs Tierney, kicking up her heels to show off her scarlet slippers. And the laughter comes bubbling from my lips, spilling from my heart that is drunk with joy. I do not mind them now, they can mutter and skip as they like. A hundred days' indulgence – a thousand pairs of slippers; I do not care. I lie in my bed, eyes closed; all stones upturned. 'The judgement day must first be nigh ere you shall fade, ere you shall die,' he called, stumbling in the corridor, 'my own Rosaleen.' But Rosaleen was Ireland.

It was Ireland that would not fade, that could not die. And my mother's name was Mary, Mary Elisabeth; she knew that.

The hawthorn taps at my window and shakes its clear blossom. How often did it warn me? I have asked Nurse Kenny to lay a white cross under its branches, as we used to in Galway, after a death. I have given up my coat and scarf, my patent leather shoes, my hat with the violet trimming. I will not need them now. I have kept the photograph. Her face in its silver frame; where she sits on the banks of the Royal Canal, the water flowing smooth under its bridge; where she went for safekeeping, with Lily Kavanagh. The wind plucked their voices and blew them far behind, but her green eyes smile at me over her shoulder.

I lie in my bed, and the pictures dance before my gaze; the brilliant pictures that have returned to me. Sister Josephine approaches: 'Well, now, Miss Callaghan – isn't that the wonderful smile?'

My jaw does not stick and I can say anything that pleases me.

'Isn't that grand? Would we like a few of the lovely daffs round our bed?' I stretch my fingers to their yellow light and the laughter bubbles like champagne from a wide brimmed glass:

'For oft when on my couch I lie in vacant or in pensive mood they flash upon that inward eye which is the bliss of solitude and then my heart with pleasure fills and dances with the daffodils.'

'Well indeed, Miss C. Aren't we the great one to remember it now?' she says. 'Are we quite ourself, at last? Aren't we the proud girleen?' She takes my hand, her smile is wide and calm as the walls of my room, and I say, 'Yes Sister Josephine. Yes.'

Flowers for Easter

He stretched out his arms, Oop la baby, he caught your hands and pulled you up. You climbed his tall, loose body that was the branch of a tree blowing. You climbed his knees, his thighs, his chest until you stood high on his shoulders. Oop la baby, you swung on his shoulders. Eat up your porridge, pick up your heels, blow your nose, do what you're told, time for bed baby, upsa daisy, mind your head, ba.

At five to six his train came in. You watched at the window. Bars of chocolate stowed in the pockets of his mackintosh. Lucy set his slippers by the fire. He read to you a bedtime story – blood and thunder – just to please you: fee fo fei fum I smell the blood of an Englishman, drop it stranger, thar she blows. When he was finished, your mother came to carry you and Lucy up the stairs. Upsa daisy baby, two girl girls ha.

Once you ran away from home. You ran away because they had beaten you. He woke you in the night and slapped you pulling up your nightdress. You had punched your brother's nose and made it bleed. You hated everyone. You ran all the way up the hill. They ran after you. Their feet beating the road, their breath panting. A flying tackle, they caught you round the waist. Bad bold brat, cry baby sissy. They held your kicking legs, they bore you home. You

107

locked the bathroom door, you blocked the keyhole. You promised yourself, cross your heart and hope to die, you wouldn't run away again until you were big enough to run faster.

No one slapped Lucy. No one needed to. Thin and frail as he, with his solemn sober eyes. Daddy's good girl. He taught her the names of the flowers and birds of Ireland. He taught her to do the crossword puzzle, though she was only seven years old. Old enough to travel by herself on the bus to school (you trailed the house after your mother, she sang you songs, you tied a red bandanna round your neck), old enough to go alone to visit him in hospital. She took him pansies from the garden and his favourite polo biscuits. Oop la baby, you staggered in and drew from the left. Come here to me my little drunken soldier. You held up your hands, but he was too tired then to let you climb.

Your father's clothes still hung in the wardrobe, but you were afraid to open it now.

'Will you get out my red dress pet; the one with the long sleeves and the buttons down the front?'

Your mother was sitting at the dressing table, a cardigan over her shoulders, brushing out her hair. You did not want her to see that you were frightened. She did not know about the wardrobe.

She had left all his things in their usual places: his books and magazines in the livingroom, his silver cigarette case on the chest of drawers, his shaving brush on the bathroom shelf. You picked it up sometimes and held the cold metal handle to your cheek. But you never opened the wardrobe.

You used to hide in it once, drawing back the small steel bolt that fastened his door and climb inside. You would crouch in silence behind his long coat while your mother searched the house downstairs calling your name.

His clothes were in there still; his shirts and jackets and ties shut up in the darkness just as he had left them. You could see them without looking. Broad-shouldered on their wooden hangers: his good suits

108

for the office; the grey one and the brown one and the blue one, their creased legs dangling, the shoes lined up beneath them, leather stiff and gleaming.

'Hurry up love, I'll be late for the shops.'

You opened the door on your mother's side carefully. You lifted down the red dress that she had worn the first day going to the hospital. You closed the door without looking in the mirror. That was the other thing. You did not want to see his face. It would be there in the glass still, as it had been every morning when he stood before it; his shirt collar open, his sleeves rolled up to shave for work. You crept behind to watch. When he caught sight of your reflection, his lips grinned through the foaming lather and, rolling up his eyes, he drew the long blade across his throat.

It was a game he played to make you laugh.

The scream had been waiting inside Lucy since the night they came for him. You saw it huddled in her shoulders; pinched in the whitened corners of her mouth.

Coming home from school, her feet in their leather soled shoes slithered on the icy road. She held onto the belt of your coat. She taught you to say your prayers, to tie your laces, to write the first letter of your name by imagining a railway bridge upside down and drawing that. When you played highway men with Billy she was the lady in the stagecoach waiting to be robbed of her jewels, or the housewife who called you in to fix the plumbing.

It was the week after Christmas.

You were woken in the night by the noise of his heart attack. Lucy lay on her back stiff and cold beside you. You were afraid to speak or to touch her, but you knew her eyes were open staring into the darkness. Her knees were drawn up to her chin so that draughts of cold air came under the lifted blankets. You thought if you made your body as stiff as hers the noise might stop. You clenched your toes, your hands, your eyes, but it grew louder. You counted to one hundred and one and down again but still you heard it. It was not like anything you had known. Not like a human voice at all. They had told you all the words for your father's illness; they were long soothing words, you had boasted of them to your friends. Migraine, hepatitis, thrombosis. You went over them now in your mind, trying to fit them to the panting like an animal in pain that came through the bedroom wall.

A silence followed and then you heard your father speak in almost his usual voice. 'For Godsake hurry woman.' You heard the sound of your mother drawing on her clothes, stumbling in the darkness. 'What does it matter what you look like,' and her feet going down the stairs and the banging of the front door.

'Hail Mary full of grace the Lord is with thee, blessed art thou among women and blessed is the fruit.' Your brother Fergus was reciting the rosary. He would be kneeling by the bed, his head bowed, the beads dangling from his hands so that the crucifix lay along the sheet. Holy Mary Mother of God pray for us sinners, now and at the hour. The sound came round and round; a humming ring of sound that circled in the pain, the fear and the noises that broke from your father's body.

There was a new footstep on the stairs, clumsy; making the floorboard creak that your mother knew to avoid. The rosary stopped. You heard the doctor's voice. Not the usual one – Doctor McGrath who had the funny way of walking and broke a syringe once boiling it in the kettle, but another one. He spoke to Fergus, whispering and, silence again. Then a gurgling came out of your father's throat that was like water being sucked from a drain. You put the pillow over your ears.

The stretcher banged against the door as they tried to fit it round the bannister. You knew what it would look like. You had seen a body brought up from the sea, carried swaying along the pier; the long mound covered by a grey blanket, leather straps to bind it like a suitcase over the legs and chest.

The doctor spoke to your mother as the stretcher

went down the path. 'Not to worry. He'll be quite comfortable now.'

On a windy day, when the sea was big and rough, blowing gusts of spray over the harbour wall, you walked up to the bathing place. The sign at the gate said 'men only', but you went in anyway because it was winter and there would be no one to mind who came. In the summer they stretched out their towels and lay on their backs, the sun on their white skin and the fat sausage, pink or yellow curled on their thighs. Once you had climbed the cliff with Billy and thrown down stones so that they jumped up clutching their towels. But it was winter now and too cold for anyone to be dressing or undressing, except for old Mr Johnsson with the long white hair who swam every day for the good of his circulation.

You walked along the cliff path that was steep and narrow. The wind caught at your clothes and blew your hat high in the air, but your mother held your hand and shielded you with her coat. You stared down at the fierce water thrashing itself into a hundred white pieces on the rocks. You stood until your cheeks burnt and your lips were blue. Then your mother pulled you by the hand and you ran madly hell for leather down the hill, your bodies knocking together until you were both worn out and laughing.

It was a perfect day for the bathing place. After dinner when the boys had gone back to school, you asked your mother if you could go. She went on washing dishes at the sink and did not look at you. 'Have you forgotten that we have to go to the hospital?'

You walked beside her through the tall silver gates, past the parked cars of the doctors, into the revolving doors, and entered the hallway where Saint Michael,

111

high on his pillar, gazed down at you as he speared to death a yellow snake that had coiled about his feet.

Your father had been sick for five weeks now lying in the bed next to the window, his head turned towards the street so that he would see you the moment you alighted from the bus.

Your footsteps clattered on the stone floor, your voices sounded far and small. The smell closed in on you as you walked up the staircase; the thin blue odour, as it seemed to you, that rose from everything you touched: the chrome bannisters, the gloss green walls, the trolleys that stood on each landing, filled with fine glistening instruments. Why do hospitals smell like this? It's disinfectant. What's disinfectant? To kill germs. What are germs? What people in hospitals have. Why do they put sick people in hospitals then?

At the top of the stairs a woman was down on her hands and knees polishing the floor with beeswax. That was a nice smell. 'Hallo,' she said, smiling at you because she had seen you coming so often. You skated along the corridor on the slippery tiles past the old men in plaid dressing gowns who had been brought out to sit on the benches for a smoke. A nun appeared and stretched out the white wings of her sleeves. 'No running in the corridor please!' A stiff white shield of cloth stood out from her face. A golden crucifix was fastened like a dagger in her leather belt. Her long skirt made a clacking noise as her black boots pushed from under it.

There was Saint Mary's ward, Saint Anne's, Saint Joan's and Saint Brigid's – that was where your father was, three pillows behind his back to help his breathing. He put out his arms. How's my little drunken sailor? How many pirates have you killed today? He pulled you to his chest. He had on the same blue striped pyjamas that he wore at home when he slept in the big bed with your mother, but the feeling of the cloth against your face was different now. He cleared books and papers from his chair, your mother sat down and you sat on her lap. There were one, two, three, four, five, six, seven other beds in the room with a man in every one, a locker beside it, with a water jug, a tumbler and flowers in a vase. They lay on their sides, only their heads showing as if they were sleeping but you saw that their eyes stayed open. One man with a bald head sat up reading the newspaper. That was Mr O'Connor, a great man for a game of chess.

'The dandelion lights its spark lest Brigid find the wayside dark and brother wind comes rollicking for joy that she has brought the spring.' You had learnt it to please your father. You said your ABC and counted backwards from a hundred. When the nuns got hold of you they would have nothing left to teach you.

'How is the garden getting on?' he asked your mother. She told him everything she could think of, about the snowdrops, the crocus and the daffodils that had bloomed under the forsythia. It did him good to talk about the flowers. He worked in the garden every Saturday, and after work when the evenings were fine. He took up the bulbs of the tulips and stored them in the coalshed wrapped in newspaper for the autumn. He cut lengths of bamboo and used them to support tall flowers whose heads were too heavy.

They told you not to stare, but you did when you heard the curtains drawn, rattling round the corner bed, the scurrying of the nurses' shoes, and the doctor giving orders in the low, urgent whispers you remembered from home. Brought in last night, poor lad, not much chance for him.

Will we open the treasure trove? That was what he called his locker. There were books and magazines, grapes, apples, bananas, boxes of chocolate; Milk Tray and Black Magic brought by visitors who did not know he had to watch his diet. He took out a mandarin orange and peeled it with his penknife. He pierced one section with the blade and held it out to you. You put it in your mouth, but you did not want to swallow it. You had the idea that his sickness might have got under the white pith as he sliced it and would run down your throat with the sweet sticky juice.

Like water washing in a basin, the nun's habit made a swooshing noise as she strode into the ward. You knew visiting time was over. Your father wiped your mouths and hands with a handkerchief from under his pillow. Don't give your mother too much trouble. She bent to kiss his cheek and he said something into her ear. You ran to the end of the room, as you passed the last bed you looked through a chink in the curtains. A man with a red face was lying on his back, plastic tubes trailing from his nose.

'Whose little girl are you then?' The nurse put her warm hand on your head. 'A caution, Mrs Moore, a caution.'

You were getting away with murder, Brian said, with your father sick, you did what you liked. You left the table when your tea was only half finished, you went to bed at all hours. You stole his school tie and left it lying on the grass in the rain. He was twenty minutes late for class because of you. His face was pale, a little muscle bulged at the side of his jaw. He caught your wrist under the table and, putting both hands around it, twisted the skin in opposite directions the way he said the Chinese did in the war. But your mother did not notice. She sat at the bottom of the table holding a cup of tea but not drinking from it, staring out the window at the sea that was rolling slowly in, the sound stirring the seaweed that grew on the rocks.

Fergus said Brian was a sissy. He was weak and thin and had no muscles. He had no friends either and was always being beaten up by other boys. That was why he was mean to you. Once they kidnapped him, and tied him with barbed wire and left him on the pier with the tide coming in. Fergus could knock him down with one punch. At the dinner table he would put out his fork and pinch potatoes off Brian's plate when he was finished his own. He called him Queeny. Brian looked up the dictionary to find long words that people would not understand to insult them. He said cruel things to everyone to get his own back. Your mother did not have time to read to you before bed. She asked Brian if he would instead but he said, let her learn for herself like everyone else and mocked you with his new name: 'Infantile Paralysis'.

He came home from school with a bloody nose. He said he had fallen off the bike on the way down the hill but you knew he had got it wrestling with Fergus in the park. Your father had forbidden them to fight, to use bad language or to stay out after dark. When they wanted to go up to the hill to play football your mother let them, though it meant that they came back with their clothes covered in mud, and she would have to wash out their shirts, and have them dry and ironed again for the morning. But she said anything for peace and did not mind if it was dark when they came home.

Was Fergus your mother's husband, Billy asked you, now that you did not have a father anymore? You were on the swing you had made, that hung lopsided from the copper beech; you were swinging high in the air, feet and eyes tilting to the sky. You told him you did have a father, that he beat all the other men in his ward at the crossword puzzle, you said he was suffering from migraine, indigestion and coronary thrombosis and that he would be home for Easter.

Billy McNally was your best friend. He called for you every morning. He climbed the apple tree that grew between your gardens and pressed his face between the boughs to watch you having breakfast. With a plank over the gravel path you were Robin Hood and Little John meeting on the bridge in Sherwood Forest. You brought dead crabs up from the harbour and roasted them on a spit; lighting a fire under the bushes and stuck earth worms on the wire fence to dry. When you had collected enough empty jam jars you stacked them in the pram and pushed them up to the town. A penny for the pound jars; a halfpenny for the halfpound.

'People were very good, it was wonderful how they

rallied round.' On the days that you did not go with your mother to the hospital you went in to play with the McNallys or the Stephens. The Stephens kept pet rabbits in a hutch at the bottom of the garden. Jockser and Daisy. They were always having baby rabbits that Mr Stephens killed by putting them in a biscuit tin with rags soaked in chloroform. You poked handfuls of grass through the wire of the hutch and they rolled back their long ears and stuck out their noses that quivered as if you were going to sneeze. Do you know how they get their babies? If you waited long enough you would see them doing it. But, though you waited for hours sometimes, you never did.

Would you like to stay for tea, they asked, when it was getting dark and your mother was not back yet. You said what you had been told to say, 'if it's not any trouble'. 'Of course it's no trouble.' They brought out the high stool for you and you sat round the table in the kitchen that was warm because of the Aga cooker. Welsh rarebit, flapjacks and peanut butter on your bread instead of ordinary. You could have as many helpings as you liked because there were no boys in the family. Mrs Stephens made chips for you, knowing you could not have them at home.

'Fried food is bad for the heart. It gives you indigestion.'

'Children can not get indigestion'.

'Can they get thrombosis?'

When Mr Stephens came in he kissed Mrs Stephens on the top of the head. How is my girl? He read aloud the bits from the newspaper that made him laugh. He took Barbara and Geraldine on his knee. 'Mareseadoats and doeseadoats and little lambseadivy, de doudiny doudin doo, wouldn't you?' He swallowed a penny and brought it out through his ear. He made an Egyptian pyramid with a pack of playing cards.

'My daddy can turn his eyes inside out!'

'Can he now? And how is he getting on,' they asked and Mr Stephens said your mother was a wonderful woman.

'For as long as you need it, Sheila – please God that won't be for long.'

Fergus helped your mother to carry the bathchair upstairs. It was too wide to fit round the bannisters so they had to lift it over them. When they got it into your parents' room they set it down next to the bed on your father's side. You wanted to know why it was called a bathchair. It did not look like a chair. It was a square shaped chest of dark wood and it looked like something to keep clothes in. Yes, yes, it was for washing more easily your mother said. But when you lifted the lid you saw that there was a wooden seat and inside it a white porcelain toilet bowl exactly like the one you had in the bathroom. Brian sneered. It should be called a commode not a bathchair. They had to move the table, where your father kept his books and tablets and cigarettes, to make space for it. The room looked strange with all the furniture changed about. What does he need a commode for, you asked. Your mother opened the chest of drawers and put your father's tablets and cigarette packet inside it. When he comes home from the hospital at first he won't be strong enough to be going back and forth to the bathroom. You imagined his legs being too weak to hold him up. He had special exercises to do for his circulation. He lay on his back and waved his legs in the air as though he were riding a bicycle. But even so they must have got very thin and white lying under the covers for all those weeks.

He used to go for a walk in the evening after work. His constitutional. He would go to the pier and talk to Mick Maguire or Mr Costigan when they were mending the pots. You went with him and stood by the drain where the rats came up from the sewage pipe – great black furred water rats that would scuttle across the rocks, jump in and swim across the harbour if you threw stones at them.

'Will he be able to go for walks when he comes home?'

'Not at first, love. Not until after Easter and then only for short ones.'

Lucy said that Easter was on the seventh of April.

And that it was one week, six days and seventeen hours away. Every night before going to sleep she marked off another day with red pencil in her diary. It was a blue, leather covered book with gilt edging. When closed it formed a case that you could lock with a small key. Beside every date there was a space for writing and a poem beside it. You wanted to know what she put down in it, but she wrote it in code so that even if you found the hiding place she had for the golden key, you could not understand it. You reminded her that you could not read ordinary writing, but she said that did not matter. She read out to you the rhyme for the seventh of April. 'But green leaves and blossoms and sunny warm weather and singing and laughter all come back together.' You said that when your father came home from hospital you would all have to do homework again at night. You asked did she remember the time he had slapped you for punching Brian in the nose and making it bleed. He had got you out of bed in the middle of the night and put you over his knee with everyone watching. That could not happen while he was in hospital. God will strike you dead, Lucy said. She would tell your mother. You begged her not to, but she said she would. You pinched her arm. Cross your heart and hope to die. She called you little savage and kicked your shins. Your mother came in to turn off the light. Have you said your prayers yet girls?

It was early morning in the garden. You sat on the front steps in your red windcheater and boxer shorts, your chin resting on your knees, and contemplated the tulips. A blackbird on the sycamore sent a peel of song across the hedges. The petals of the flowering cherry fell to earth in a spray of white and pink. The sun was everywhere. It shone on your cheeks and on the bare skin of your thighs. It drew the oily smell of tar from the black pebbles of the road, it beat on the blue water lying in the bay until it glistened like silk.

The tulips had opened in the night. In rows three

118

deep under the cherry tree, they rose on tall green stems, a blaze of colour, the delicate curve of their sides held wide as a cup to drink the light. You gazed at them in wonder. No other flower could equal them; proud and valiant they stood; a battalion of infantry drawn up, shoulders pressed together, their petals grouped in a brilliant shield of satin.

Billy's face appeared between the boughs of the apple tree. His glance travelled from you to the flowers and back again. He watched in silence to discover what you were thinking, his eyes squinting against the brilliance of the sea light. You stood up and walked slowly to the centre bed. You took hold of one bright stalk and put your face into its bowl of petals. The sweet dusty perfume washed over you. You fingered the fine black tongue that rose from the heart. You looked up and saw that Billy was smiling, an intent, fleeting smile of comprehension. He had understood exactly. He crossed over the fence and came to stand beside you.

Slowly you moved about the clipped edges of the bed, smelling, touching, tasting the flowers, the pollen blowing in your faces. Then the idea came to you, the best idea of all. Imagine if you made a carpet for the little hut. Imagine them spread like a gleaming cloth under the bushes, you would lie in them when it rained, or sit buried to your knees. Imagine the feeling of them on a hot day under your feet! Billy hugged his arms about his chest and his breath escaped in a long whistle. Imagine! No one anywhere would have a hut to match it.

You touched a red petal tentatively with your fingertips; it felt like the inside of a cat's ear; furred leather. You plucked one and held it to your mouth. You stroked your lips with it. Then you held it to Billy's face and he laughed because it tickled the fine blond hair that grew along his cheek. He plucked a tall white one with pink streaks and he put it to your face, tickling your ear. And then you plucked another, a red one and he plucked a black one, and you plucked a yellow one and he plucked a striped one, and you plucked a white one and he plucked a

119

scarlet one. Soon they were falling in drifts behind you, each one snapped lightly from its stem with a sharp cracking sound as the head broke free. Treading cautiously on the edge of the soil so as not to trample the primulas, you began to gather the tulips from the inner row. The pollen covered your fingers with its golden dust and the smell of them rose in waves that made you giddy. And then you had come to the final one. It was red. You touched the tip of the black tongue, it quivered at your touch, you smoothed the stiff curve of its petals. It was yours. You plucked it.

Billy held out his arms rigid in front of him as if they were the prongs of a fork lift truck. You caught up bundles of the glowing blossom and piled them into his grasp. When his arms were full, he carried them to the mouth of the hut between the fucshia and the rose bush and, dropping on his knees, wriggled through the narrow tunnel. You watched while he let loose his cargo. He ran back to join you and it was your turn to stretch out your arms and be loaded. Billy gathered up handfuls and spilt them over you. The petals were cool and soft on your bare skin. When the load reached almost to your chin you heard the window opening behind you, the whirring sound as the sashcord slid upward. Your mother was standing in the front bedroom, gazing out to sea with a vague dreaming expression in her eyes that were the pale, clear, green of the water as if they had soaked up its colour. You waited for her to turn to you, for her praise when she saw the treasure you had collected. 'Look – look – we are making carpets,' Billy sang out. And her eyes moved reluctantly from the sea to the garden. She was smiling. 'Flower carpets,' Billy called. But she was not looking at him or at the brilliant petals strewn about his feet. She was staring at the flowerbed where the sharp green stems of the tulips rose three deep under the cherry tree. 'Hundreds and thousands,' Billy cried, jumping up and down on the rug of blossom, pounding it with his white, leather sandals.

Your mother clapped her hand to her face. It covered her smile, but not her full, staring eyes. Tears came up in them. She shook her head from side to side but no sound came. Your stomach clenched with fear. What had happened? You turned from her pale, stricken face and looked behind you at the bed where the stalks of the tulips rose raw and jagged from the brown clay. You clutched the bundle of flower heads close to your chest. What had you done? What terrible mistake had you made?

Your mother wore her best clothes visiting the hospital: her wine red dress and coat and her blue, silk scarf that she fastened at the neck with her foxhead brooch. You sat beside her on the warm plastic of the bus seat. You put your hand into her pocket and closed your fingers round the dimpled leather of her purse. Neither of you spoke. You understood what you had done. She was not angry with you. She had not slapped or scolded you. She sat sad and still, looking out through the grime of the closed window at the men and women who hurried past on the street, who were smiling and calling to each other because of the sunshine and the fine day.

They had let Lucy out early. She stood waiting by the hospital gate in her brown and beige school uniform with two yellow bows tied in her hair. You went first through the revolving doors, pushing hard with the flat of your hands so that the swooshing noise it made was louder. At the foot of the stairs your mother paused. She brushed the hair off your forehead and reset the slide. Whatever happens, she said, do not tell your father, it would kill him. You knew what she meant. You remembered then that he asked every day how the garden was coming on. You remembered that they were letting him home on Sunday and that the tulips were his pride and joy. What has she done now, Lucy asked. You looked down at the bare stone feet of Saint Michael where the yellow serpent was coiled, its tongue darting. You touched the head, it was smooth and hard and cold.

You passed the woman who was polishing the floor.

'A beautiful day, thanks be to God.' 'Will it hold out until the holiday, do you think?' your mother asked her. You did not feel like sliding in the corridor. Instead you walked close behind Lucy, taking short steps so as not to tread on her heels. At Saint Brigid's ward the nun appeared in the doorway. She stood with her arms folded, her hands hidden in the drapes of her sleeves. You saw a line of black hair growing out from under her veil. She looked from you to Lucy and made a tut-tutting noise with her tongue on the roof of her mouth. 'It would be best if you did not take the children in today, Mrs Moore.' You glanced around her skirt to see into the ward. The bed next the door was empty, the sheets and covers had been stripped off and only the lumpy grey mattress remained. Was that the reason you were not to go in? Your mother took hold of your hand and drew you past the nun. You walked hesitantly with your head lowered. You saw the twinkling diamond pattern the sun made on the linoleum covered floor. Then you heard your father's voice. 'Come here to me my little drunken sailor.' You looked up at him. One of his legs was sticking out from the side of the bed. They had wrapped a pyjama jacket round it and propped it on a stool. You wondered why that was. The bones of his cheeks stuck out and his skin was the pale waxy colour of the candles that burnt in the nun's chapel. It was his eyes that frightened you. They were sunk into his head, and it seemed to you that all the blue had faded from them so that only the white was left. You had the idea that he might have gone blind. But he turned his face to your mother's voice and whispered something as she drew near. She went ahead of you and lifted his stiff leg from the stool and put it back under the covers. She put the cigarettes she had brought and the bottle of Mi-Wadi barley water on the top of his locker. His own chair was piled with fruit and papers so your mother took the one Mr O'Connor offered. He patted the sheet for Lucy to sit beside him, but you thought of his stiff leg lying under the blankets and you climbed up on the window ledge to sit next to the statue of Saint Francis. 'Are we sitting comfortably?' he asked with a slow smile when you were all settled.

Your mother laced her fingers through his and their hands rested together in her lap. His voice was weak and tired so she did most of the talking. She told him about Brian getting ninety nine percent for algebra and geometry and how Mrs Molloy's new baby had been born two months premature, and they were both in the nursing home still.

Nurse O'Reilly came in to take his temperature. She had a silver-faced watch strapped to the starched breast of her uniform. You liked the way she had of drawing the thermometer from its sheath and shaking it in the air as if to cool it. But she did not do it this time. She looked at the chart at the end of the bed. 'How are we getting on so?' Your father said he had a surprise in his locker and would she get it out for him. It was the turquoise blue box with stars carved in the lid that you had glimpsed every day behind his library books. Terry's Starlight chocolates: a new kind you had not had before.

'Can I tempt you Joan — I have been saving them for a special occasion.' But Nurse O'Reilly laughed. 'We haven't all your luck. Some of us have to watch our figures,' and she said she would come back in a bit for the temperature. Your father opened the box and then laid the sweets in their brilliantly shaded wrappings across the sheet. Lucy took three for herself and passed three to you. But your mother did not want any and kept hold of your father's hand. She had stopped talking. You wondered why she did not finish the story about Mrs Molloy and the incubator. Your father squeezed her hand in his to make her smile. But it did not. You thought he must have pressed the rings into her fingers again because she jumped slightly in her seat and glanced up startled.

'How is the garden looking,' he asked and then rested for a moment, leaning back against the pillows until he had enough breath to go on. 'Are the tulips up yet?'

Your mother sat silent. She moved her eyes slowly towards the shaft of sunlight that came through the high window and fell in a pool at your knees. You curled your tongue round the sweet you were sucking and held it in the back of your throat. You swung your feet faster; to and fro so that they knocked loudly on the wall beneath you.

'Yes,' your mother said, 'they opened this morning. They never looked more beautiful than they did this morning.'

You could not stop the blush that rose in your cheeks, that came always when you told a lie. But your mother did not blush. Her face stayed still and white and her eyes rested on the blue flowers between you and the feet of Saint Francis.

Your father began to cough, holding his handkerchief to his mouth. When he took it away you saw that he was smiling.

'I'll see them at Easter,' he said.

'Yes, please God.'

It was time to go home then. You kept your head lowered while you stood behind Lucy, waiting to kiss him goodbye. He kissed her forehead as well as her cheeks and held her tight against him so that the buttons of his pyjamas pressed into her flesh. You thought he must have seen the fear in your eyes because he put the box of Starlight into your hands and said you could take them home with you. You wanted to ask him if he would finish reading *Bitter River Ranch* the next day, but you were thinking about the flowers and did not say anything. He reached out to tousle your hair and then his arm was too weak and fell back onto the sheet. Your mother stayed behind for a moment. When you reached the door you looked back and saw that she lifted the covers and put his stiff leg out again on the stool.

For three months afterwards your mother dressed in black. You did not have to. You wore all your usual clothes. You did not go with her when she took the suitcase from the top of the wardrobe and went in to collect his belongings. You did not see what she took out when she came back. You did not go to the

124

mortuary or to the removal of the remains. You did not see him lying in his brown cassock, his hands joined on his chest, his face in the dark hood, his white eyes closed from sight. They sent you to stay in the country instead, to the farmhouse your aunt lived in, to play in the fields, the hayloft, the stables. The food was better for you in the country and the air, and you would get to know your cousins. They taught you to ride a horse without a saddle, holding on to the shaggy mane, bounced on the sharp backbone; to bring in the cows for milking, the long teats held in your hands, the pimply skin, the shooting of warm liquid between your fingers. You collected the ducks' eggs, finding all their places; buried in the straw of the pigs' stall, the hedges and ditches, the burrows dug under the henhouse. They asked you about your own home, about going out in boats and fishing and swimming. They wanted to know what it was like to live beside the sea.

When you came home you went with your mother to choose the headstone. You sat in an office with a venetian blind, a man in a striped suit behind a desk asked what you wished to have inscribed on it. You had to decide how many words you needed. It was like sending a telegram. You paid by the word. You could have in memory or in loving memory.

You were measured for your new school uniform. You were going to the nuns in the autumn. You stood at the shop counter in front of everyone in a starched white petticoat while a woman with a bun of grey hair knelt and stretched a tape measure round your waist. It was a girls' school. A convent. They wore a blouse and red gymslip, nylon stockings or knee length woollen socks. They would laugh, Brian said, when they saw you, with your scarred and battered legs. One of the girls from the class you were entered for, you knew already. She had a beautiful name. Elinor O'Rahilly. She had blue eyes and a long black ponytail. You would make a terrible pair, your mother said. She was worse than you were – wild as a march hare!

In the garden the lupins had bloomed, the sweet

william and aubretia. They grew in profusion around the centre bed. But they did not hide the tulips. The raw green stalks rose headless from the earth. You saw now how ugly they were. The petals you had gathered had rotted in their carpet under the bushes to a dark, dank-smelling mulch. You wished the stems would wither too and die. You would have liked to go out and pluck them, to tear them up, one by one. You did not want anyone to see them and remember. You did not want your mother to look at them and think what you were thinking. She had said, do not tell your father whatever you do, and you had not. And could not now. It was something he would never know. You had thought of that when she came into the bathroom and asked you to pray for him. The evening after you got home from visiting him; when he had given you the chocolates to keep, the last evening, though you had not known it.

The wind had been blowing spray against the window, sending the rain bubbling along the wooden frame where your mother had set cloths to catch it. You had finished your tea and you were getting ready for bed.

'Lucy and Katherine.' Your mother stood in the open doorway with her hands hanging at her side. She lifted one and rested it on the doorknob. She was looking into the room, gazing at nothing. Her face was stiff and her eyes looked out of it without seeing you. It was not like any expression you knew. She might have been listening rather than looking. You strained your ears to hear what she heard; the wind sucking at the trees, the waves that would be swilling into the harbour, black as they rolled in, white as they scattered on the steps. Lucy was washing at the basin, dipping her blue facecloth in the soapy water. You were sitting on the toilet waiting for her to finish. You had torn a stretch of paper from the roll and bound it round your arm.

'Lucy and Katherine.' It startled you when she said both your names together. You looked up into her eyes and you saw then that she was frightened – afraid of you; because of what she had to say. You wanted to console her. You wanted to ask her not to speak. But she did.

'You must pray for your father tonight,' she said, 'you must pray that he won't be home for Easter.'

The blue flannel fell from Lucy's hands into the water. Her head jerked back and her mouth opened wide as though someone had pulled it. The scream that came out was the one that had been coiled inside her since the first night. And when you heard it you understood what it had been waiting for.

In the morning, when you woke, your mother was not in the house. It was Mrs Stephens you heard downstairs cleaning out the fire. The blinds were drawn in the front rooms. The radio was off. Mrs Stephens said she would stay until your mother came home, that she had a lot to attend to at the hospital. She said God was good; that Brian and Fergus had been with him at the last. She gave you the two chocolate eggs that were waiting on the kitchen table. A blue one for Lucy and, in the box shaped like a fort with a cut out window, in red foil paper: the one you had asked for.

Mrs Stephens made your breakfast. She poured hot milk on your porridge instead of cold.

It was Easter Sunday.

'Will you get out my green dress, love, the one with the long sleeves and the buttons down the front.'

Your mother was sitting at her dressing table, brushing out her hair, her back to the wardrobe where your father's clothes still hung, shut up on his own side, just as he had left them.

You were getting ready for school. You put on your pleated red tunic and fastened the blue sash about your waist. You pulled up your socks and folded them once below the knee.

'Have you learned your English for today?'

You had reams of stuff to learn off every night: tables, spellings and poetry. Mother Magdalene had said everyone in the class must choose the poem they liked best and commit it to memory. 'Sea Fever', that was a good choice. 'I must go down to the sea again, to the lonely sea and the sky . . .' Why was the sea lonely, and in what year did John Masefield die? 'To the gull's way, and the whale's way, where the wind's like a whetted knife.' Whetted had two ts, not one, and meant sharp. When the wind was in front of you, you were late for assembly; when it was at your back, you were early. That was no excuse, Mother Magdalene said. She read in sing-song voice, her veil bobbing, beating time with the glantoir on her open palm: 'and all I ask is a merry yarn from a laughing fellow rover.' When she came to the last verse her tongue made a hissing sound on every s: 'and a quiet sleep, and a sweet dream, when the long trick's over.' It was a beautiful poem; it taught acceptance of God's will, she said, and reverence for the wonders of the world he had made. But when you gazed out the window to watch the gulls playing with the wind or the waves spilling on the pier, filling and emptying the rock pool that was the nuns' private bathing place, she rapped the handle of the glantoir on the blackboard and called: 'Katherine Moore – day dreaming again.'

'Have you learned your tables?' your mother asked. Yes, you had. You had done addition and subtraction too. You did not care for them. But you liked the rhythm of the words 'multiplication tables'. You asked what they meant. You imagined a huge classroom, bigger than your school, filled with tables, stacked one behind the other, table after table, stretching on forever. The way you saw reflections of yourself in the distorting mirror at the Fun Palace in Bray. Was that Infinity, you asked.

'Hurry up, love, or we'll be late again, and don't forget your beret.'

You had a dream that he came back. You saw him standing at the window above the stairwell, the one with the panes of coloured glass that made it look like

128

the window of a church. He stood like one of the saints in a painting – Saint Francis of Assisi; barefoot in his brown cassock, white flowers drooping from the crook of his arm. His face was pale and tired, his cheekbones protruding from the skin. He did not move or speak, but you knew why he had come. He was your father but altered; he could not draw near to question or to reprimand. He could do nothing but stand still, his eyes sorrowful. Staring down from Heaven – longing for you.

But he was dead, and you had stayed alive.

Introducing Nessa

The traffic light had changed to green but she sat still, her foot pressed to the brake, her hands gripping the steering wheel so tightly the knuckles showed white under the skin. She looked at the telephone kiosk. A bulb in the ceiling filled it with light. She saw the beige paint peeling from the door, the tattered directory on the shelf, the black receiver gleaming on its metal cradle. Her fingers reached into the pocket of her coat and played with the smooth rim of a tenpenny piece. She had only to cross the street. In a few moments she might hear Nessa's voice again. But supposing it was not Nessa who answered. Supposing she was not in Leeson Street after all? Supposing it were to wake Sheila instead? What excuse could she give for calling at two in the morning? She would look ridiculous and start them talking.

She pushed the car into gear and swung the wheel roughly to the left, down the sharp incline of Ardmore Avenue to darkness and the sea. The road emptied behind her, speeding back between the smooth lawns of Hillside and Beech Heights, the houses staring after her blank and unseeing. At the foot of the hill she turned onto the seafront; drove past the station and the coal harbour until she reached the carpark. A row of cars was drawn up by the grass verge. As she pulled in, her headlights illuminated the windscreen of a blue Cortina. She glimpsed for a second a young woman's face, her eyes wide and startled; her head pressed between the seat back and her lover's shoulder. Saturday night and all over the city in locked cars men and women were clutched in one another's arms. She switched off the ignition and rolled down the window. The sea blew up to her: the small, nudging sounds of water against rock. As on that first night. They had walked here arm in arm along the dimly lit pier, the blue-black water heaving beneath their feet. Why else was she here now, if not clinging to the memory, as though it was already all that was left her? If she had guessed then how short the time ahead was to be, she would have tried to impress on her mind every moment, every last detail. As it was – drunk on cheap wine, careless – she had talked too much and whole hours of the evening were lost to her.

She lit another cigarette, gripping it between tight lips, sucked warmth from it. She was tired now, weary of pain, of anger, of self-pity. She knew there was no one to blame but herself. Not even Ben and Karen. Least of all them. She had seen them off tonight with presents and kisses – set them on the plane content in their image of her: good old Anna, never changes. She had given them a last pleasant evening, the one they wanted; one fit for retelling in Vancouver to any old friend who might ask, and to Harry. Was it for Harry she had done it? Was it for his sake she had lied? A lie no different from the others; one she would scarcely have noticed except for the mischance of it being overheard. And even tonight she had gone on with it, having nothing more to lose; gone on lying to make them happy. Ben had sat in front, his arm draped over the gear stick to fondle Karen's knee – smug and boastful in this new role of contented family man. Would it have pleased him to know what havoc his visit had caused? But he had no inkling of it. Shrewd, worldly wise, he noticed nothing. He made only one comment on Nessa, and that on the night of the dinner as she drove them back to the hotel. 'A nice looking kid,' he had said 'but a bit of a wall banger.' And Anna had smiled as though in agreement.

She took a pair of leather gloves from the dashboard and, turning up the collar of her coat, stepped out of the car. As she locked the door, she heard a stifled grunting from the Cortina beside her. She walked down the wet slope of grass, the dank acid smell of shore rose to meet her. She could see in the distance the glassed dome of the lighthouse, the shaft of white light flung out on the black bay of sea. She walked close to the wall past the ferry with its yellow portholes shimmering on the oily water. Nothing stirred; even the gulls were silent. It was dangerous to come here alone – asking for trouble. But what did she care? Physical danger was a comfort to her; the clear, undemanding fear it aroused; distracting. She wanted the night and the wind in her face, the great blank emptiness of sky, it could not be dark or cold enough. She walked quickly, head down, hearing the ring of her heels on the granite paving stones. She remembered Nessa saying that she hated the sound – the vulnerability of it – a woman's footsteps leaving a trail through the darkness. Nessa! She felt the old constriction come back into her chest like a steel band tightening around it. What did she want of Nessa? Forgiveness? She could not ask for that. What then? Understanding – was that it? The newly discovered luxury, the last thing she could bring herself to give up? But how could she explain to Nessa what she did not understand herself. There were no words left to them; they, who once had so many, thousands of words written in love, strewn on paper about the house: on table tops and pillowcases, in drawers between the folds of a shirt, pinned on the inside of a cupboard door, hidden in the pages of a book – my darling – my lover – my only one. What could she call her now? Every phrase was bankrupt. She could no longer tell even where it had begun. The love and the lying were bound inextricably together, so that to surrender one was to lose the other. And yet there had been a time when they were not. A time before fear and caution; at the start, whenever that was.

The night of the party, that first night when I kept you in conversation for hours by the fire while other women danced. Afterwards persuading you to come here with me, to walk by the sea in darkness and silence, a windblown, starless night.

We walked as far as the old boathouse, the invisible water beating against the flags of the pier. I remember our talk – dreamlike; fluid and luminous as dream. My voice predominating, in wandering anecdotes, telling the secrets of years and more than that. Discovering places I had not known – the gaps between one event and the next that are the real happening. You said we remember the past like a street seen at night; the pale, globed lamps strung in orderly procession behind us. But it was not in the light we lived, but in the spaces between – in the darkness. You seemed most at home in those unlit spaces.

You walked with your head down so that I hardly noticed how intently you listened. Smiling every now and then with that ironic, worldly wise smile of yours. At the end of the pier we climbed down the narrow stone steps to the water's edge. Standing one lower than me, the black fronded seaweed washed lazily at your feet, you looked up:

'You have set a lot of store by sincerity, haven't you? It's going to be hard for you when they start demanding lies.'

I did not know what you meant then, and did not ask because you had retreated a step to stand beside me, and I wanted only to preserve this moment of intimacy forced on you by the erratic gushing and seepage of the sea.

I remembered it later when you teased my trick of easy confidences; the innocence of my face – a privileged habit you called it – the careless, unthinking response of respectability.

And enjoying it as you did, this 'old world charm', you could hardly have foreseen how easily I would lose it. How quickly I would trade one habit for another; how soon the pattern would build: one deceit leading to another until at last they were stacked like bricks around me.

Was it I who invited you back for a drink, or did you suggest it? Either way you came home with me. You were impressed by the house, and critical because it was elegant and suburban or because my salary alone could not pay for it? You wandered about the kitchen while I made coffee, running an eye over the shelf of cookery books, fingering gadgets on the sideboard: the blender, the juice extractor, the electric breadknife – the remnants of middle class marriage. I chose the old brown earthenware mugs from the rack and set them down on the table, the milk still in the bottle.

'Harry pays half the mortgage,' I told you, 'it's no more than fair while I am bringing up Sally.'

'Sure, why not?' you answered, your voice coming to me from the sitting room where you were putting a record on the stereo, 'you have worked for it after all.'

I do not know why you made me feel I should find excuses. Perhaps it had nothing to do with you.

You stayed the night because I was too tired to drive you home; in my bed, because it was too late at that hour to make up another. The light off, it was I who reached out a hand, saying 'goodnight, to ease the tension I felt lying so close to a stranger. The rough wool of your hair startled my touch, the curls springing back from my fingers. You stretched your hand to mine and drew it to your mouth. I felt the warm deliberate pressure of your lips. We might have fallen asleep that way, side by side, our fingers interlaced, but at that moment a car drove by sweeping a yellow arc about the walls. I saw your face lit for an instant; your eyes glittering like a cat's; wide with alarm. It was you, Nessa, who first showed fear. Was it that gave me courage? Or was it a caprice; arrogant in its naivety – did I want to show you how little I was disturbed – how broadminded? I kissed your mouth. After that there was no turning back and no stopping place.

We slept for a few hours after dawn, light returning, the sounds of morning rising from the street, and it was the first time, Nessa, in almost three months that I slept without dreaming of you.

But that was not the real beginning was it? For me at

least it started somewhere else entirely, long before that night. In those shabby unheated rooms beside the river when I went to my first Thursday meeting. You hardly remember that afternoon, I suppose, a cold wet day towards the end of December. I had read a letter from one of you in the Times advertising a debate on the divorce campaign. I do not know exactly what prompted me to go – curiosity in part, wanting to see for myself how women at the centre of so much controversy behaved among themselves, and the half acknowledged feelings of anger and frustration I had known since coming home. It was a shock coming back after five years of married life in Canada. I had forgotten how women were treated here: the patronage and contempt that were a part of daily life, how the smallest social exchange could become a set battle. It infuriated me to have half grown boys call me 'dear' and 'love'; to tolerate the gauntlet of innuendo and abuse one had to run ordering a drink in a pub or simply walking down a city street. I had forgotten all this. I had not realised that I could be made to feel a schoolgirl again because I had taken a ring from my finger.

We were halfway through the meeting when you came in. You stood leaning your back against the door jamb, hands sunk in the pockets of your jeans, smiling with that curious, upward, catlike tilt of your face. And your eyes were feline too: brilliant and wary as a cat's.

We were sitting on the floor in a circle discussing welfare discrimination against married women. When you spoke, the first emotion you roused in me was resentment. You accused us of trading in power by association, quoting Shaw: 'any woman who reads the marriage service and goes through with it deserves all she gets.' You said we collaborated in our own oppression. Of course, you were being intentionally provocative but I felt injured, aggrieved. As a single mother, working to keep myself and my daughter, I had expected support and sympathy from feminists not denunciation. As you talked on, developing your theory of right wing women policing each other to win male approval, I recognised a depth of feeling that

135

eclipsed mine completely: an anger carried so long it had been honed to a smooth, gleaming weapon. My hostility evaporated. Listening to you, I felt restored to my old self image of balance and moderation. In a strange way (and this should appeal to your love of irony) that was the origin of your fascination for me – you made me feel safe, normal again.

From then on I went to the meeting every week. Sitting in that cold draughty room in the company of women who were self sufficient, self directed, who took each other seriously and who, in the intensity of their conflicts, bestowed on each other an authority nowhere else given to women, I felt an amazed elation, the sense of coming home, though it was a home I could not have imagined. Experiences I had thought too private, too petty to be spoken of, shared in that room became politics so that I lost the burden of them and found them transmuted into tools of liberation.

So many marches and meetings, so many drunken debates afterwards in pubs up and down the city. And always for me, your voice passionate and eloquent: inspiring, provoking. Anyone familiar with these things could have predicted, I suppose, that I would fall in love with you. But what was it that drew your attention to me? You have given me many reasons, but I still do not understand it. Was it just the old pull of opposites? Or was I a challenge to you, or perhaps even a kind of reassurance?

I thought twice before going to Sheila's party. It would have been easy to find an excuse. I think I knew, without allowing myself to know, what was likely to come of it.

Do you remember how awkward I was at the beginning, visiting your house in Ranelagh? Five women living together, sharing one another's clothes and bedrooms, walking about the kitchen half-naked, rolling joints for breakfast, making love at all hours of the day and night: shamelessly, as though it were the most natural thing in the world, Robyn and Joan so loud they could be heard from the back garden. I had not realised how many women were in on this extraordinary secret I shared with you.

It took me a while to work out who was lovers with whom. I imagined communal orgies. I thought that, living as you did, you would have a total disregard for the usual romantic conventions. The day you introduced me and we sat in the kitchen drinking bottled Guinness, with photographs and posters from the movement staring down from the walls, I felt ridiculously out of place; for the first time what I suppose I looked: a suburban housewife. But if I did, no one else seemed to notice. None of you was puzzled by me. Not even when I began to call four or five times a week. You went about your lives blithely unaware while I shed my orderly habits as so many superfluous clothes at the end of winter and no one asked questions or showed the least surprise. Had you seen it all before?

You must have, of course, and must have been through it yourselves at some time. You said I was coming clear from years of camouflage. Out of the closet, as you all called it. But to me when I forgot to be self-conscious, it felt more like emerging from a chrysalis – a slow, laboured, sensuous process of self-discovery. Every day casting off layer by layer the outworn pretences: weakness, passivity, dependence on men – centuries of artifice sloughed away – the quick, vital core released.

In your room on those long March afternoons, the window looking onto a jumble of small gardens and the yellow brickwork of the old bakery, in bed together: the strangeness was only that there was none. Where had I learnt my knowledge of you? In what hidden part of my being had I stored it? Each nerve woken by your touch remembered you. Your lips on my skin were my own, or yours in some other life. My hands became the flesh of your thighs, the arc of your spine. Our names came spilling from some source more secret and magical than childhood. And when I reached inside you and felt the push and suck of your womb, it was as if my own body was birthed again, hurled through the singing flesh and bone.

How long was it before I persuaded you to move in with me? That was the first mistake. I should have left

137

things as they were, spontaneous and undefined. But I could not bear to be parted from you, not for a morning or a night, I wanted you near me and all to myself. I had no way of reckoning the cost even if I had wanted to.

One night driving back to my place from a party at Barbara's, you asked if I did not mind living alone after so many years as one of a couple. You knew only too well how much I missed Sally. There was no need to go into that. But I had told you very little about Harry. I had not talked much about him to anyone since the break up. Perhaps it was because I had felt none of the expected things: no guilt, no fear of the future, no half regrets. So I told you then what I had not dared tell the others, that for weeks afterwards I had been conscious only of a sublime relief – a shameless rejoicing. I woke in the mornings an hour earlier than usual, my heart pounding with excitement, and I would lie there not able, for a moment, to remember the cause. And then it would come back to me – flooding my nerves – the realisation that I was alone – free. Free of the exhausting games of reproach and self-justification I had played for years with him, arguments that were incapable of resolution because they had no starting point. I would get up at once without waiting to dress and hurry down the cold uncarpeted stairs of my new house, wanting to sing with pleasure because there was only myself to make breakfast for – no one waiting to be served, no complaints, no disputes over the newspaper, no disputes at all, not even the need to make conversation.

And you smiled and said you knew exactly: 'going into the bathroom – dry towels and no hairs in the basin.'

You named it with your usual mockery – the bliss of recovering solitude after years of submergence in another life. Yet, seeing it so clearly, you did not wonder at my impatience to surrender it again.

You moved in with me, it must be said, under duress. You had fallen behind with the rent because Robyn had lost her job and the landlord, to whom you had been suspect from the start, seized the chance to get you out. It was a temporary measure, we told each other, until you found another flat in town. That was three months ago. How long would it have continued, I wonder, if Ben and Karen had not come to dinner?

Our life was nearing a crossroads anyway with Sally returning home in two weeks' time. Not that you thought so. You were looking forward to it. You seemed to imagine she could be slipped into our world with no more disturbance than a dog or cat. You loved my stories about her; you encouraged me every time I talked about her, which I did far too often: all the hilarious times and the sad ones. You dragged them all out of me, and we laughed ourselves awake in the morning, drinking jugs of black coffee and swapping stories of our own upbringing. It was as if you returned me, briefly, in those hours to the simplicity and spontaneity we think of as belonging naturally to childhood, but is perhaps only experienced, recalling it, years later, when we have escaped its captivity.

Part of me longed to introduce you to Sally. I wanted to show each of you off to the other. But when I thought of the questions she would ask, what she would say when she found a stranger sharing my room, little hooks of ice seemed to fasten themselves about my heart. Was it only coincidence that she had stayed so long with her father, a month more than planned, or had she detected something in my letters already, some unconscious signal that deterred her? I tried to explain to you, but you said that at eleven years of age she was no longer a child and would understand my need for a life of my own. I said that eleven was exactly the worst age. They understood enough to be vulnerable but not yet enough to be understanding. She would not begrudge me a life of my own, she was used to that. But it was the kind of life that was the problem – something she had never encountered before. 'How on earth was I to explain you?' I asked. And you said that there were no words, only actions. That she would see for herself when the time came – see my happiness and be glad of it. And then you would kiss me and we would make love again. I would forget my doubts, forget just what it was I needed to make clear.

So it was always: the hunger of our bodies subverting us, distracting us from all necessary discussion. And so it was that I never got around to telling you about the dream.

You said she would see my happiness. It was true, she would have. No one with eyes in her head could have missed it. I was absurdly, immeasurably happy. I would catch sight of myself in a mirror and, with astonishment, see my brilliant eyes, my cheeks flushed like a schoolgirl's, and think: so this is what they mean when they say radiant with happiness! All the clichés made true. All that my mother, in her innocence, had thought I would discover in marriage and motherhood, I discovered in those weeks with you. I would stare back into the glass and slowly shape the words: love, lover, in love, rehearsing them as though they were not the most commonplace in the language, but rather phrases of initiation to some secret rite.

In those first weeks I lost altogether the usual sense of human separateness, of being a single, selfcontained entity in the world. When I think of that time, I think of our bodies – our hands, our mouths. Every nerve in my being fused with yours so that we were like one creature, drawn taut with desire, and love was something that moved over us: air or fire, and we trembled together in its force. Away from you, my flesh hurt as though cut from your bone. Spasms of longing might grip me at any moment: having a drink with friends, leading a prayer in class, standing at the checkout in a supermarket, and the thought of you – the smell, the taste of you, would overpower me so that it seemed my heart would batter its way from my chest. On such days when I got home to you at last it was with a kind of desperation we made love. I felt possessed by a deadly fever; felt I must be consumed utterly, burnt to ashes before I could regain sanity, self-possession. It frightened me. I had not known such desire was possible. With men sex had been effortless – like the pleasures of food and drink. Once gone from their bed, I lost all memory of them, except for a certain satisfied ease that gave me more energy, not less, for the things of the world. With you, lovemaking carried me so far I feared the struggle it cost to return. There was no end and no beginning. Only longing. I could not have enough of you. I remember the first morning, lying in your arms I asked was it always like this? Like what, you said. So sweet – so devouring? And you smiled your mischievous, enigmatic smile and said why else do you think they hide it from us?

I wanted there to be no more hiding. I wanted to announce it to the world, I wanted to run through the streets calling out my love for you. But I did not. Oh no – from the first day I learned to conceal it. The first time I was tested – back at school on Monday. That morning, after two days and three nights in bed with you, I went into work and felt like a sleep walker who wakes from some marvellous dream to find herself at the open window of a tower block. It was Peggy Keogh who woke me – Peggy with her red, greedy lips opening for gossip. Peggy bringing me over a mug of coffee and asking in that tone of lazy curiosity:

'What did you do for the weekend – anything strange or startling?'

I felt my heart beat, the blood coming into my cheeks. How was I to answer her? Only a second's hesitation but she caught it.

'Well,' she said, running her eye over my face. My stomach tightening, I snatched at an answer.

'Yes, as a matter of fact,' and I gave a quiet little laugh of mockery, 'I met the love of my life.' That was it. As simple as that. She looked away at once, ladling sugar into her cup.

'Is that all,' she said, 'I didn't have such a great time myself.'

I had hit on it quite by accident – the perfect strategy – to lie by telling the literal truth so bluntly they could not believe it!

After that it came with frightening ease. I discovered a hundred ways. I lied to everyone and everywhere. Inventing stories that nobody asked for – imagining suspicion where there was none, and forestalling it with every trick of dissimulation. I learned with amazing speed. I found that lying was something that engaged the whole body, eyes, mouth, hands, even the way one stood could be put to service, and that its skill depended less on what was said than on carefully chosen silences. You would not believe how many opportunities came my way.

It hurt most to lie to my mother, who loved me, who had faith in me, who only wanted my happiness – who had said it so often I had almost come to believe it. The Sunday I went to visit her – the Sunday after the first week spent in bed with you, I had a wild fantasy of confiding it all; of taking her in my arms and telling her that I was happier than she could ever have imagined possible. The instant she opened the door to me I was returned to reality. She wore her sad, wistful look when she greeted me – a smile that conveyed all she wanted for me; the depth of her disappointment and her determination to go on hoping, in spite of all. We sat in the dining room for dinner. My father carved the joint at the head of the table. He talked about the mess the country was in; the new bill they were introducing to give an allowance to unmarried mothers. It would make a laughing stock of us he said, every whore in the place paid by the state to raise her brats. I lost my temper.

In the kitchen later on, doing the dishes with my mother, she put a hand on my arm and begged me to be patient with him; to remember his age, that he did not mean half of it anyway; it was only that he was annoyed with them for taxing his pension.

They were the usual words, but there was a special tenderness in her appeal. She had picked up, of course, with her unfailing eye, the change in me. She saw the new energy, the excitement I was trying so hard to suppress which had burst out in my heightened aggravation with my father. She wanted the reason. I would not help. So at last she had to ask. I raised my eyebrows and gave a look of perfect surprise. And she gave back a small knowing smile – a smile that would not be denied.

'It's Harry, isn't it. Is he coming back with Sally this time? I knew it would only be a matter of time before you two got together again.'

I turned my back on her. I told her not to be so foolish. That it was nothing of the kind. And she changed the subject and went on with the dishes for my sake, but the pleasure stayed in her eyes.

It wounded me that, ridiculously. That she could be so wide of the mark, wilfully, almost. I saw that she would never let herself confront the truth, even if it was staring into her face. It would take a battering ram to break down her defences, her dreams for me. And I had not the strength of one word.

She asked, as I was leaving, if I would be alone on Wednesday – would she come over as usual after her golf? I heard the pause that I left between us, as if it was the noise of something opening. I felt the shabby pretence of struggle with myself before giving in and with eyes down, telling her, yes I would be alone – to come over as usual. She kissed me. She had got the reassurance she wanted.

I began then, on the way home in the car, to think of an excuse. Some way, that you would not notice, to get you out of the house for the night.

And so it started – hiding you like a stray dog I had brought in from the streets which had to be kept from polite company. They compelled me to lie, Nessa. They forced me to conceal my love for you as though it were something contaminating. Every name I had heard used against women like you – like us – came back to me. Every insult that made us seem corrupt or pathetic. Away from you I had no guard against them – no dam to keep the poison from my heart. It shamed me to hide you: to deny you, every hour of the day, if only by keeping silence – silence when they asked how I had spent the weekend or what was it that had me looking so pleased with myself? For of course they all nosed it out. At work, even those I hardly knew sensed something, felt the presence of some private source of happiness hidden from its rightful place in their gossip. I lied, Nessa, for both of us; I cut myself in two, but what did it matter, it was a superficial thing, was it not, no more than a social tactic? I lied to them, and I lied again to you so that you would not know how I betrayed you. I denied everything I had discovered, denied it to strangers so that they might allow me a little corner in their world.

And all the time I was haunted by the fear of exposure. The more I concealed our relationship, the more I dreaded its discovery. There were dangers everywhere. Do you remember the day we went to Wexford and, imagining myself safely miles from anywhere, I was kissing you languorously in the car park of White's Hotel when, over your shoulder, I saw John Fogarty walking towards us up the street. I tried to pull you into the car out of sight but you stood obstinately staring back at him. You wanted to know who he was and when I told you, asked did I not think he looked suspiciously macho for a music teacher. You forced me to wait, and then he had seen us and I had to speak to him. I blurted out some rubbish, blushing, about a change being as good as a rest which made everything worse. You began to laugh helplessly and he looked at you in bewilderment and did not notice that you were not introduced.

You thought it all a great joke. I tried to make you see the seriousness of it. What if he had seen us? What if he went into school on Monday and told Peter Walshe or, worse still, Peggy Keogh? And you said he would just think we were nice affectionate girls and if he thought anything else it was because he knew too much and could not afford any gossip. Needless to say, no one I knew could be gay – nobody normal – so that did not persuade me at all. I think you felt I was playing it up to amuse you. Whatever it was, you were strangely patient.

How often did we go through my check list of fears? And, after a show of dissent, you would acquiesce reluctantly when I said that, being a teacher in a Catholic school, I would certainly lose my job if anyone in authority knew I had a woman lover; that I could not tell any family friends or relations because they might tell my mother; and that I could never, in any circumstances, let my mother suspect it because the shock might kill her; but you would not agree, whatever I said, that if she knew she was capable of going into court to testify against me if Harry ever tried to get custody: you would not think so little of her. And when it came to acquaintances and strangers, you said I had run out of excuses.

You teased me – made me see the absurdity of it. You said I was going through a phase – growing pains – that every girl had a difficult period between adolescence and maturity. And I agreed, yes, it would all come right with time.

You loved sending it up, reversing all the usual saws about sexuality. You made a game of the elaborate strategems to which I resorted to allay the neighbours' suspicions: making sure that they saw curtains drawn in two bedrooms, that we did not always leave the house together, that we had a record playing when we made love. It seemed a novelty to you. Like a child's game of making secrets, lending a thrill of the illicit to every ordinary activity. Was that the source of your patience? Did you believe your own jokes, believe that I would in time develop your courage and self-confidence, become at home in this underworld? I think you must have.

That was why I could not tell you about the dream, a pathetic trivial thing, brutal in its lack of subtlety. I am embarrassed even now to confess it. Night after night – almost from the first day you came to live with me – I have been haunted by the same predictable little fable. I am taking Sally to school. Her hand is in mine, warm, soft, confiding. We walk as far as the cloakroom door. Children are playing on the lawn to either side of us. Birds are singing, the sun falling on our upturned faces. Images of spring. Mother Ignatius is standing in the doorway. As we draw near her, she does not greet us, or step back to let us pass. Her white plump hands are clasped together across her black apron, she stands rigid, barring our path. She looks at me, and her eyes are two hard blue stones that will not meet mine, but have fastened themselves to my breast. 'I must ask you, Mrs Munro,' she says in her clear, thin voice, 'to take yourself and your daughter away from here and not to return again. We have the other children to consider.' And as I stare at her, bewildered for a second, I see that the pale stiff face under the white veil is my mother's and the eyes confronting mine now are my mother's eyes, staring in dull horror. 'There is a word for your kind I will not sully my lips by repeating.' And I hear the word she will not speak banging inside my brain. I turn without answering and pull Sally alongside me away down the wide gravel path to the gates. We walk with our heads lowered, Sally's quick stumbling footsteps following mine, her cheeks flushed, afraid to run. The children on the grass are laughing, pausing in their game to call after us. And Sally lets go of my hand.

That was the dream, Nessa. You see, it was too tawdry a thing to confide to you. You who stopped to meet me on that crossroads from another existence. You who asked always why we should cripple ourselves to protect their ignorance?

It was that foolish secret that has destroyed us.

You know well my love of parties. I do not suppose we missed one in those weeks. Crowded, noisy rooms full of dancing, drink and music; strangers cheek to cheek, or small intimate celebrations; a familiar group around a table. I loved them all. Even more than going to them, I liked to give them – to draw people together; to share my friends; to bind them in an atmosphere of candlelight, good food, wine and conversation, in a room that might be anywhere. To bind them to one another so that they forgot themselves and talked of things they had not intended and might regret when remembered.

So that when Ben called, his voice bouncing across the line to announce their arrival, wanting to meet right then, my first thought was come over to dinner, I cannot wait to see you. Thinking how you would enjoy them, the laughter and talk we would have, sharing you with old friends at last. It was not until I put down the phone and you called to ask who it was that I remembered: remembered who you were, and what I had become, and knew that they would see only the common image of the thing and pity me or sneer. Oh, to my face they might be pleasant enough, after the first stiff shock, careful, polite liberal words. But they would begin immediately to withdraw from me, to hide their lives from me as they would from a stranger. For this is what they do, I know, if you will not lie to them; if you force them to acknowledge it, they begin to lie to you. They conceal themselves behind good manners; seeing in you a threatening, unpredictable outsider who has rejected their standards, their common life – an outsider with an ugly name.

There was no way to ask them not to come and no way of asking you to leave. The next day, all through the preparations with you, shopping, cleaning, cooking this special meal for my oldest friends, I made a show of excitement. Knowing that if you guessed my thoughts it would be worse, wanting at all cost to avoid your questions, your anger: rightful anger. I bought four bottles of wine, food enough for ten, and rolled joints in advance to last the evening. You took it all without comment, noticing nothing strained in my high spirits, not curious, not wanting to know what they were like, these emissaries from my husband for whom I was taking so much trouble. It is one of the things I like most about you: your unself-consciousness, your way of taking things as natural and uncomplicated. So in your easy trust of me – wanting to share my pleasure – you did not notice, did you, that an hour before their arrival, while you were bathing, I took down from the wall the picture you had given me: two Victorian ladies on a balcony, bows in their hair, long flounced skirts, their arms about each other's waists, one turning her head to stare in arch defiance at the camera? I took it from our bedroom wall, and the photographs of the two of us

147

lying drunkenly in the garden on your birthday. I took your clothes and books too and made up the bed in the spare room, putting your things about it as though it was lived in. I made these alterations with a thief's stealth, checking a mental list of precautions to make certain that I removed every trace and hint of our relationship. I would not have believed myself capable of such furtive caution.

When I went into the bathroom I carried a bottle of champagne, wanting you drunk early so that you would be unwary; wanting to make you happy with me in this last hour alone. And you drank to the success of the evening, understanding exactly my need to impress these friends, to show them how well I had done; how much I had achieved since leaving Harry. You kissed me, the wine spilling warm from your mouth to mine. Lightheaded with fear I caressed your shoulder and the soft fall of your breast. Lying across the bed on the woollen counterpane, we made love. Stretched on the white cover, I held your dark head between my hands and was glad that your eyes were hidden from me while your mouth drew its path of fire across my skin. And then, for the first time, the dream came to me, filling my mind with its spiteful image. I wanted to break from you and, calming us both, confide my dread so that you might dispel it. But our bodies moved us beyond consciousness and when at last words broke from me, they had nothing to do with guilt or fear but a fierce, sweet joy.

And so it was that at eight o-clock, when we went downstairs dressed and groomed to greet our visitors, it was as two lovers that we opened the door. They should have seen it. Our eyes were bright and full with it. But people only see what they have heard of.

A middle-aged man held out his arms to me: a man with hollow cheeks and a greying beard. Karen beside him, thin, nervous as ever, smiling at me. Standing in the hallway, we all said how good it was, how long it had been, how little any of us had changed. And then you stepped forward. And they waited hesitant, a little surprised, for the introduction. Was that my chance? Was it in that second I should have made everything clear? Should I have taken your hand and said I would like you to meet Nessa – my lover? Is that what you would have done in my place? And I suppose then they would have kissed you too and smiled while I took their coats. But I cannot ever know what they might have done because I did nothing like that. I stood a little to one side and, without looking at you, said, 'Nessa: Karen and Ben,' and they shook your hand in turn and said how pleased they were.

And so we sat together around the sitting room fire and I poured out the drinks. And they were so easy, flattering and humorous. I showed them around the house and they said how lovely: the space, the light, envying me the garden, the lawn, the roses, the little glimpse of hills behind the roof tops. And you, setting the table, lighting candles, did not guess that I showed them the spare room and said Nessa likes to sleep at the back, it's quieter.

We gathered about the long table with its flowers and embroidered cloth, and Ben talked, and I talked, and mostly you listened, knowing none of the people or places. And I filled every glass to the brim before it was emptied and ladled out dish after dish against all protest. And they said delicious, marvellous, a feast, a banquet: I had lost none of my touch. And Ben, sinking his small sharp teeth into cream filled pastry, said that Harry had been crazy to let such a paragon out of his kitchen. And we all laughed, except you, but then you did not know Harry and no one found it odd that you did not laugh. And I poured brandy over the crêpes, and the flames leapt from the centre and ran blue and yellow round the pan, and they cheered and called bravo and said how wonderful it was to be together again, it had been much too long.

I passed round the joint as we sat by the fire and Ben said that Harry was off it completely; did not drink or smoke, had taken up jogging and healthfoods; and I said how extraordinary, Harry of all people! And Ben chortled, and looked knowing, and said, yes, Harry of all people; he is an utterly changed man. And I poured coffee into the blue-grey pottery cups you had given me. And Karen exclaimed how lovely they were and demanded to know where I had bought them. And I told her the name of the shop and the street, but not that you had given them to me for my birthday, spread them on the sheet between us, spoils of love, and, choosing one, running your fingers along its rim, had said: 'the colour of birds' eggs, the colour of your eyes.' Lounging by the fire, legs stretched to the heat, his hands cradling the broad base of his glass, Ben began to talk politics, about the left in America and the women's movement. And you saw at once how I steered him off with irony and wit and a sudden impassioned eagerness to know how Karen's exhibition had gone in the fall. But Ben saw nothing and did not notice that I had been selecting the talk all evening; nudging and shunting us from one topic to another. He did not see how my eyes reached for yours across his shoulder and begged you to be patient; saying I love you, trust me, say nothing. But you did, and dropped your gaze from mine. You took the bottle of brandy, and filled up your glass again, and sat, watching and listening, and kept silence. And were you waiting, confident I suppose, that sooner or later I would say something real, while my nerves were stretched taut, my eyes straining to catch the least gesture, to anticipate danger and draw us from it? And you had never seen me so gay, so frivolous, my conversation so insistent. You know you have changed after all Anna, Ben said, so laid back, and Karen agreed. My heart raced, my hands shook as I poured more coffee. And so it was I made my first mistake letting Ben take hold of the talk, sucking at his pipe, his tone suave; a long wandering monologue of his travels in North Africa and Asia, with self-satisfied indignation telling us of the oppression of women in these countries; the barbarous system they subjected themselves to. And I listened, tired suddenly, and thought how much he had altered, even more than myself in three years. Or had he remained exactly as always and it was only my vision that had shifted, transforming him, opening up a chasm between us? I listened, waiting for the word or phrase that must inevitably come, the question or joke that would

150

shatter my defences, pitch us into territory from which there could be no retreat. And you were bored, unheeding now, and perhaps you thought that when the time came I would stand my ground, assured, uncompromising, and say what needed to be said.

But it was not Ben who crossed the line at last. It was Karen, almost at the end, while we washed dishes in the kitchen and I had started to relax a little, imagining we had passed safely to the last half hour, to the last drinks, the last drowsy words of thanks and then bed and your body and a thousand ways to explain, to apologise. Karen stood by the sink, drying the coffee jug you had given me too, and, as if by instinct, spoke your name and asked so casually, with such lack of emphasis, her voice a little husky from smoke and alcohol,

'When did Nessa move in?'

I could not have willed myself to move or speak, though my hands went on mechanically scouring cheese from the pan.

'You know in Canada,' she continued, 'if two women of our age live together, everyone thinks they are queer. Isn't it absurd?' And she laughed that pleased chuckle of the sophisticate at the credulity of others. She laughed and I heard myself laugh too, a kind of high pitched rasping noise made into a laugh, and our joined laughter seemed to run about the walls, rattling the plates and cups, shaking the flowers in their vase, quivering the candle flame, and I said,

'Yes, that's Canada for you!' my words linking with the laughter, 'we do things differently here. In Dublin, if two single people live together it's only to halve the electricity bills!'

My back was to the door and I heard nothing above the shrilling of the kettle but I knew, the blood beating at the base of my throat, I knew in that second you had come into the room and that you were standing in silence behind me. I knew that you had overheard every word spoken. I bent forward over the sink, my hands plunged in the soapy water, and waited for someone else to speak, for someone to lift the burden from me. Karen turned, opening her lips, and then

151

closed them again because you had gone, left us
without so much as a goodnight. I heard your
footsteps across the hall and up the stairs muffled by
the carpet and the door of the spare room opened and
shut. I stood rooted, gripping the rim of the sink. Then
Karen spoke again, her voice flung into the vacuum as
one in fear rushes down a darkened passage way
sensing but unable to locate the danger.

'Well, what was that about?' And then, with a quick
brightening smile, 'I guess it must have been the
dope,' she said, 'I guess it got to her all of a sudden.'

'Yes, I suppose it did,' I replied, seizing at once on
the brilliant simplicity of it. And when we went inside
for a last coffee she told Ben and he agreed with her –
the dope, the drink – all of it suddenly too much. And
we laughed again and had another drink ourselves.

And lying upstairs alone, Nessa, perhaps you heard
us. And if you did, was it that final cowardice that
decided you?

Shortly after that I drove them back to their hotel.
When I returned an hour later, the house was in
darkness; and checking the rooms, I found them all
empty. You had taken your bike, a few belongings:
clothes and books in a rucksack, and without bothering to leave a note on the table, you had left my house.

She had reached the pier's end, the water, the glowing
glass dome of the lighthouse.

She leaned against the stone parapet and looked out
to sea. She watched the waves break in the harbour
mouth; break and, turning, beat their way out again
through the incoming swell: each white bank jostled
by another. She looked past them towards the open
bay, the dark waste of water that lay beyond. She
thought of all those compelled to live at sea. She
wondered how they endured it; to live for months on
end in exile from land. There were even some who
chose to – who set out, voluntarily, on lone voyages of
discovery. Harry had envied them – the last great
adventure left to man, he called it. Well man could
have it and gladly, as far as she was concerned. The

sea, to her, was no more than an immense vacancy; a glittering mirror, which no matter how far travelled could give back nothing but one's own reflection. But that was perhaps just what they sought in it.

She was cold. Her hands in the pocket of her coat, she drew it close about her and rocked herself gently. She should go home. In a few more hours it would be time for work.

She turned from the sea, from its cold and dark, from the repetitious noise of it, the white froth left clinging to the rocks. She turned her eyes towards the shore; the houses flung like an arm around the bay, the neon signs of the seafront hotels, the yachts at anchor; each one moored rattling to its buoy, the metal bridges arching over the railway. This was what she loved – this was her security: where the amorphous wash and spill was given shape and meaning by the grip of land. The reassurance of the everyday: the solid human world; her world, of work, friendship, family.

How often had she tried to explain it to Nessa? With no success. How could she have hoped to? Nessa had faith in people – she believed in good intentions, the power of conviction, the capacity for change. She could never understand women like Anna, anymore than she could understand cowardice or admire hypocrisy. Anna had said often enough, that it was easy for Nessa to confront the world – she had so much less to lose. But that was only half the truth. Nessa was brave; to a fault at times, careless of opinion, and above all sure of her cause. But for Anna there was no cause – no lofty vision, no banner, no battle cry – nothing to fight for but love – the right to give her heart where she pleased. And in all the world was there anything less free than love? anything more subject to social coercion, more vulnerable to envy and malice? She had known this before ever meeting Nessa but in the last few months with her she had learnt more. It was this very love that had stripped the veneer from things, shown her people as they really were; the rage and vindictiveness that lay just beneath the surface, in wait for anyone guileless enough to break rank. And once seen it was not easily forgotten.

Nessa had mocked her middle class privilege, her complacency, but even she did not see how deep the roots went – cut them, it seemed, and the whole structure toppled.

For two days now Anna had put off calling Nessa. She had told herself it was because she feared her reproaches, her anger, but there was another reason, deeper than this and less easily acknowledged. She had been aware of it in the first second of waking, of finding herself alone. Something even a few days ago she would not have believed possible. Shocked, she had pushed it below surface. But there it was again. She could not deny it. Relief was what she had felt, then and again tonight, a shabby, reluctant dawning of it, but unmistakable nonetheless. Having lived for so long on a precipice; it was an immense release from pressure to have reached an end; to know that one way or another, the struggle was over.

At the rim of the sea, light was creeping into the sky, staining the grey a muddy yellow. Seagulls set up their harsh wail along a line of black weeded rocks. Nessa would be in bed still, wherever she was; in Leeson Street, at Sheila's or Claire's, in whatever household she had taken refuge: sprawled across the sheets in the fierce abandon she had in sleep, her dark head pushed into the pillows, her skin breathing heat and fragrance. If Anna could go to her, she would steal in beside her, and without waking her, draw close; kiss her neck, her shoulders, the long indented path of her spine, she would whisper some of the old words – my darling, the most precious thing in my life, nothing I would not do for you – some soft loving lie to add to all the others.

But she knew even as she imagined this what it was she feared in appealing to Nessa, what had made her postpone calling her all these days. She was afraid not of obduracy but of forgiveness. Yes, she was afraid that she might be pardoned but on condition. Forgiven but asked to change; to begin again but differently. And which would be more painful, which would take more courage in the long run? To live without her? or to live with her — without the lies? Had she the strength for either?

She turned from the sea and began to run; running towards the shore; the dim outline of houses huddled about the bay, the clatter of her heels echoing in the waking silence. She ran without stopping until she reached the carpark. The Renault stood alone on the black sweep of tarmac, the courting couples, hours ago, gone home to their separate beds.

As she drew close to the car she noticed a door opening in one of the terraced houses on the far side of the road. A man in grey striped pyjamas stood in the hallway, stretching his arms, yawning, the white drawstring of his trousers dangling under the sagging wall of his belly. She watched him bend and lift four milk bottles from the step, scratching at the seat of his pants as he straightened up. She looked at his worn cloth slippers, the ashen stubble shading his cheeks. A woman appeared behind him cradling a crying baby on her hip. Catching sight of Anna, watching from across the road, she stepped back hurriedly, pulling her husband after her, and closed the door; not wanting to be seen in her nightwear. What hypocrites people were, Anna thought, with their petty decencies and respectability: with their right times and their wrong times, their shaved lawns, their concrete walls; their little censorious minds set straight. And their furtive pleasures behind lowered blinds and closed curtains; on Friday nights and Saturdays, the thin partitions of their rooms shaken with it; in the name of God and country, spawning babies. Shamefaced in the morning. How absurd it all was. She stared at the door of varnished teak that had closed opposite her, with a strange fascination, as if beholding something never seen before. Was it for these people — these solid citizens and all like them, was it for their good opinion she had sold herself? Was she prepared to trade everything she had discovered, to keep a little corner in their world? private, safe, accepted?

She got into the car and started up the engine. She drove quickly along the seafront and turned into

Ardmore Avenue. The phone booth on the corner was empty. She parked the car, stepped out and walked across the street. When she lifted the receiver and placed the coins in the slot, it was Sheila's number she picked at random. For thirty seconds the phone rang uninterrupted. They must all be asleep, she thought, after a late night or perhaps had left early. And then, abruptly, the ringing tone stopped and Nessa's voice took its place; sounding muffled, half asleep, as if she were still in bed. Of course – she would be in Sheila's room with the phone beside her.

'Hallo?'

Anna wondered if Sheila was there too, listening, or would she be on her way to work by this time? What was she to say now, she asked herself. She could not think of one solitary thing she had planned; she could think of nothing at all, but to say stupidly, forlornly:

'Nessa.'

'Oh . . . it's you.' The voice was cold; indifferent. Or hostile? She could not tell which.

'Nessa . . .'

'Yes?'

She wanted to say, I have missed you, but she did not. She wanted to say, I am sorry, but she did not. She only said them in her head, deliberately, as if counting the words, assessing their suitability for some other occasion.

'I am sorry if I woke you,' she said at last, to say something, anything before the silence hardened to stone between them.

'Oh, it doesn't matter.'

'Is Sheila there still? I'm sorry if I woke her.'

'No you didn't,' the answer came out flat, merciless, refusing to give her any help at all. So she was not going to be forgiven then. She would not be asked for explanations, apologies. This voice was not going to ask her anything whatever. It would go on replying in polite, bored monosyllables until she put down the phone.

'You left your dole card in the house. I thought you might need it.'

'Oh yes, I will. I'll want it on Tuesday.'

156

The next step obviously was to offer to bring it over. Anna could do it now, before work, if she hurried. But it would have been as easy at that moment to grow wings as to suggest it. Her right hand was gripping the receiver that smelt of stale aftershave, her left hand was picking at the directory open beside her. She had torn the first three 'Murrays' from the top of the page when Nessa spoke. Anna was so startled she gave a little nervous jump the way her mother did when the doorbell rang unexpectedly.

'By the way, I thought you might like to know . . .' Was the tone reproachful now or scornful? 'That one of your friends thinks we seem very happy together.'

'Who?'

'Karen.'

'Karen?' What was this about? Was Nessa taunting her, or was this intended to be funny?

'What do you mean, Karen?'

'Just what I said. Karen thinks I must be good for you. She says you seem altogether different.' Anna felt a cold anger rising in her. But whether it was towards Nessa, Karen or herself she did not know.

'When were you talking to Karen?'

'That night. She came up to the bedroom before leaving.'

'I see,' Anna said, though she saw nothing. She could not follow any of it. She did not know how she was supposed to respond. And she did not know why she felt angry.

'Why?' she asked at last.

'Why what?'

'Why did Karen go up to you?'

'Oh, she just wanted to apologise.'

'Apologise? For what?'

'Because of Ben. She thought it might have been something he said that offended me. She was worried when I left so suddenly.'

'And what did you say?' Anna could hear the irritation just barely suppressed in her voice. She was angry with herself for asking these questions. She felt they were drawing her into some trap she should be

157

able to see but could not. But neither could she prevent herself from speaking them.

'I told her it had nothing to do with Ben, or nothing of any importance anyhow. I said it was you who was being offensive.'

The detached, controlled cool of Nessa's voice struck a little flame of fear through Anna. What else had she told Karen? If she could not manage to stay absolutely calm herself she might never find out.

'And what did Karen say to that?' she asked, at last, when she felt herself ready.

'She said yes, she saw what I meant. She said it was a pity you seemed to think it necessary to hide our relationship. She said there was nothing Ben would have enjoyed more. It would have capped everything.'

Anna was slammed into silence: a tense, angry, humiliated waiting. There was nothing she could say. She had absolutely no words for this. It was beyond her wildest fears.

After moments of suspense, Nessa spoke again:

'Poor Anna,' she said, 'all that hard work for naught. You see, it seems there was something they wanted to tell you. It seems that, along with health foods and jogging, there's something else Harry has taken up. But neither of them knew how to tell you. It's quite a crisis for him.'

'What, for Godsake?'

'Men.'

'Men?'

'Yes . . . men.'

And then Anna heard the last thing in the world she had expected. A sudden explosion of sound came through the phone so that she had to hold it out from her ear. It was a second before she realised that Nessa was laughing. And not in derision or scorn but a giddy whooping and bubbling of mirth.

'Men,' Nessa said again, the single word struggling clear to be engulfed once again by a wave of laughter, so that after a moment Anna found she was laughing too. And so there they were, no more than five miles apart, in the early hours of the city; holding tight to their receivers and carried over the distance; bouncing, gushing like water, unstoppable, laughter ran along the wires that joined them.

Sweet, Practised, Endings

Ah well, it was a comfort then, to be in her arms: embraced in the heat of her soft, unknown, echoing flesh – different from all you were used to and so, comforting, yet familiar, plangent with memory. You felt your heart beating and re-knew its urgency; beating to free itself, to explode the confines of the reasonable. You looked at her neck, found the pulse that throbbed at her throat, saw it hopping as if it might burst from the skin and remembered that, too – the old signs and emblems. And what else, after all, have we to go by? To what other evidence can we trust?

Her hands and mouth told the same story, tireless in the retelling, though you were revelling in lassitude and were reluctant to abandon it to an orgasm that would distract you from the intensity of the last. These well-worn, astonishing actions carried out with such fervour; taken for granted, as inevitable, as though life were easy, delight a thing freely available – requiring no more than harmony of the senses and the readiness to forgive. Ah, it was nice to see the smile on her face, the way she bit her lip with the pleasure of you; of giving pleasure and you gave yourself up to it; assented to this confidence and simplicity. And perhaps it was all that you needed, the only oracle. Your body thought so anyway, gushing into hers, pouring out response and gratitude. You would come again now, in a moment, mind taking flight, soaring from the known, hovering weightless, loosed from time and then, the void, the stillness, the dark, and the return: the waves receding, the womb opening and closing in great, violent shudders as if it had given birth to something. And her mouth was so sweet. That was what gladdened you most – the corners of her mouth when you put your tongue to them – so hot and sweet. And the way she kissed. So few have that way; such a lovely, easy, ardent rhythm to it.

Why are you telling all this? It makes it seem a mechanical thing and it was not. No, that was the joy. For that while life was alive, blood taking over, in its pulse and flood making it seem all was well. Is that not the most extraordinary part of it, for five minutes or hours; what a sensation to produce by the friction of skin? But not without her eyes smiling at you. That was it. All in the eyes. You wish you could see them now: ripe and dark and glowing, little lights flickering in them. And a depth, a radiance that made you feel you were looking into her mind and heart – a long, bright, warm passage into the very heart of her. Not like others. So many others – almost all in fact, with eyes no more than pale, hard stones fastened in the skull. No surprise to learn that they were glass – everyone of them. Her eyes were like her flesh; succulent and enveloping. And then they laughed at you and the whole of it, as though it was not such a serious business, when it came to it, trying to be happy. This great tedious straining that absorbs our days and makes each one of us lie to the other, this sad, silly straining after happiness. And then when discovered for a moment in the midst of it: her fingers drawing streams of joy from you, dissolving in you, her voice crying for you; at this moment her eyes smile – see, it is not so very serious after all, an easy matter that might happen anywhere, to anyone. Were you to believe her. Ah, were you to believe her.

You did then, you know, for that short time, up there in the attic, with the roar of cars below and the smell rising of newly baked bread from the patisseria and the Italians making a tremendous clamour as usual about filling their stomachs; choosing exactly the right substance to put into them that day. Always the same fuss and significance, day after day, enthusiastic as dogs begging for a walk, wagging their tails – the same walk day after day, the same yapping and excited beating of tails, the eyes rolling up in eagerness and goodwill. Comforting, that.

You stayed in bed all day and talked until the light dimmed and your throats were dry. Exchanged histories and later got up and, on the small stove in the alcove, cooked something together in one pot: pasta. She made a pesto sauce, the best you had had. You returned to bed and ate it there, sharing plates, sucking the juice from each other's fingers; all the usual things – the small homely, familiar gestures of lovers being happy together: swopping stories and laughing, eyes searching the other's face; every scrap of it, the smell of food on your mouth, kissing and starting all over again until once more you were hungry and went out for something to eat. You know the kind of day, so many known before, almost forgotten, had not thought to find one again. And for her was it the same? Or different? In some way new, untried? Disquieting that. You would prefer no division of that kind. Trouble later. Trouble anyway but worse if started off like that from different starting blocks, different expectations. But not worth worrying now. So separate anyway, all of us, no more than illusion: understanding, similarity. Sundered soon enough, thrown back into antipathy, self-consciousness, criticism – why can't you be more like – why are you so – I wish you would try to – and all of that. Making over the image. Do not want to think of it now, bask a little longer in this softness. Close the eyes, say the words, a great comfort: my love, darling, little one, sweetheart; old as the hills, the mother words, the child words, dark and sweet and comforting.

And what had brought you here into the sound and sweetness of this bed, this small white room under the sloping roof, with its green painted furniture, the mattress on the floor, its ochre quilt, its brown sheets?

What had brought you to lie together facing its high square window, in its green frame the blue spring sky, tiled roofs, the cries and clamour of the converging streets, the warbling and wing beating of the grey doves and the brown? What had brought you here? You had no answer or several. Destiny, design or accident, one guess was as good as another. You could take your pick from any number. At any rate you met, eyed and fell into lust. At a party you danced together, once only, but enough to reveal the unnerving sympathy of hands, feet, voices. You listened to a Jamaican band in a garden by a river, lambent with the orange glow of homemade lanterns, pumpkins hanging from the apple trees, candles shining through their teeth. A high pale moon. Later you stood by the river bank, the boats rocking and whispering in the light, knocking their sides. She asked if tomorrow you would come and row with her here on the slow, weeded river. You saw the long, slender oars, the wide, curved blades. You felt them under your hands, heard the squeal as they turned gently in their spurs. You said yes.

And now, so soon, you were bound here together in the damp sheets, her blood on your hands. And those old sweet words sounding round your ears. How easily they slipped from her tongue, with such smooth grace. You knew it could not be long since they were last used. A month ago at most, at the airport, a week perhaps in a letter, the same day if she had been to the telephone that morning. She had gone down to the street before you were awake to buy cigarettes. You did not ask who she was calling. Soon she would want to tell you about her lover. These words always aroused that business. Always someone lurking in the background behind such warm practised phrases. Everyone you met over thirty one half of a couple, yourself, half a lifetime, included. Wisest to make it clear from the outset. And you would. Establish name, place and duration. Would not care to go beyond that. Indiscreet, nearly impossible to find any words about the matter that meant the same thing to two people. Love, fondness, trust, security, infatuation, in love, like minds, kindred, familiarity, empathy. Hard to say yourself what you meant by any one of them. Misleading, consciously or not.

She was looking out of the window her hands resting on her thighs, strong square hands that were given a vulnerable look by the bitten nails. You leaned your head on her shoulder, wide beautiful shoulders in the black sleeveless tee-shirt. Have you sisters and brothers you asked? Time to begin. So much to discover, the difficult, laborious process of establishing friendship. Were you happy at school, what does your mother look like, how old were you when you first made love to a woman, a man, how was it? All this to be gone through yet. The afternoon before you had postponed it. Enough to lie in the sun, to row on the wide, shaded river, to swim in the reeded, brown water, to eat baguette, anchovies, cambazola and apricots. You drank beer because of the heat and because you were thirsty from the work of rowing. You dived from the dipping bow, splashing her face and neck. You wanted to swim well to impress her though the tide was strong, the wind running with it. She drank red wine from the bottle, the entire bottle in the end. When she lay stretched to dry later, on the deck of a barge moored to the bank, the dark curve of flesh at the belly, the deep breasts, caused some boys to throw stones, taunting from the tow-path. A woman's body, too luxuriant to be displayed half-naked in public. You looked at her enthralled as they whistled, not sure why it was you were in such a hurry to be in bed with her. For that was, of course, already what you wanted. And then she spoke, without opening her eyes, her low brooding voice that seemed to play with the words like fruit between her lips before letting go of them. You hoisted yourself out of the water, gripping the rail of the deck so that your eyes were level with hers. Leaning forward, you put your mouth to a line of dark freckles on the bone of her shoulder.

And here you were now, the sun spilling through the high window, licking crumbs of blue cheese from her breasts, sipping white wine from her mouth. She

164

asked you then what love meant to you. You thought
of it: all that it had meant, all that you remembered.
Certainly you had known the state in all its guises. But
one picture only presented itself to you now. Two
bodies on a floor naked, sweat on their backs, their
arms about each other, their lips smiling, their legs
entwined. You heard the noises they made; the harsh
panting, the whimpers, the sighs and cries of ecstasy,
yes, transport; borne up onto another plane. But that
was not love was it? That was in love, lust, you were
remembering, a different thing entirely, surely. But
how else could you think of it here? And afterwards,
you remembered of course, such as now, the delicious
sloth, lassitude, all the limbs bathed, scented. When
you talked about other people: trifling, light, entertaining slander. It was a very good time to speak of
someone you hated, someone who made life wretched
normally; you could be generous then, detached, as
though it were a frivolous matter, liking and dislike.
Magnanimous, one became at such times. You confided
terror and anxieties too and laughed over them. It was
also the time to recall childhood when all was safe
and sound, a thousand miles from the territory of
youth.

So you exchanged the parent stories, the stories of
father, mother, but mostly mothers. Hers one kind,
yours another. Whichever way of loving probably the
wrong way, seen in retrospect by son or daughter as
first cause of all subsequent hardship. Her mother had
wanted the best for her, not having had it herself. She
wanted the right associates, discipline, elegance, a
sense of purpose. Her daughter wanted something else
but was not asked. And so she was consigned to the
religious mind, deep in the forest, beside the lake, a
medieval fortress of stone and stained glass where the
Sisters of Mercy held captive the daughters of the rich.
From the first day she knew herself in exile. Once and
once only her mother took pity, summoned by tales of
refuge sought in fainting fits and palpitations she
came, sombre eyed, solicitous, arrayed in silks and
fur, bearing flowers and Swiss chocolate. But when
she departed at evening, the mist thickening on the

lake, she left her daughter behind her in the odour of
tallow candles, the dereliction of hourly prayer. She
had not been forgiven for many years, perhaps not yet.
That was why, or probably why, the daughter felt as
she did; craved affection while rejecting it and must
fret every evidence of it with a thousand small tests of
constancy. Something like that. Everyone has her
reasons. Yours contrasting but no less exacting. One of
a tribe, end of the litter, appreciated because you were,
not for who you were. Love given not won, an ease
and simplicity that made other attachments obtuse or
demanding in comparison. Loving too little or too
much, the right one, the wrong time, one way or
another, the thing left its mark.

Well, it was all over now, well behind you. The past
another country. You kissed, you sighed, you held
close, you took sanctuary deep in the recesses of one
another's flesh. The body held all tenderness and
candour. Suffering was behind you.

She dressed for the street in orange culottes and
black cotton jacket. You were standing by the window
feeding the pigeons that clustered on the narrow sill,
knowing you were strangers and that you would not
know that it contravened the rules of the area to
encourage them. She stood behind you. Do you want
to go out to dinner or to make love, she asked? You
drew up her hands and kissed them, you leaned back
against the heat of her thighs, her hair falling along her
cheek. Both, you said, and in that order, hunger now
growling in your stomach adding weakness to the
ravaging of desire.

Before leaving you must change the bandage on
your leg. She would help you. She filled the enamel
basin, brought the jar of aloe cream and the roll of
white gauze. You sat on the floor, she knelt beside
you. Was it the prompting of contrition or the sight of
your helplessness that lent such skill to her hands,
that kindled such heat and radiance in her glance, that
bathed you in the caress of a sister, a mother, a lover,
all these loves bound together as her fingers carried
out their task, but for how long? Guilt inescapably she
felt, seeing that it had been her car that struck you and

she driving it. In such impatience to be with you she had not braked, had not changed gear as she rounded the corner. And you, no less oblivious, had stepped off the pavement as you crossed to the appointed rendezvous at precisely the second she turned into the street. An occurrence so absurd, so unaccountable as one lover (or would-be lover) driving into the other on the way to their first assignation, seemed to hold a significance and portent you were unwilling to decipher. But, undeciphered, unmentioned, they cast their weight nonetheless on everything that followed.

No harm done then, or to the body only, your knee gashed and bleeding. But the sight of you lying laughing, tearstained in the gutter, unleashed such a storm of solicitude; words and names that an instant before would have been exaggerated, precipitous, now swirled about your head as she clasped you in her lap and staunched the pumping escape of your blood. The wine and coffee drinkers converged from their counters and assaulted you with such happy distress and indignation, such calls and counter calls for doctors and ambulances, that you rallied at once. Waving aside alarm and advice, she supported you across the street to the door and courtyard of the apartment she had borrowed for you and up the five flights, leaving a trail of your blood, to the room and the bed, the white walls and brown sheets and all the physicking that human hands can provide.

All for the best, in the best of all fantasised worlds; the shutters fastened, the candles lit, a baptism of fire.

And so you were dressed at last and into the street, your bodies frail and new, assaulted by the crush and uproar, the light dazzling, thirty six hours since you had left it.

On the bus you sat with knees and shoulders close; she took the hand that lay between your thighs in hers so that your three hands nestled captive there. As each new passenger arrived you were stared at, estimated, covert or blatant, before their eyes slid back reluctantly to the snarl of traffic, the oily, slow moving sky.

A woman took the platform, with scarlet rouge and scarlet headscarf, swaying as she gripped the roof strap, a madwoman, tramp, wino, baglady; lost or found, at the ring of the bell, she threw back her head and let loose in wavering soprano the woeful defiant chorus of a Piaf song, and again and again at each scheduled stop. And in the anguish of determination not to notice, all eyes swung back to the lesser evil of your joined hands.

She led you through a labyrinth of backstreets, old yellow stone that might have crumbled at your touch, cobbled pathways, the smell of warm dust lifted by your step mingling with tobacco and the sweet pungency of food prepared in a hundred small eating houses clustered together, sleek grey cats in the windows, at their open doors white shirted waiters smiling, beckoning to win you for their tables. She led you to the last one, pressed between a bookshop and the windows of a Jewish bakery, red and white check tablecloths, a basket of newly risen bread on each table, a terrace, a balcony opening onto the river.

She had come here years ago with Zelda. She would tell you about her another time, another night, so many yet to be gone through and only one left to hold them, her profile turned to the lit street, your jacket over your shoulders, the breeze blowing in off the water, candles lapsing and beating up again. Your hand stretched along the table, finding its path between the flowers and the glasses to take hers. And too long the waiter took with the changing of plates and cutlery, the pouring and tasting of wine, his eyes hungry to tell you about this city that was not hers and not yours though it had been yours and had been hers. You had both lived here once but at differing times. And what if? Ah yes what if — that old entertainment lovers play wishing they had flown as the crow flies to the place that has come to be theirs; lamenting the devious, distracting routes they chose in ignorance. So much would have been altered, made simpler even, if. You would not have lived through A or B, she would not have dealt with L or even R, and you would not be leaving tomorrow night on separate

168

planes carrying you back to your lives. You poured the wine.

Zelda would have ordered endives salad, asparagus tips she told you. She came here, to this table and ordered swordfish every night for a month when she was breaking up with Theo. So it was time then to talk of lovers, of the ones left and the one who left, too late or too early. And so many there were in twenty years or more of loving. To begin with, then, you elected to speak of men known, to keep at least to chronological order, though it was not because her first lover she had met at school, a woman, or a girl as she was at that time. Never mind, all in good time, a herstory of good times.

But first you spoke of men. Life with them different in most ways but most striking of course in the matter of sex, nature or attitude or whatever it was, making them always out of rhythm. Mechanical they were in their habits, tedious for you. The day long, week long indiscriminate wanting of it, senseless; anywhere anytime, always starting up: in the small hours of the morning, eating breakfast, cutting the grass, in a storm at sea, watching a movie, waiting for the lights to change, anything at all likely to set them off. Like a cuckoo clock with its hours confused. Or dogs. The one you passed in the street yesterday, the alsation having a shit; straining so that its prick came out, with the red inflamed look that makes you feel sorry for them. A crap and a hard on at once. One thing leading to another, all sensations confused. That was what you remembered best, or worst, you told her. Ben at night turning to you when you had just fallen asleep. His penis prodding your back, waking you. Pushing, wriggling as though it were trying to escape from him. And he hiding behind the urgency of its carry on, pretending it was some kind of emergency, as if it did not happen a dozen times a day for no reason. Shamefaced, conscious of deceit. It was all such a drag, you said, keeping a straight face when he went to brush his teeth and up it sat waving about through his pyjama flies. (Flies – odd term, or maybe not when you came to think of it.) Worst of all pretending to be complimented, the mutual game that it had something special to do with you, because he touched, smelt, looked at you, and all the while knowing it would have happened if he had been walking along a street and knocked into a lamppost. You said did it not bother her, the silly confusion and repetition of it all? But she did not like to think that way, piling incidents together to get a principle. She liked to keep things separate, self-contained entities in a hazy, pleasant wrapping of vagueness and half knowledge. And who could blame her?

You had reached the main course. You ate sole and she lobster. You averted your eyes from the tank where they crawled, lumbering over polished stones, twitching angry red eyebrows displaying themselves to advantage, had they known it; their fitness and eligibility for the pot. But why suffer for crustacea while pulling the spine, blithely, from another creature because it lacks legs or wears eyes on its back?

Her experience of men quite different, she told you, smiling at you, tenderness for your qualms at the proximity of death and digestion. Married at twenty-three. Less travelled in that respect than you. Her husband impotent or something very like it. From the first night on, needed help. And when he did get it up it did not last. Not for long at any rate. Boring for her, frustrating. Though successful enough to breed the three requisite children. She tired of his diffidence very swiftly. Began to dream of men she supposed were otherwise: truck drivers, sailors, not having encountered them. Dreams she could not admit. How could she leave a man who meant so well? It was not his fault. No never that, no one's fault ever; that was her way. Too gentle, too respectful of women, that was the reason; heterosexual intercourse demanding, he considered, a certain brute violence, aggression on the part of the male. Who could blame him for not being equal to the task? She did leave him, needless to say, but not for that cause. That was the least of it. She left him – why? Because he drank or snored, because he read the newspaper at the dinner table, because he preferred football to her or his team mates, in the end, to her, because she could not talk to him, because he did not talk or when he did it was something quite different from what she wanted to talk about. One of those reasons no doubt. But some years later she discovered women and realised that none of it; none of her sense of something missing with men had anything to do with them.

And at last, dessert ordered, all others in between described and categorised, it was time to talk of present lovers; their unspoken presence now beginning to build little heaps and pitfalls of silence. Hers first. Yes, called this morning, as you had thought. You took the bottle of wine and added an inch or so of the pale greenish liquid to her glass and filled yours right to the brim. Not that you were jealous. Alas no, never that – jealousy of the absent, temporarily abandoned lover never entered into it, only discomfort, unease that the woman once – still – loved must be fitted into conversation; estimated, credit given, measure taken. However it was done, injustice was done. Circumlocution no good, bluntness worse. She went on holding her glass to her lips after she had drunk from it, the yellow candlelight reflected from it casting a little pool of sun on her palm. Finding the right words, the right note. Leaving aside the question that, if she loved her, what was she doing here now with you, and if she did not love her, what was she doing there until now with her? Imponderables – unspeakables anyway.

And you? It would be your turn soon. What could you say? How to define, explain it? Say that it was over, say that you had no lover, that you lived alone recuperating, indeed, convalescing from the last attempt; the longest and the last that had nearly finished you off altogether? Too dramatic that, if even half truthful. Would it not inspire a desire to comfort, to console, to prove that all can be made over again in a new and different image; the haunting of the right, the true one, the one unlike any other; never far from your own fantasies, not to be aroused now again in someone else? And yet easier that than to say flatly that you did not want love. Easier to invent a phantom lover than admit that you did not want the demand,

171

the intimacy, the concern, the knowing, the not knowing, the questioning, the silences, the trusting, the doubting, the arguments, the light on or off, dishes washed or left, to watch television or to go out, to be confiding or discreet, monogamous or other mess, the expectation of passion, reliability, giving, humour, the unreadiness to sacrifice pleasure, adventure or anything much to secure them. Ah where were you to begin?

You took from your bag a photograph. There she was: A., sunbathing on a blue towel on a white beach in Greece. Or at least the image of her body was there, a body that might be posing for some magazine advertisement, the very picture of health and sensuality, but for her hand at the corner of the frame reaching for a cigarette packet yellowed by the sun and her gaze turned to you, meditative, mischievous. All that you had wanted, all that you had dreamed her to be before you ceased to dream. And you told then the stories of this time and that, with A., and she saw the laughter in your face, the joy and the sorrow; the moments lost and not forgotten that you had not wanted to reveal. You lifted her hand where it lay derelict beside the candle. Over, all that, long ago, you said, all forgotten. And you set your mouth to the inside of her wrist where the fine blue veins conceal the colour of blood. You kissed the heat of it, the urgency. You ordered cognac.

A ferry boat sailed down the river, its decks strung with red and yellow bulbs, the eager crowd pressing forward to watch the land sail by them with its boulevards, cafés and restaurants, its throng of gaily dressed diners of which you were a part, being gazed at while you gazed. You watched it swallowed by the last bridge. Some of them save up half a lifetime to come here, to make that trip she said. Can you imagine it? You looked at her lips and saw that they were dark red and swollen from your days of kissing, her sharp white teeth glistened between them. Can you imagine waiting that long? And you asked her then, though first you moved your eyes from hers and out to the water, if Karen – for that was her name – would come by train or car to pick her up at the airport (did she have the flight number?), arms outstretched for her cases, for herself; welcoming her when she touched down into real life tomorrow at midnight? You asked only to make clear, as though it needed making, that the complexity was not all of your doing; to shift the blame squarely where it belonged to those inescapable abstracts: time, life, circumstances, which can be relied on to make innocents of us all.

And she too had a picture to show you. The coup de grace, you might say: three children stacked on the bonnet of a Fiat 127, smiling, of course, photographs preserving nothing but gaiety, three blonde curly heads; after their father, smooth cheeks – though teenagers now – old enough to fend for themselves but nonetheless a tie. And what was worse you wondered, the ties or the lack of them and how quick we were to tie up any loose ends we came across, all of us, no matter what we claimed. Is not this what business men do, you said, as the image was slipped back in her jacket pocket – on conference weekends – swop convenience cards of spouse and homelife? Yes, but to each other, of course, not a lover, she said, and then neither of us has a wife. No, nor husband, nor any easy excuse. The rules every day self-made. The definitions re-drawn.

And people came in she had known years ago, the man tall in white jacket and tie, the woman swathed in some red silk-like fabric, silvered toenails on show from her sandals. A couple she had known long before when this city had been her home. She knew them at once, though changed. Do you mind . . . you said, almost aloud, as they made their way to a corner table, not having seen her, or seen and not recognised, and she stood up and would have called after them but not now you said – do you mind, not now. Let's go, let's walk by the river. And you took her hand to persuade her, not wanting to talk to strangers, not wanting to talk to anyone, but to be alone in the night with the crowds all round you in the hot charged air, to feel her skin along yours to the shoulder, naked in summer shirts, wanting already this exclusion and private territory while the lights grew brighter in the dark of the water, and from all about rose the laughter and murmurs of other lovers alone in the night.

Walking back, almost home, thirsty again you stopped in a café, a place she had liked as a student. The waiter the same, the flat chest encased in its white jacket, the black brows, the long narrow hips. All these years, while she had been half way over the globe, more than once, here he had stayed; pulling caps and corks from glass bottles, clenched between thin knees, his towel flourished, sieving through change in the small cloth bag on his belly. Content it would seem; great pride in the work, gliding between chairs, pirouetting around tables, singing his orders at the bar. King of his castle, get down you dirty rascal, clear in the eye to each customer accosted. Respectful, you took your places at the corner of the terrace, backs to the wall, and ordered one brandy, one cointreau. She played a song on the juke box and another without speaking, choosing the most clichéd she could find, twice as rich on the pleading, extravagance of a latin tongue, the phrases spilling over you, cream and honey, making you sick with laughter, baffling the straight couples around you, her deep sudden laughter, staccato as handclaps, making a joke of it all; of the seriousness and embarrassment – the first – of the talk that had gone before. But what did it matter any of it now, together or separate you were united now, borne up, on your own plane, transcendent in this new unlooked for joy, this well-being that had commandeered your bodies, self-generating, absolute, so that the exterior world was a dream only, a sweet projection of your vitality.

Another cointreau, another brandy and another and at last another so that when you resumed your walk – having emptied your pockets to the last silver coin – the river was rolling wildly under its bridges like waves of the open sea and the stars went off and on in the sky like Christmas lights. You clung close to each other. Men passing winked and whistled and called after you and you laughed and called back as though it were all in fun, no offence meant and none taken.

Desire beating up between you, creating a space, an electric field around you, warding them off, protecting you in a hot inner cell, untouchable.

You had observed this, sober before, watching two women walking in love through the street, at their most exposed and vulnerable, inviolate. Curious thing. You went home. You climbed the broad wooden staircase, five flights to the room she had borrowed for you, the room with the sloping roof, white walls and green painted furniture. You turned back the quilt, the brown sheet, you lay down together. The stars were at the open window and the night noises of the street; unlike the continuous low humming of the day, came up, now soft, now raucous; the laughter of lovers, the shouting of prostitutes and their clients, a car engine bursting suddenly into life and from the café on the corner the Arabs singing: their high trembling lament, their low drumming reaching its way up to your closed ears.

And so, it is hard to know what followed then. There are so many possible endings. You have lived so many various and dissimilar conclusions. Unalike and yet, as time separated you from them, beginning to take on an air of similarity, some common link between them all, that was perhaps only that time allowed you to see that they were not endings, but merely one of the things that happened, before the next event that you chose to see as a beginning.

Perhaps you lay side by side, still, leaden with consciousness, the fear of parting making your belly ache. The abandon, the unthinking, the simplicity gone, leached from you. Did you listen to your own breathing and then hers that came slowly, almost sighing. We will not get up tomorrow you said, until it's time to go, you thought but did not say – the unspoken things crowding again, loading you; building a wall between your bodies that were less than an inch apart.

Perhaps you made love, loving one another until the sky grew white at the window and the singing went out on the street below; loving in a last pitched battle against time and distance as though flesh itself were your enemy – these too solid vessels of sinew and bone that had first led you into each other's power and would now betray you; transporting mind and spirit as so much registered freight to another time and place. And so you railed against each other, straining to break down the barrier that was her life and yours.

And in the morning? For the morning must have come, as thus far it has always, whether you woke in terror an hour after dawn, or late when others had already completed breakfast and begun once more the forage for lunch and you cursed sleep for cheating you of that unthinking pleasure.

You threw open the shutters to the bustle, the roaring of traffic recommenced, the scurrying back and forth to the bakery, the smell of hot bread wafting up, the calling of voices shrill and birdlike from piazza to piazza; the whole frenzied affair begun afresh.

The pigeons strutted in line along the sill, their chests swollen with carolling, their bright eyes cocked, impatient for their illicit feed, when you phoned the airline company to discover if they might extend the ticket that lay in its white and red folder on the shelf above the bed. The line busy, they put you on hold; an electric jingle played out to keep you occupied. Listen, you said, stretching the earpiece towards her, they are playing our song – Home on the Range. And the querulous mechanism piped out: where seldom is heard a discouraging word and the skies are not cloudy all day. That made her laugh, but not as before and not for long, the angles of her face beginning already to set into the etched, unyielding lines necessary to become the woman who would no longer be with you; a woman waking while you slept, sleeping while you ate breakfast, talking to others, laughing without you, washing, dressing, working, going about her life as if there was no other. It would take three hundred pounds, you were told, to alter the date of flight. So that was that, then, as it always is and has been. A thousand lira in her pocket, five hundred in yours. For want of a nail and so forth. Money speaks all languages but the language of need and its silence is incontestable.

You put your hand to the nape of her neck where the hair was cut short and the skin exposed under the dark, soft down. Let us go down to breakfast before the bread is cold.

When you climbed the stairs again it was to begin the ritual of packing; the division of belongings, fused in these last days – the clothes, the books, the incense, the leather sandals that you had bought for a song at the Porta Portese, two jars of pesto sauce, the last bottle of whiskey. Would she take it or you? Her back was to you for an instant while she fetched her toothbrush and towel – almost forgotten – and you lifted a magazine from her luggage and concealed in its centre pages a last note to be discovered when she opened it by chance to read in some place you were not and would never be. And when she closed her case finally, did she unlock it again to take out the white cotton shirt she had worn on the first night, when you danced under the hanging lights by the river, only once but long enough to uncover that sudden sympathy of skin and blood, and give it to you to take home? Did you sleep in it for weeks afterwards?

Of course there are other possibilities. Perhaps she persuaded you to stay. Perhaps she called the airline company and, arguing with all her charm of voice, achieved a stay of sentence for a week, or two or three? Perhaps you gave up, as they say, everything. Caution to the winds. Perhaps you absconded with your lives, abducted one another and made no demand for ransom. Perhaps you found money in the street or learned to steal it; lifting visa cards and travellers checks from the pockets of rich business men made careless by expensive drink or sex, and rented an apartment somewhere in Tastevere and sequestered in the city's core, until at last, almost sated, you would venture out each day in search of a few hours of remuneration: cleaning the homes of wealthy housewives or teaching English to their husbands in early evening offices: husbands who had earlier, unknown to themselves, with a largesse beyond their dreaming, been the benefactors of working women – yourselves or others like you. You might

177

have lived for years there, happy as any lovers are, living together anywhere for years.

Or did you stick to schedule, the pre-designed, duty, the dictates of the practical world? Did you arrive at the airport at the appointed hour, paying off the taxi driver with your last note of the currency, and board at the call your respective planes to your respective destinations? And a small boy who sat opposite you in flight, having beheld you, cheeks wet, laughing, kissing, over and over at gate B13 − your number announced before hers − embracing as if someone's life depended on it, stared at you transfixed through every trolley of distractions passing: coffee, lunch, tea, dinner, coffee and God knows how many whiskeys, while repeatedly he asked his father (who contrived, with phlegmatic propriety, to ignore him) why the lady was kissing the other lady like that with their mouths?

Once home you pinned her photograph to the wall (the one taken that morning/evening, drinking beer on the Spanish Steps by the American girl with the polaroid who asked you if she might − why you did not know, but readily agreed.) And then letters. Oh such letters! Written every day or twice, on scraps of paper torn from notebooks, serviettes, the backs of used envelopes, writing pads lined and unlined, scented and unscented, airmail or surface, any shred available was pressed into service used to transport the tried and tested banalities of love − faith, hope, charity.

You wrote every day for a month, two, three? Discursive outpourings which gradually grew shorter, less frequent and eventually were written on pre-stamped airmail paper only, as memory and fantasy were frayed, eroded by the ceaseless washing of time and physical space. Or perhaps she tired of letters in the first week and, borrowing money from her sister, sent a one way ticket for you to come and join her. Perhaps you did.

All of these things have happened and will again to you and to others in this place or that. Any one of them probable, none remarkable in itself.

One possibility however, you have not mentioned: one more than possible, likely even. Something so often experienced, and so faithfully recorded there is hardly need to consider it. Nonetheless, having troubled thus far. It is this . . .

You went home then to your separate nations and resumed the lives that had been so weirdly interrupted by the chance encounter of your flesh. Without doubt, for a while you dreamed and woke shivering at night. Without doubt you wept and made telephone calls at dawn and promises. But at last and maybe not so very much later after all, life, as we name it: daily existence, the necessary or at least repeated goings on of mornings, afternoons and nighttimes ensnared you, drew your flickering attention into their clutter and oblivion, and thus securely webbed in the physical exigencies of breathing, eating, sleeping, working, talking, going out and about, with this one or that, when you looked back (and it was undeniably already retrospective) you saw that this miraculous event was no more or less than others that had gone before it: a temporary entanglement of self-interests and mutual need, a conflagration of the senses from which you had risen wraithlike, charred but reason intact. And you came to speak of it as people do with that special note of pride and self-deprecation adopted by those who have survived disease or a passing loss of sanity.

Yes, indeed, what other outcome could be at all probable? Liaisons – affairs – what you will (and you will hardly object to its inclusion in these broad, loose terms) in countries foreign to both protagonists, foreign to their work and companions, whether of several days' or weeks' duration, could scarcely be expected by any reader to progress otherwise. Might as well leave it at that.

But supposing . . . ah that word again. Never one to let well enough alone, and, is it ever enough? Perhaps . . . the adverb haunting, as it always does in any recalling, raking over the ashes; past meetings, friendships or lovers; even now, so far from reach of any of them, even the last, the most long lasting.

Perhaps, then you say to yourself – that was not

quite the end of it. Not the full finale. Perhaps it seemed so only to an imagination grown lazy, dispirited, skeptical. Perhaps you took it for truth having no reason to doubt it until one night or day, dawn or dusk, walking or driving the streets of a city familiar or foreign, at an airport arriving or leaving for home, entering a room full of strangers; a surprise party or conference hall, feeding bread to ducks (pigeons?) from a park bench, going up on a lift to the thirtieth floor or down, sitting next to one other in an empty picture house, skiing, caving, hang-gliding (on safari – were you that kind of woman) on an all night sleeper to Marseilles, buying flowers from a stall, taken into custody in a provincial jail, stoned in the aisles of a Ginza department store, at an open air concert in Central Park, a mass rally in Trafalgar Square, holding a banner . . . yes, alright. However, wherever, you would catch light – a gaze – for one instant and feel that miraculous quickening of nerve, that heat at the base of the spine, or hearing a voice before seeing; that slow, plangent, winnowing voice that seemed to laugh at you and this silly straining after happiness, and looking into the eyes then – those warm, bright channels that seemed to lead to the very heart of her and beckon you closer; saying, you see it is not so difficult after all this business. Perhaps you borrowed a room, right then, high above the city, a mattress under the window. Perhaps you are there still, hidden deep in the interstices of the flesh that promise all pleasure and transcendence.

Ah yes, yes; the old, sweet, practised endings, tried and tested.

Comforting that.

Nights Underground

'Attention – attention, please. May we appeal to members of the public standing on or near a main staircase to facilitate the arrival of others by moving further along the platforms into the body of the shelter. May we also ask those in possession of seats or benches to surrender them, when and if necessary, to senior citizens, young children or their mothers. Thank you.'

'Appeal – surrender – possession – would you listen to the language,' Juno muttered. 'Where in the name of God do they think we are? The Ballroom of Romance?'

They were down in the air raid shelter – well, not quite a shelter, but the basement platform of a north London tube station on the Piccadilly line; a thousand feet or more below ground level and it was the first night (or early morning now) of the Civil Defence exercise in damage limitation and crisis control. They had been alerted without warning just past midnight; woken by the wail of police sirens (or it might have been ambulances), the noise of doors slamming, voices shouting all through the corridors.

'Shite,' said Juno, pulling on her clothes, not knowing what was going on; nor expecting to – and where the hell were her shoes and socks? and why were they never where she'd left them? 'What unbelievable lunacy,' said Aoife, who knew exactly what was happening but did not feel any better. And was there or was there not, they wanted to know, time to have coffee or something to eat? Grumbling, they made their way down the fire escape and into the wet, cold November night, with all the other angry, half-awake, half-dressed people, stumbling and pushing; children crying, husbands swearing, and the wives, (clutching hastily gathered provisions), soothing both, shepherding them through the noise and dark to the garish radiance of the station lights.

'Hurry up now, please – we haven't got all night. This is an emergency operation.'

'What the bleeding hell is the bleeding rush for? You'd think the bleeding thing had dropped already.'

Once below ground; penned in with all the other bleary-eyed, fretful residents dragged from houses and flats from every part of the district; a curious calm descended, almost a suppressed joviality: 'Better safe than sorry,' they called to each other, 'Nice to know someone's looking after things', 'There'll always be an England – eh?'

'Shite,' said Juno again, who felt even worse now that she did know what the fuss was about and had just realised that she had forgotten to bring anything to read or drink.

'You can say that again,' a short redfaced man answered, pacing beside her, a duffle coat pulled over his pyjamas. 'What a convenient time to choose, don't you think? One in the bloody morning. How bloody intelligent.'

'It's got to be inconvenient, love,' said a woman in a white plastic raincoat, 'I mean, that's when it will happen, isn't it? It'll always be inconvenient.'

'The Russians aren't going to hang about 'till you've had your Rice Crispies, are they mate?' a thin balding man who might have been her husband chipped in.

'Who said anything about the Russians?' said the first man, 'what about the protectors of the free world, the bloody Americans?'

The station seethed with human flesh, the stale indoor air rank with the smell of it; skin lurid under the fluorescent light: pink, black, white, brown and anything else going. They sat crammed together on the few available benches or bucket seats, lounged against the tiled and postered walls or strode restlessly along the platform edge. It might have been any rush hour crowd, made plaintive by a delay on the line, only that now they were talking to each other: strangers approaching strangers, swapping complaints or information, borrowing a light or even a cigarette, as if they might be people anywhere and not in London at all. The men were telling one another what they would do and how quickly if they were in charge, the children were chasing in and out of tunnels; or firing paper pellets at small brown mice startled from their nocturnal forage through the litter on the tracks. No one knew what was to happen or how long it would take: 'What's the bloody point of herding us down here like a lot of headless sheep if they can't decide what they want to do with us?' said the redfaced man in the duffle coat.

'Just wait quietly until the all clear sounds, I expect,' offered a young woman who had heard something from a steward on the way in.

'Well, it had better be bloody soon,' the man replied. 'I'm not putting up with this silly nonsense much longer.'

'Well,' Juno said, turning to Aoife, 'I hope you're satisfied, at least.'

'Why?'

'Now that the worst has happened.'

'It hasn't,' Aoife said, 'not yet anyway.'

'Oh come off it Aoife, what could be worse than this?'

'A lot,' said Aoife, and sank deeper into the collar of her long black woollen coat.

She was concentrating her attention on the children, to console herself as she might on a plane trip; a long night flight at the moment when they ran into turbulence and passengers were bounced like balloons in their seats, glasses went sliding and stewardesses, blanched and tight-lipped, strapped themselves in while assuring their charges that they had nothing to worry about. Aoife at such times would stare at the children chattering and giggling, spilling orange juice or chocolate down new holiday fronts, or sleeping with superb peace in their mother's arms, and would tell herself that whatever else no God could ever let so many innocents suffer. She thought this though she was an agnostic and had taken a great deal of trouble to avoid children of her own. But she had her priorities right. She looked at the milky eyelids, the plump limbs and assured herself that while she was certainly dispensable not even an omnipotent Christian deity could fail to be moved by their vulnerability. She went on thinking it even while she considered that he was forever failing in exactly this manner. How often did one read about children killed on a school outing; bridges collapsing under their buses, drunken drivers swerving off cliff tops, paraffin heaters overturning in holiday caravans, summer waves sweeping them out to sea, police shooting them dead, war planes dropping bombs on their school playgrounds? And why on earth were the children always out playing in them as the bombs fell? Could not God be trusted with even that much?

'You'd think nothing too awful could happen with all these kids around, wouldn't you?' she asked Juno, who was sitting bunched beside her on the bench like an animal about to spring, her features handsome and furious under a mane of dark red hair.

'What are you expecting to happen? It's only an exercise you know.'

They had quarrelled earlier in the evening and Juno was still feeling bloody-minded. One of those stupid arguments that begin with nothing and go on to everything. They were not lovers but they had been, once, and they still argued like lovers: petty and persistent with a memory of every grievance and secret confided over twelve years. There could be no resolution to the first part of their dispute: their whereabouts when they learned of John Kennedy's assassination, because they had not met until years later. But it was the kind of thing people tell each other and Juno knew for a fact that Aoife had been at

184

the cinema and not, as she now claimed, in bed with Craig Gillespie. She had known Craig for as long as Aoife had, longer, and she would certainly have heard about it from him before now. So why on earth was Aoife wanting to lie to her? 'I'm not lying,' she had said. 'In that case,' Juno replied, 'you have been lying to me for years, twelve years to be exact.' 'You can talk,' Aoife had said, 'what about Zoe?' 'What about her?' 'Why did you lie to me about her?' 'I didn't.' 'Well, why did you not tell me she had been in touch with you then?' This question Juno was not ready to answer, so she swung out of the room slamming the door behind her and had not spoken to Aoife again until they were dragged down to the station.

'How do you think they'll manage at home?' Aoife was asking now. 'They haven't even an underground, let alone shelters. Where will they put people?'

'What people?'

'Everyone. The nation. The citizens they are supposed to protect?'

'At least they'll be spared this carry on. They'll have great fun tomorrow when they read about us in the papers.'

'But if it was the real thing,' Aoife said, 'if the bomb was dropped? What then? They'll have nothing prepared. They never do. Where will they go? Under the kitchen table, as they advised us in that government pamphlet? Or block up the doors and windows with sandbags? They'll be decimated. They haven't so much as a gas mask between them. You know in Sweden they build a fallout shelter with every new house?'

'Sounds optimistic. Maybe you should emigrate?'

'Oh no, if you think of it they'll be even worse off.' Aoife refused to be cajoled: 'It's the ones in the shelters, after all, who will really suffer. Just imagine it. Imagine what they'll face when they come up, if any one does survive on their tinned beans and bars of chocolate. It's beyond belief. The air poisoned, the water poisoned, the stench. People mad with fear. You know the film I saw about it that time; I'll never forget it: they came crawling out on all fours, skin burnt off, their eyes blinded, scavenging for scraps like rats in a sewer and then . . .'

'Oh for Godsake Aoife, give me a rest! It's bad enough being corralled down here in this hole without having to listen to you. Can't you think of something else to talk about? Tell a joke or do a funny turn or something?'

'I only know old, bad jokes. Racist and sexist. You wouldn't laugh.'

'Try me.'

'Well, let's see,' Aoife paused. 'Okay then. There were three men walking up this mountain right?'

'Right.'

'Paddy the Scotsman, Paddy the Welsh man and Paddy the . . .'

'Oh Jesus,' said Juno, 'I don't believe it.'

Aoife had thought it all out. There would be no crouching in subterranean shelters waiting for the fallout. If she wasn't somewhere hit by a first strike she would take her own life; put a bullet through her head or swallow an overdose. But when she considered further, even suicide was fraught with problems. She could buy a gun for instance, but she could hardly carry it with her everywhere she went from now until the big day, and the same was true even for pills – how could she be sure of having the damn things with her when she needed them? She could of course do it in other ways; she could jump off a roof, or throw herself under an express train. But would the trains be running? Would there be any building left standing to jump from? What if she was blinded by the light flash and couldn't see to drag herself across the room? What then?

When she went on like this at home people thought she was crazed. They all adopted Juno's stance – the 'ah sure' attitude. 'Ah sure, we'll take off to the west coast; the prevailing winds will blow it all eastwards.' It had not happened after the last disaster; on the contrary, the rain had brought more of it down there than anywhere else. But that fact didn't bother any of her Irish friends. They did not – unlike the English – believe in wise planning and sensible precautions. If the worst was going to happen it would happen, what was the point of worrying?

Maybe they were right. Maybe it was their awful history.

'May we appeal to those in charge of young children to exercise proper restraint and prevent them from endangering their lives and the lives of others by running uncontrolled about the platforms. Please do not allow any child to stray beyond the warning light at the tunnel mouth. We thank you for your continued co-operation, and ask you to remain calm until the all clear sounds.'

'Remain calm,' the red faced man in the duffle coat stammered, 'what the hell do they think this is? The Second World War or what?'

'The Third,' the woman in the white raincoat answered, 'it's the Third we're practising for, isn't it?'

'Maybe it's started already,' said the balding man who might have been her husband, 'and they're afraid to tell us.'

'It started years ago, didn't it?' demanded a young woman with pink hair and dangling earrings, 'for the last forty years, more than half the world's population has been at war at one point or another. But does anyone notice? Does anyone care? No. And why? Because they're not white, are they?'

'Well, it won't only be our lot if this balloon goes up,' said the balding man, jerking his head towards a group of rastafarians to his left, 'we'll all be in it together – black or white – then, won't we?'

Black as sin, the black death, blackguard, black-list, black-sheep, black mail – every phrase was infected by the thing, Juno thought – black magic, black Protestant, white Christmas, white flag, white knight, white lie – why had Aoife lied about Craig? Was it a real lie or just one of omission? Was there a difference? Well, her own was only a white lie – letting Aoife think that Zoe had called her. She could hardly admit to Aoife that she wouldn't have known, even, that Zoe was back in London if she hadn't heard it from Jean Stockwell. If she had complained, Aoife would have said, 'What do you expect for, Godsake – why should she get in touch, with the way you dumped her?' And she would be right. Juno knew that she had no reason at all to expect anything of Zoe. But she did. She expected, at the very least, that Zoe would phone her when she was back in the country and not leave her to learn the news from Jean Stockwell. It wasn't like Zoe at all – not the Zoe she knew – who couldn't bear a grudge for more than ten minutes.

'Half the people down here are coloured,' the woman in the white raincoat was saying. 'Where are they going to find room for them all – that's what I'd like to know. I mean in a national emergency you'd think we would get preference, wouldn't you?'

'There are an awful lot of Irish about too,' said the man who might have been her husband, 'all that lot down from the flats.' Juno turned towards them, smiling encouragement: 'And you know what the Irish are like – didn't even fight in the last war. Let them into the shelters – drunk and singing – and they'll use up all the air in a night.'

'Oh, I hadn't thought of that, dear. It might get very unpleasant if we have to stay down much longer.'

'When Irish eyes are smiling,' Juno sang out raucously, reeling on the bench, waving her arms like a street drunk with a bottle of sherry, 'sure the world looks bright and gay, but when Irish mouths are singing, sure they'd steal your air away!'

'Nice to see someone's cheerful,' the balding man said, 'have you Irish friends or something?'

'Oh nothing to speak of – just the odd aunt, cousin, sister, mother, that sort of thing . . .'

'I see,' said the woman in the raincoat, taking quick nervous steps backwards, drawing the balding man by the sleeve, 'it takes all sorts, doesn't it? That's what I always say to Ron – don't I – it takes all sorts.'

'That got rid of them anyway,' Juno hissed, watching them retreat into the crowd, 'it's at times like this, I wish I was back in Dublin.'

'Yes, dear old Dublin – not much chance of racism there. Who have we got to threaten us, after all?' Aoife was scornful, 'a couple of hundred Jews, some Indians at the College of Surgeons and a handful of Italian ice-cream families!'

'I still wish I was there.'

'So do I.'

Aoife, in fact, had been thinking of going back for some time. Sounding people out about jobs and so on. Not that there would be any – there never were. That was the problem. Everything twice the price and no chance of work. You came over here to make a living, to escape the neighbours and the Catholic church and then, before you knew it, you had become an emigrant – crying into your pint and singing 'Comeallye'. But you couldn't go back. When you went for a visit you felt like a foreigner – the place seemed so small; a parody of itself – or was it just that you grew too rigid for its inquisitive, garrulous ways? Aoife had seen it happen to so many – half her friends were living in London or the States, talking of going back when they had enough money or the right skills or whatever. She and Barbara had come for a summer – four years ago! And Juno and Zoe too. Zoe had moved on, but to Paris, not home. And now that her mother had died she'd probably never return. Would any of them, come to think of it, even manage the annual Christmas pilgrimage if not for mothers anxiously waiting?

'Is Zoe going to Dublin?' Aoife asked.

'I don't know.'

'Has she brought the kids with her?'

'Don't know.'

'How long were you going to wait before telling me she'd phoned?'

'I wasn't waiting,' Juno said, 'I just forgot.'

It was hard to believe that Zoe was really trying to avoid her, Juno thought, but if not, what was she up to? Just playing it cool maybe. After all, she was sure to have heard by now that Juno had broken up with Ulla. Would that make things better or worse? Would she gloat? Or might she feel that it trivialised everything she had been through, to discover that Juno

189

had cast off so lightly the woman for whom she had cast off Zoe, so painfully. At least she would now feel that she could talk to Juno again, without fearing that everything she said (as it had more or less) would go back to Ulla. Nor would she have to put up with Juno appearing in Ulla's extravagant, as she called them, and attention-seeking coats and hats, in which Juno, she said, looked plain ridiculous. Best of all she would not have to watch Juno feeding Ulla's cats every time she came to visit. That had been the last straw – the very last – having to hang about waiting while Juno drooled over that woman's cats as if even her bloody animals were more important than she, Zoe. Which in a sense, at the time, they were. God, what treacheries were perpetrated in the name of love! And the forgiveness pleaded for in its wake, never sufficient. No wonder Zoe would not . . .

'Did I tell you about the dream I had the other night?' Aoife looked impatient as if she was asking the question for the second time. Maybe she was. Anyway the expression in her eyes was one all too familiar to Juno.

'No, I don't think you did. But if it's anything like your usual . . .' Juno was growing every day less anxious to hear about Aoife's dreams, heading her off discreetly when she seemed on the point of confiding one. Her night life had always verged on the macabre but lately it had become downright horrific. She would wake in the small hours screaming, from some fantasy she had been telling herself of flood, fire, or famine, and refuse to be comforted. 'It's because you sleep so much,' Juno told her. 'If you ever got up in the morning you wouldn't have time for these nightmares.' 'I only sleep in the morning,' Aoife would reply, 'because I can't sleep at night.' Which was true. She had a growing terror of sleeping when everyone else did, of leaving the world to its own devices in the dark hours – unguarded, as it were, by her watchful, ever anxious consciousness. 'Think of night pilots, nurses,' Juno would urge, 'telephonists, night watchmen, shift workers, ambulance drivers, long distance truckers, doctors on call, lighthouse men, the queen's bodyguards – they're all out there, keeping an eye . . . doing their thing. Who needs you?'

'That lot!' Aoife's scorn was absolute, 'What possible good could they be? They're the ones who got us into the mess in the first place!'

'What mess?'

'This mess.'

'Jesus – what a pessimist!'

'And what an unbelievably complacent, myopic . . . you're like one of these awful German spiritualist women . . .'

'What awful women?'

'You know the ones – with their crystals and magic charms and mantras – thinking they can stop plane crashes and earthquakes with the power of positive thinking.'

'And what about you?' Juno snarled, 'what does all your angst come down to? Protective cowardice! You anticipate the worst in every situation, to make sure you're never disappointed.'

This was an old argument that never got them anywhere. In the old days it hadn't mattered. Having nowhere they wanted to get; they had been content to disagree, to savour the conflict, the scoring of points. Each one's temperament a lure and provocation to the other. That was then. Now was a different matter. They had begun to grate on each other's nerves. Now, when every news bulletin sounded like one of Aoife's better dreams, Juno could no longer afford to be profligate with her optimism; learning to hoard, to ration sympathy and listening time. And when she did, Aoife rapped out, exasperated: 'Come off it – who do you think this stoic act is fooling? You're as nervous as everyone else.' Now she regarded Juno, sprawled beside her, in her brown leather jacket and blue jeans, hands in her pockets, legs stretched out; her look of lean, poised, obstinacy, and demanded:

'Why are you being such a bitch, tonight?'

'Bitch? I thought that word was off your list. It's sexist remember?'

'So is every word you need in a crisis!'

And so it was, thought Juno, but it was not like

191

Aoife to admit it. Aoife was careful with words; exacting, using only those she wanted, only when she wanted. She was forever taking Juno to task for her lazy dependence on a few, well worn phrases. Not to mention Zoe! Zoe's language was foul – for a semi-respectable mother of three, she could get more out of an average swear word than any sailor. That was why she didn't store anger, of course. She went off like a fire cracker for ten minutes and then forgot all about it. Or at least, she always had in the past. But maybe Paris had changed her. Juno hoped her message on the ansaphone had been suitably conciliatory while hitting the right breezy tone. She had invited Zoe over to the flat for dinner where they could have a whole night of talk in peace and quiet. On Thursday, when Aoife would be at the Centre. Not that Juno needed her out of the way. Zoe liked and trusted Aoife entirely – in fact, at times; many times – she had liked her better than she did Juno. But, then, Zoe had never been in love with Aoife, nor was likely to be. It was easy to like and trust most, or many, people one was not, nor ever had been, in love with. But was it easy, or even possible, to like them afterwards, freely, without rancour? That was the question. After all, it was going a bit far, as Zoe had told her once, to expect others – as she did, with her awful vanity – to go on caring for her while she was busy dumping them! So she had set aside vanity and made herself hateful and Zoe had hated her. And now, could she ever come to like her again? Well, Aoife had, and plenty of others, but there had been less blood and bitterness in earlier partings. But where there was loathing, wasn't there always love lurking somewhere under cover? And no greater malignancy was possible than love without outlet. And why was it so little use could be found for the thing, once its physical expression had become redundant?

'Aoife?' Juno asked.

'Yes?'

'Do you think Zoe really wanted to get in touch with me?'

'Why not? Didn't you say she rang you? She still

cares for you after all.'

'Do you think so? I left her, remember, not the other way round.'

'So what? You leave all your lovers – don't you? and they go on caring about you. You're that kind of person. Don't know why. I mean look at me! And I know you better than Zoe ever could.'

'Thanks,' Juno said.

'We would like to announce that members of the local Civil Defence force will presently be passing among you to distribute light refreshment. We would ask you to facilitate their passage by remaining in your current positions until they can reach you. Those requiring tea should raise their right hand. Thank you.'

'Oh my God – can't you just see it,' Juno moaned, 'five minutes left to live and British Rail will be offering light refreshment!'

'Yes, I can see it.' Aoife felt sweat running down her arms. Her throat was dry and her heart was beating with an odd lurching motion. She detested the Underground at any time – the confinement, the pressing of damp human flesh, the rank breath, or cloying scent, the sickly swaying through dark tunnels, the sudden unexplained halts. It was a nightmare to her. Rebirthing – that's what you need, her friends declared, to relive (or was it relieve?) her birth trauma. But Aoife did not want to. As it happened, hers had been a painless birth. Slipping from the womb as cleanly as a seal into water. Or, so her mother said – smiling, she had come into the world. Well, coming into it was one thing, Aoife thought – staying in it, quite another.

'Why haven't we done more?' she asked Juno now, staring away from her angrily, down the tracks towards the dark of the tunnel mouth, 'Why haven't we taken it seriously before this?'

'You have surely? You've been worrying about it since the year dot. Long before anyone heard of Cruise or Trident, there was you and Bertrand Russell. Right?'

'Yes, but I haven't done anything. I just stayed home and worried. We should have done something.'

'Like what?'

'I don't know. But there must have been something possible.'

'The peace camps – you could have joined one of them.'

'I couldn't,' Aoife said. 'Never. Rounded up like a lot of sheep for slaughter. Worse than here. Sitting about in the mud behind barbed wire just waiting for it to happen. Thinking about it all day, everyone around you thinking about it. I'd have gone mad. Even if I had believed for one moment that it could make any difference. Can't you just see the boys from the military-industrial complex turning round and saying, ' "Sorry girls – we didn't know you felt so strongly!" '

'I hope they don't keep us waiting much longer for that tea,' said a short, stout woman standing next to them, who might have been the woman in the white raincoat but wasn't because her hair was more tightly permed and her coat was blue: 'I'm dying for a cuppa, aren't you?'

'I could do with something a bit stronger actually,' Juno said.

'Oh yes, but you couldn't expect that from Civil Defence. I mean they couldn't very well go about handing out free G and Ts – especially with all these foreigners about.'

'Oh but I thought they weren't letting them in?' Juno looked worried: 'I thought I saw a notice on the street – no Irish, Blacks or dogs?'

'Did you dear? My neighbours won't like that – half of them are coloured. Same everywhere now I expect.'

'Not for long, it seems. They're flying them all out – part of this emergency drill – flying them home courtesy of the RAF.'

'Well, that's alright then, isn't it. I imagine they'll be glad to get out of it and all,' the woman's face was bright with relief. Aoife gave her a long considering look and spoke very softly:

'I wouldn't mind myself. Ireland is neutral, you know. Best place to be.'

'Oh, how's that then?'

'Simple. We just told all the superpowers "we're neutral", so no bombs on us!'

'That's nice,' said the woman. 'I always thought Ireland was a nice quiet country. None of this immigrant problem there either, have you? I always meant to visit some day. I have relations there, you see – on the south coast or the east – Tipperary, I think. Or is that just because of the song?'

Aoife was watching the young couples. They wore their usual air of quiet superiority in the company of anyone too old or too young for their self-absorption. But for the occasion they had added a special consciousness of the demands of gender. The men were being protective – solid and paternal. They stood feet planted wide apart, shoulders back. The arm about their partner's shoulder was clamped tight: custodial and anchoring. The women, in immediate response, made themselves fragile, uncertain, crouched a little, knees bent, and, leaning into the male torso, their upturned face was a clear pool in which he saw reflected his brave impassive gaze.

'I told you, you should have made some sandwiches and brought the sleeping bags,' a tall blonde north London type was saying to his girlfriend. 'We could be here for hours.'

'I'm sorry,' she said, 'it was my fault but I didn't like to make a fuss with so many people waiting.'

'Why shouldn't they wait? What else have they to do? You women are all the same – one glimpse of a uniform and it's, "Yes sir, no sir, three bags full sir!" If I hadn't been there I don't expect you'd even have had the sense to ask where they were sending us, would you?'

'Listen to him,' Aoife said, turning up her eyes, 'the original man of conscience!'

'Yes, and it's always the big mouths who are first

195

out! Give his kind one glimpse of uniform, never mind "your country needs you", and they'll be falling over themselves to get to the front, polishing up their puttees and singing a soldier's song.'

'And some of the women are as bad,' Aoife sighed, 'do you remember the Falklands when they were flooding down to the quays? Not content to wave their men off, they had to pull up their tee-shirts and waggle their breasts. Remember all that hysteria?'

Aoife could still see clearly the newspaper pictures of the time – smiling, war-crazed young women – and remembered the stories of how the ships were loaded with porn videos to maintain troop morale on the tedious sea voyage. Well that was war for you. It had always brought out the worst in the sexes. That was one of the reasons for having them, of course – to make boys into men and girls into wives. Keep them off the streets and the home fires burning. And wasn't it much the same thing with the peace camps? she thought. Another reason she had stayed clear of them. What had it got to do with Women's Liberation – as she went on calling it long after everyone else had adopted the bland 'women's movement' – How does it liberate us? she demanded of her friends who were deserting rape crisis centres and radical newspapers to imprison themselves behind wire fences, acting out the time-honoured role: protecting the species, praying for peace, clearing up after the male mess.

'I wish to God I'd thought of bringing the Walkman,' she said to Juno, who seemed to be falling asleep beside her.

'The Walkman! If only you'd reminded me to bring some whiskey!'

'Lord yes – I could do with some.'

'You!' Juno made a face of exaggerated horror, 'Whiskey! The Russians would have responded to the first strike before you got a spoonful swallowed!'

'Ha, ha. Very funny!' Aoife swung her head away and glowered into the distance. She looked intensely childish when she was angry, Juno thought, with her round cheeks and pouting mouth, her hands closed into fists. And for all her fretting and anxiety, younger than any health freak.

'Come on,' Juno coaxed her, suddenly contrite, 'cheer up – this can't go on much longer.'

'Why not?' Aoife growled, 'most things do.'

So Juno asked about the dream Aoife had wanted to tell her. She said she would listen to the whole thing now if it would make Aoife feel any better. But Aoife said, 'no, it was boring. Nothing out of the usual.'

And it wasn't. It was just the kind of awful thing Juno had grown used to. A dream of terror and disgrace. But, huddled now in this terrible place, it seemed to Aoife prophetic. It would not be the first time she had dreamed her own future. It had started innocently enough. They were all three, Juno, herself and Zoe at a circus; sitting under the big top, eating popcorn and chocolate and watching the trapeze artists fly through the air, when Aoife thought she caught the smell of cloth burning. Then the scent switched, as it usually did, and she found herself on the deck of a great liner that was sinking, bow first, inch by inch, into the night sea. And the smell of burning, well, it was the flames gushing from the engine room. The air was filled with hideous screams. She was trapped at the top of a stairway leading from the lower deck, a terrified crowd milling in front and behind her. She could not find Juno or Zoe anywhere. She shouted their names but nothing could be heard above the uproar. She watched the lifeboats launched one by one, rocking like paper hats on the black water. The mob surged behind her, lifting her off her feet. And then the cry went up, 'No more room in the boats. Mothers and children first.' An officer with a gun stood in front of her, forbidding her passage. Behind him, sitting on a stanchion, she suddenly caught sight of Juno and Zoe. They were playing a game of cards with an absurd expression of contentment; smoking cigarettes and laughing, happy as if they were down in their local having a pint. She shrieked to them to help her, but they ignored her completely, either not seeing her or not wanting to. She saw the last boat hoisted up over the rail. She kicked her way forward savagely.

197

She trampled over the bodies fallen before her. She crawled over the body of a woman. She felt the soft flesh of the stomach give beneath her heel. She heard a bone crack. But she was nearly at the boat. It was almost at arm's reach. She heard herself wailing frantically: 'Save me – save me!'

'Pack up your troubles in your old kit bag and smile, smile, smile . . .' the woman in the blue coat was singing now in a small quavering voice, her pallid face assuming an expression of arch music hall cheer. 'What's the use of worrying – it never was worthwhile oh . . .'

'If you had listened to me,' the north London type was saying to his girlfriend, 'we could be in Hampshire by now. None of this is going on outside the cities, you know.'

'I'm sorry Paul,' the girlfriend said with a nervous laugh, 'but I just didn't feel I could take your father at present.'

'And what's wrong with my father, I'd like to know?' "Paul" was standing in front of her now, his fists clenched at his side as though he might strike her. 'If I can put up with your bourgeois shit of a mother dragging round Harrod's looking for matching bathroom towels . . .'

'At least that's one thing we don't fight about,' Juno said. She leaned over and took Aoife's hand between her own. How was it, she wondered, no matter what the time or circumstance, Aoife's body always held this lovely, steady heat. She squeezed her hand: 'Come on love,' she appealed, 'give us a smile. I'm sorry.'

And Aoife smiled. She was sorry also but it was too early to say so.

'At least we don't fight about what?' she asked.

'Our mothers.'

No, certainly they did not and never had. It was one unshadowed area of pleasure in their lives. In fact, Juno considered, knowing Aoife's mother was one of the best things about knowing Aoife. She loved Juno with a special fascination and indulgence and was loved in return. Having been used to such empathy made it all the more difficult to deal with Zoe's mother. Not liking her and not being able or willing to hide it had made trouble between Zoe and herself from the start. It did not help that Zoe's mother liked Juno even less. She considered that Juno had ruined her daughter's life, invaded her home, estranged her husband and abducted her children. She wasn't far wrong. Juno did not care to argue the point. When forced to meet each other they were polite, but distant – very distant. Fortunately, Zoe did not at all resemble her mother. Or at least only now and then, the slightest bit, and when they were arguing Juno liked to tell her so. Taking it back afterwards. Once they had split up, of course, it comforted her to think that Zoe was, in truth, very like her mother – growing more like her each week. And she persuaded herself she had made a timely escape.

Aoife was slumped into silence. She was scratching at a rash on the back of her hand that would have healed weeks ago, Juno told her, if only she would leave it alone. She was thinking again about her dream. Haunted by that image of herself, demented with fear, crawling her way over the injured. Is that how she would be if it came to it? Is that the best she could expect of herself? Better not to say anything about it to Juno.

'Why are you so quiet? Are you still sulking, by any chance?'

'No, just thinking.'

'Well why don't you share it then?' Juno asked, nudging her sharply in the ribs, 'say something to entertain us, come on.'

'With what?'

'Stories, gossip, anything, even that old dream.'

'I don't hear any gossip. I don't see anyone these days, you know that.'

'You must see someone.'

But Aoife refused to be goaded. After a pause that

199

seemed at least five minutes to Juno, who was growing fractious with boredom, Aoife sighed:

'I was thinking . . .'

'What?' Juno asked desperately.

'I was thinking – that if this thing is going to get serious – wouldn't we be better off at home?'

'Why? It wouldn't be any safer. I don't think the super powers – whatever about this poor woman beside us – really appreciate your story of "no bombs on us".'

'You don't say?' Aoife was sarcastic. 'You know what I mean; we'd be with our families, my mother, yours, our friends – old friends.'

'All our friends emigrated years ago.'

'You know perfectly well what I'm saying – I mean that if we are going to snuff it, do you want it to be here, in this city – in exile? Do you want this place to be the last thing you see on earth?'

'Oh, for God's sake! Can't you stop talking about death for five minutes? What *has* got into you?'

'Alright – you talk then.'

So they sat in silence and said nothing at all.

Why in the name of God, thought Aoife, should she exhaust herself trying to make Juno face reality? It would catch up on her soon enough. And why the fuck, Juno asked herself, should she give a shit whether Aoife came out of her macabre doomsday fantasies or not when she so clearly preferred them to reality. She was getting more neurotic every day. Why else would she invent that ridiculous story about Craig? Craig Gillespie of all people! Juno would have liked to ask about it again – get to the bottom of it, but when she thought it over, it did not seem likely that she'd get very far. She could just hear what Aoife would say: 'I didn't tell you a lie – I just had no reason to mention it before.' What Juno could not understand, was *why* Aoife would want to keep secrets from her. Everyone had secrets of some kind, of course, but not Aoife. She was outspoken and guileless to a fault. Suddenly Juno remembered something Aoife had said a few weeks ago after some other small act of concealment – she had paid no attention at the time –

but now she remembered Aoife's defence; she had said, 'It's just nice to have something for once that you haven't commented on! Everything I do, everything that happens to me, you have a remark to make, an attitude, an opinion. And the worst of it is that half the time you're right!'

'Aoife?'
'Yes?'
'You know this thing about Kennedy?'
'Oh you're not starting off on that again, surely?'
'No, I was just wondering why . . .'
'Look, how on earth can it matter who I did or didn't sleep with – it's more than twenty years ago.'
'It doesn't. I didn't care who you slept with, even when I should have, if you remember. All I want to know is why you didn't tell me all these years – why you should want to keep secrets?'
'Secrets! My God you don't ask much, do you? Haven't you ever heard of the right to privacy?'
'Privacy for whom, that's the point.'
'Oh for God's sake Juno can't you drop it? Can't you ever let sleeping dogs lie?'
'Sleeping dogs?' Juno's voice soared in indignation, 'so you mean you did sleep with him after all!'
'Oh Lord, you are tiresome.'
'Hallo – oh. Hi there!' They looked across the tracks to the opposite platform and saw Nick and Sarah, friends from Juno's last flat, waving to them. 'Hullo, how are you doing?' they called back. Nick made great sweeping movements with his arms, like an injured bird trying to take flight, and shouted something back to them before they were both swallowed from sight by a sudden heave of the crowd.
'What did he say?' Juno asked.
'Don't know – sounded lke "Picnic at Chernobyl". Oh by the way, that's some gossip I'd forgotten,' Aoife laughed, delighted with herself.
'What?'
'Guess?'
'About those two?'

'Yes.'

'Oh come on, tell me. I can't imagine.'

'She's pregnant.'

'Sarah?'

'Yes, I met her in the library a few days ago, looking rotund and self-satisfied, getting out baby books. And she told me.'

'Is that all?' Juno sighed. 'I thought it was something interesting.'

It was all you heard these days, she thought. Everyone was doing it, for want of anything better to do. Gone were the days when you bumped into an old friend and the first news was who had come out last, with whom, and who had run off with whose wife. Now it was all "was it a girl or a boy – home delivery or hospital?"

'I suppose she had it by insemination, just to keep it radical?'

'I don't know,' Aoife replied, 'but whatever it was, she's delighted. She said she did it just in case she regretted not doing it later on.'

'And what if she regrets *doing* it later on – what then?' Juno almost shouted.

'You're very vehement, all of a sudden. You're not in love with a mother again, by any chance?'

'I gave that up after Zoe.'

And she had. Once bitten twice shy, as they say. She had loved those children as her own. Better, far better. Never having wanted children of her own flesh – the burden and reproach of heredity. But Zoe's children, borrowed as it were, ready made, were a perfect, painless gift. Until they were taken away. That was the drawback in loving other people's children. You had no rights of possession. Not even of viewing. Ironic. It was Juno who had fought for them in the first place; stolen them from under their father's nose from the house to which he had entrapped them. In a rented car she and Zoe had swept them off at dead of night, for a holiday – a magical mystery tour, as the kids called it. It rained and blew for two weeks; icy Scottish rain. They slept in damp tents, draughty youth hostels, once in a disused goods train. Cold, poor and hungry, life had never been so good. The children played and sang in the back seat of the car, ate baked beans from the tin and slept noiselessly at night beside the lovers' fevered bodies and never wanted to go back to their cold father in cold Edinburgh again.

'It's so selfish!' Juno said, 'having children when nobody needs them – egotistical and capricious.'

'Their parents need them surely?'

'Yes, as playthings – consumer luxuries for the liberal who has everything. I mean society, the community, has no need for them. Not in the west. We're so artificial and fragmented. No one knows what to do with them anymore – what to teach them.'

'Well feminists should, they're . . .'

'Aw! They're the worst of the lot.' Juno was scathing. 'They raise little monsters who blackmail them from the first day they can talk, for being different.'

'What amazes me,' Aoife said, 'is that anyone still has the courage to bring children into this world. Do they never think what lies ahead of them?'

'No. If they did they couldn't do it. That's what it's all about, isn't it? Flying in the face of fate – an offering to the Gods.'

'Hostages to fortune, more like.'

' "There'll be blue birds over the white cliffs of Dover, tomorrow . . . just you wait and see . . ." Was that the Second World War girls, or the First?' the woman in the blue coat, who was singing to herself again, asked.

'Vera Lynn anyhow,' Juno offered.

'"Goodbye Piccadilly . . . farewell Leicester Square . . . it's a long, long, way to Tipperary . . . but my heart lies there." That one was the First,' she smiled triumphantly, 'definitely the First. Going off to the trenches, that was, with their knapsacks on their knees.'

The crowd about them had grown weary and subdued. The children, tired of playing, had fallen asleep in arms and laps; heads thrown back, mouths open. The young couples had given up the act: they lay sprawled about the platform, the men resting their heads on their girlfriends' knee, the latter stroking the men's foreheads with the soothing, abstracted motion of mothers with young children. Old people sat huddled on the benches, heads drooping. There was a continuous, low murmuring of voices, broken now and then by spasms of coughing or laughter, quickly suppressed, as it will be by travellers sleepless on a long night journey, fearful of disturbing the others. The smokers had run out of cigarettes and turned hostile and taciturn. Those who had thought to bring food or drink had long since finished it.

'Are we all going to die, Mummy?' a child woken abruptly asked her mother.

'Of course not dear.'

'Then why are we all waiting here?'

'To learn to protect ourselves.'

'From what, Mummy?'

'We don't know yet dear, they haven't told us. Go back to sleep for a bit, there's the good girl.'

Juno was thinking about what she would do when she got out. She would phone Zoe, she had decided, and ask her simply if she would come over and have breakfast with her. It would be like old times. On the way home she could buy flowers, croissants, Columbian coffee and all the papers. Everything Zoe used to love. A real Sunday morning – a whole lazy day of it.

Aoife was considering what she should have done, and trying to decide what she could do in the future. She could join that underground group, for a start: the ones who went round sabotaging power stations, intercepting computer networks, decoding their messages and fucking up the system. She was sick of all this passive resistance and self-sacrifice. She wanted power and action. She wanted to get someone before they got her.

'God it seems so long ago, doesn't it?' Juno said suddenly with a groan.

'What?'

'The old days. When you were with Moya and I was with Justine, and we were running all over the country, falling in love, drinking ourselves to death and changing the world!'

'Yes incredible. The innocence of it – all those occupations and sit-ins, pickets and marches. Who ever thinks of changing the world now? We're all just happy to save it!'

'What happened to it all?' Juno looked round lugubriously at the despondent, listless people huddled about them, too weary now even to mutter complaint. 'What happened to all the fire and conviction?'

'They just wore us down, I suppose,' Aoife said with a half-hearted laugh, 'with recessions and lay-offs, poverty, the bloody murderous right-to-lifers, and the war maniacs: "Arming for Peace". They just wore us out. With fear.'

'Yes,' Juno said. 'After all, look at you. You used to be an average, normal manic depressive. You had swings – one day high as a kite, the next flat as a burst tyre. You don't have swings anymore – you just stay flat.'

That was one thing they had succeeded with, she thought, even if the thing never went off – they had succeeded in keeping Aoife and millions like her in a state of terror. They had kept them all divided, bickering among themselves. Passive. That was their triumph.

'It's all been a huge smokescreen, hasn't it, all these years?' Aoife spoke in a low, weary voice, almost to herself: 'Do you remember in the camps when women thought they had won a victory with the withdrawal of Cruise? And then they found out it was only because they had come up with something better? They made us victims of our own idealism. The real world is just too horrific for women to accept – that's our problem – we just plough on with this woolly utopianism. A hope and a prayer.'

Prayer. Aoife was so lightly contemptuous. She despised it all. But then she had not been caught early, like Juno, infected with belief; the need for divine intervention and last minute solutions. Juno thought she had cast it all off in adolescence, but in the last year or so she had felt it creeping up on her. Not the traditional stuff – Christ and redemption – but the new hotch potch; Buddha and I Ching. She practised Aikido, she lit candles and meditated. That reminded her of lighting the votive candle for Our Lady as a child. What was the difference? Passing a church one Sunday morning in Kilburn and hearing the Irish voices of women at the gate she had gone in. Since then she had returned in secret a couple of times, lured by incense and a statue of Joan of Arc. She went to synagogue to keep it balanced and twice to an Anglican service. The calm secular air amused her, the dark, polished wood, the golden eagle for a lectern; the comfortable air of a gentlemen's club on ladies' day. But it was the Catholic ritual that held its grip on her. She loathed above all mankind; priests and clergy, especially Irish ones; their oily pomposity, their vanity and self-interest. But what was the fascination for her in the voices of the women praying? Some old wound first cut by them, a vacancy into which they poured in equal measure guilt and glory. This scar in the psyche that could only be healed by their faith.

'Well even prayer, I suppose, is better than paralysis,' she suggested.

'Prayer? A load of maudlin hypocrisy!' Aoife burst out. 'The curse of an Irish upbringing – distracting us from doing a single hand's turn to help ourselves. Still . . .' and she sighed deeply, 'anything is worth a go if it can cast out fear. And better, the fear of fear.'

Fear – that was why Juno refused to admit to their scaremongering. She would not allow herself to imagine it – to let in the possibility, even for a moment. She would not go about cringing; biting her nails, crouched like a rat in a hole.

'Wouldn't you think,' the woman in the blue coat said, 'that British Rail would do something about all those mice, rummaging about through the litter. It must be insanitary!'

206

'Saves them clearing it up themselves, doesn't it?' said "Paul" contemptuously, waking for a moment from his girlfriend's lap.

'But you know,' Juno said to Aoife, persisting with her theme, 'the women in the peace camps may have been naive, but at least they were putting up a fight. It might only have been symbolic but it *was* protest. Standing up to be counted.'

'Yes, standing up to be counted by them you mean,' Aoife shrugged impatiently, 'All part of their divide and conquer routine. Look how many of us they got up there. All rounded up nice and orderly. No one left to complain about anything else.'

Juno looked up and down the platform, at the old people sleeping, the children lying quietly in their mothers' arms, and allowed herself, for a second, to imagine the inconceivable.

'Maybe you're right,' she said, 'but what's the use of equal pay, reclaim the night, custody for lesbian mothers, abortion on demand and the rest of it, if we are all going to be burnt off the face of the earth?'

'We would like to apologise for the delay in the arrival of the second round of refreshments,' the voice boomed out once more, frightening people awake. **'This is due to unforeseen congestion on Kentish Town Road. Those waiting on the lower platforms who have not yet been served are advised to move in an orderly fashion towards the main exit signs and await the arrival of the trolleys. We would appeal to all members of the public to give prefer-ence, in the likelihood of any shortage, to mothers and children first. Thank you.'**

'Sounds like the Titanic, doesn't it?' Juno laughed.
'What does?'
'This "mothers and children first" bit. Very chival-rous. Of course, it's only in the movies it happens. In reality, when it comes to the crunch, the men panic; start hurling themselves into the lifeboats, capsizing

207

them: drowning kids and old women . . .'

'Oh stop for Heaven's sake, Juno . . .'

'Why? What's wrong now?' She looked at Aoife's stricken face and laughed again. 'You haven't developed a phobia about drowning too, have you?'

'I don't have phobias. I have perfectly rational fear!' Aoife snapped.

She was all too reasonable, she thought. And it wasn't death she was afraid of either. It was life. Of what people were prepared to do to survive. It did not take a bad dream to teach her how far courage under fire; the dignity of the human spirit and the rest of it stretched in a crisis. It was the people who came through horror and mayhem who worried her – not the ones who went under. She did not want to live long enough to witness it. Death, if it meant extinction: the cessation of consciousness, held no terror for her. But suffering, torture, the sadism necessary to save your own skin, that was something else. And the future she foresaw – suffering on a scale beyond belief; slow, agonised deaths, with no one left to comfort or ease the pain – was something that in all the catalogue of human horror had not yet been seen.

'Of course, it was different in the last war,' the woman in the blue coat was explaining to Juno, 'We had spirit then – not like now. We knew how to enjoy ourselves then. We used to come down here to the Underground with our flasks of tea, our cigarettes and sandwiches and we'd play cards – yes, gin rummy, poker . . . we'd dance and sing. Oh we did have fun! But we were all in the same boat then, you see – men, women, children, it didn't matter. We were all the same race, weren't we? That's what counted.'

Did anyone really believe in the reality of their own death? Aoife wondered. If they did, human life would be impossible. Least of all these so called 'realists' preparing for the worst – hoping for the best, running about in uniforms and silly caps. Making announcements. Juno at least was honest about the thing. She had said once, blithely, when the subject came up: 'Oh, by the time it gets to my turn they'll have invented something!' Wasn't that what everyone imagined in their heart of hearts? Science, progress, God, someone or something was bound to step in and save them at the last minute? She almost managed to feel it herself at times.

'Stands to reason, doesn't it,' the woman in the blue coat was continuing, 'It's television and all this sex education in schools that I blame. We didn't need anyone in those days teaching us what to do. You saw a thing or two, I can tell you, down here in the shelters. Young couples, you know, newly-weds, brought down in the middle of the night – couldn't blame them, could you? Just carried on as if they were at home in their own beds. Well they didn't know if they were going to be alive in the morning, did they? None of us did. Live and let live, that's what we used to say. We had to keep morale up come what might. But men were men then – and girls were girls. All changed now, isn't it. Mother Nature isn't good enough for anyone anymore.'

'Don't suppose it ever was,' Juno suggested, 'nothing very natural about marriage or churches, bombs or air raid shelters, is there?'

Aoife was staring up into the woman's pale, bland eyes, she looked at the short upturned nose, and the bright pink bow painted onto the mouth, and heard herself asking with a sudden intensity:

'But did you think you were going to die? I mean did any of you, at the time, really accept the possibility of your own death?'

'Well, it was all around you, dear, wasn't it? We all knew we were up against it . . .'

'Yes, of course,' Aoife interrupted, 'but did you *feel* you were going to – did you accept it?'

'We were frightened, naturally. Anyone would be,' the woman was becoming embarrassed now, but still cheerful, 'but you had to look on the bright side, same as ever. If your number was up, it was up. But not everyone could catch it, could they? Stands to reason – someone has to survive to keep it going, don't they, love?'

Juno was wondering what she would say to Zoe once they were alone. What could she say? What was the best approach? It would be no use trying to give an explanation. She didn't know herself why she had done as she had. She hadn't let herself think about it. These days she allowed herself only superficial wounds. And the place in her consciousness that was the leaving of Zoe, even though she had chosen it, was a territory too vast to enter. Every relationship; in its time the first and last, hurt at its end. Juno could still recall exactly the pain of her break-up with Aoife, so long ago. But it had become a fond possession: a source of continuing curiosity, to be taken out from time to time, studied from various angles; a pleasing, even a consoling memory.

'Aoife? Do you ever think about our relationship? Do you ever wonder why we broke up?'

'Who? You and Zoe?'

'No – you and me, of course.'

'Oh – us . . . No I can't say I do very much. I can't really remember it now. It seems so long ago. The usual reasons I suppose . . .'

'What reasons?'

'Politics, probably, money, other women – mostly other women, wasn't it? Must have seemed like a good idea at the time.'

'It's very nice, I must say, to know how well you remember it!'

Aoife looked sceptical:

'Yes, but it does seem such a long time ago, doesn't it?'

'Yes. It does,' Juno admitted reluctantly. Then suddenly, her face brightened, a wide, self-satisfied grin spread across it.

'But could you ever have guessed then,' she said, 'that one day, all these years later, we would be sitting together in a London bomb shelter, comforting each other like an old married couple?'

Aoife gave a quick, exaggerated shudder; like a dog shaking water from its coat: 'No, certainly not. I wasn't always this pessimistic.'

'**We would like to remind members of the public,**' the raucous voice came crackling once more from the public address system, '**that blankets are available from the duty desk at platform six. Anyone wishing to avail themselves of this service should make their way to the area as soon as possible, demand being greater than we had foreseen, and provisions consequently running low. Thank you.**'

'Now that you've split up with Ulla again,' Aoife asked, 'do you think you and Zoe will get together?'

'My God no! Why should we?' Juno looked aghast.

'Why not?'

'No one ever does, do they? Go back to an old lover? It's just one of those things. Once it's over it's over.'

'What exactly?'

Sexual attraction, Juno supposed she meant. Or the ability, the enthusiasm, the unself-consciousness to express it. And why was it that once you ceased making love with someone, even for a matter of months, you lost the knack of it – the out of mind, unstoppable passion of it anyway? Why wasn't sex, she thought, like other physical pleasures, like swimming, drinking alcohol, riding a bicycle – once learned never forgotten? Why, unless the interruption was an involuntary one, did passion require unbroken continuity? Absence certainly did not make the body grow fonder. In fact, it was very much like riding a bike, or a highwire balancing act – only possible with complete concentration and so long as you didn't think about it. Once thinking started you were lost. And it always did start during a separation. But no matter how prolonged and painful these might be at the outset, eventually, somehow or other, one survived. And wasn't that the real death blow? For could desire exist without faith in its own necessity?

'Is she with anyone else, at the moment?'

'Who?'

'Zoe.'

'Oh, I think she was. But I think it's over. Why?'

'Well, what's to stop you then?'

'Stop me doing what?'

211

'Nothing really. It's just when I think of all you went through to get together in the first place . . . breaking up a marriage, eloping . . . all that, on again, off again, waiting around . . .'

Yes, that was true enough. They had met in the old days, or at least on the fringe of them. Juno was living with Justine and Zoe with her husband. They had nowhere to make love. And they needed to make love so badly their bones ached. Their entire being hurt with the need to lie down together; to relinquish once and for all, the hold of gravity, to lie down breast to breast, thigh to thigh. It was an agony to remain upright, hour after hour. One thought possessed them – one need only – one object craved night and morning: a bed, unoccupied, which they could occupy together and remain supine and prone and vice versa for long endless uninterrupted hours. So they ran away, carrying old suitcases filled with newspaper, to a luxury hotel in the heart of the country, to a room with a bathroom en suite and a queen size bed, where they revelled in long uninterrupted hours of luxury for five days; after which they climbed down the fire escape leaving behind their suitcases stuffed with old newspaper, and hitched a lift back to the city on a milk float.

'Do you remember the time,' Juno asked, 'when Zoe and I filled suitcases with newspaper and . . .'

'Newspaper?'

'Yes, the time we went to the Glenside Hotel.'

'The time you went where?'

'Oh, well . . . never mind. It's a long story.'

'We would like to invite members of the public wishing to take part in the exhibition of emergency management to make their way to the duty desk on platform five and make themselves known to the officers in charge. Full co-operation in this exercise from all present will be much appreciated. A box will be provided for anyone wishing to tender written suggestions or criticism. Thank you.'

'At least Barbara is safely out of all this rubbish, in Yorkshire, I suppose?' Juno asked.

'Yes, more or less.'

She was safely out of everything up there in that windblown, rain drenched, Godforsaken place. If it were not for radios, televisions and newspapers. She had gone to a remote stone cottage rented from some ex-painter friend near the moors, to get away from it all; purge her mind and compose her soul. But, once severed from the city and its fevers, she grew increasingly restless and fretful. She must know what was going on. Not knowing, she felt it must be something terrible. No news was certainly bad news. She bought a colour television and ordered 'Newsweek', 'Stern' and 'Le Point'. She became, little by little, from fear of the vast silences of country life – a media junkie. She woke to breakfast t.v., listened late into the night to foreign stations and the B.B.C. World Service. She must keep in touch; hold her grip on the great affairs of men. When Aoife came to visit she had to fight her way through a feast of feminist newsprint and every political periodical in circulation, to reach the double bed and Barbara's body that was, nonetheless, growing sleek and plump on its new gluttony. Leaning to kiss her, Aoife would feel a restraining finger on her lips: 'Just a moment, love – I want to catch the one-o-clock headlines.' And however grim they proved to be, they brought a quick smile of fulfillment or relief to Barbara's eyes.

'Doesn't really matter where you are, these days, there's no escape.'

'Isn't there?' Juno looked surprised. 'I would have thought you'd have a great time up there in the rain.'

'Why?'

'Oh you know . . . country life. Just the two of you – nothing to do all day but stay in bed and . . .' Juno had been rooting through her pockets while she spoke and suddenly produced a half-eaten bar of milk chocolate with a cry of pleasure: 'Oh look – rations! Do you want some?'

'No thanks.'

Juno tore off the wrapping and, taking a large bite, began to chew noisily.

After a few minutes of this, Aoife spoke again, 'Do you mind if I ask you something?'

'What?'

'Just something I've been wondering about lately . . .'

'What?'

'Well, suppose you were caught up in some real emergency – a disaster at sea, or a fire or . . .'

'Or what?'

'Alright . . . supposing this was the real thing. I mean suppose we were trapped down here, if it <u>was</u> an air raid shelter and the bombs were falling outside and the air was poisoned and . . .'

'And what?'

'Well if it really was life and death . . . do you think you'd keep your head or panic? Do you think you'd be courageous under pressure? Supposing there was no more room and there were people outside at the entrance begging to get in . . . do you think you might have the courage to give up your place . . . to a child, say or an old woman? Would you help someone even if it meant risking your life?'

'Oh who knows,' Juno said. 'Who knows what any of us would do in a crisis. Maybe we'd surprise ourselves. Why do you ask anyhow?'

'No reason. Just thinking . . .'

'Well don't, it's bad for you,' Juno said, breaking off another square of chocolate.

So Aoife kept silence dutifully for a few minutes, her hands folded in her lap until Juno had finished eating and thrown away the last piece of silver paper.

'Can I ask you something else . . . one last thing?'

'All right,' Juno was weary, 'go on . . .'

'What would you do it if happened right here . . . tonight?'

'What?'

'The bomb, of course – if they dropped it now while we were down here?'

'They wouldn't,' Juno said, 'they always give a five minute warning. Time to launch a protest movement!'

'Oh, you're hopeless . . .' Aoife said, laughing suddenly. And Juno smiled with relief because it was the first real laugh she had got out of her since coming down to the shelter.

'But seriously,' Aoife went on, after a moment, 'what would you do . . . at the last warning?'

Juno leaned towards her, she put her arm slowly around Aoife's waist and brought her lips close to the nape of her neck:

'This is what I'd do,' she said. 'If we had anything more than five minutes, I'd call up all my best friends and former lovers and get them all together under one roof, in one bed and relive, minute by minute, the sins of our flesh . . .'

A middleaged man sitting next them, a grey army blanket wrapped round his shoulders, stared at them in horror, then jerked his head to someone standing behind him and with a hissing sound muttered: 'We could do with a war to sort that kind out, teach them what their bodies are for. Round them all up . . . bloody perverts!'

'Did you hear him?' Aoife asked.

'Yes.'

'Do you think if we had only five minutes left — they'd forgive us?'

'Not a chance.' Juno smiled.

'We regret to inform those members of the public still awaiting the arrival of the refreshment trolley that it will not now be possible to reach platforms seven and eight on the Northern Line. Those still requiring tea are requested to come to the duty desk on platform five where supplies are still available. We apologise for any inconvenience suffered. Thank you.'

'Juno . . . Aoife . . . Hallo there . . .'

Aoife looked up and saw Lizzie East hurrying towards them along the platform with her short, quick steps as though wearing a hobble skirt, which she wasn't. She was, as always, dressed for the occasion in a green combat jacket, baggy fatigues and a red French Resistance type beret.

'Why weren't you on the street with us? We had a tremendous night.'

'Doing what?' Juno had worked with her for years on the paper and knew what she meant by a tremendous night. Lizzie raised a placard she was carrying at her side and brandished it before them. In scarlet letters that dripped like blood across a white background, they read: 'Take arms – Not shelter', and when she flipped it over: 'Civil Defence – Fascist Lackeys . . . Civil Dissent – Stops Bombs.'

'Protesting, of course,' Lizzie cried, 'it was marvellous,' her eyes lit with the fire of battle, 'we had them on the run after five minutes – a dozen more or so on our side and we could have got control of the street! Where were you two when you were needed?'

'Didn't know there was anything on,' Juno answered languidly.

'Oh you never do anymore – I suppose you were in bed watching the tele? I hope at least you thought of doing a few interviews for the mag, while you were down here?'

'Nothing to write with,' Juno held out empty hands in a gesture of supplication, 'Sorry.'

'Well, I did, luckily. Listen to this. You wouldn't believe the things they're coming out with! It's like a re-run of an old war movie. Listen, and no marks for guessing age, race and sex of speaker. One: "I think they need to get their priorities sorted out. They can't expect to save everyone, can they? With limited resources decisions will have to be made as to how they should be allocated and to whom." Two: "My mummy says we're going to have to stay underground for weeks and weeks like moles. We'll have all our favourite things to eat – like baked beans and biscuits and peanut butter – and that when we come up the whole world will be different. There won't be any buses or trains or houses. And we won't have to go to school ever again." Three: "I tell you, I have been living half my life in this country while they tried to

216

get rid of me. And now, just when I'm going home, they tell me I've got to stay. Well one thing is for sure – I may not have lived like a British citizen but I'm sure as hell going to die like one. I'll be as good an English corpse as any white one, won't I dear?" '

'I like that.' Aoife laughed.

There was a sudden commotion at the far end of the platform. A group of men in bright orange astronaut-type suits with helmets and face masks were pushing their way down the main staircase, carrying some swaying cargo between them. The crowd receded like a wave as they passed. The men came to a standstill about twenty feet from where the women sat and laid down their burden – a stretcher, Juno saw now – a grey blanket covering an unevenly shaped mound held in place by leather strapping. One of the bearers knelt down and undid the wrapping to reveal the hideously charred and blackened body of a young white male. A gasp of horror rose from those watching and they inched a little closer. One of the suited figures began to spray the form with some transparent liquid – possibly water – from a plastic cylinder, while another knelt and, clamping open the mouth, brought his own down on it and breathed lungfuls of air into the throat.

'Oh no . . .' Aoife wailed, 'look at the state it's in . . . look at its hands!'

'Don't be an idiot – can't you see it's only dye and paint – can't you see it running off?'

And it was – trickling in muddy, red brown streams from the white rib cage and along the furred belly. One of the men then took up position to the left of it and began, like a steward on a plane, to intone a commentary on the actions of his colleagues, accompanying it with stylised wavings of his arms and hands: 'You will note the severe burns of face and chest; third degree where the flesh has been seared from the bone. The skin of the legs and arms, however, has received more superficial damage, second degree burns only. This pattern of injury will not be uncommon among victims living a hundred miles or more from a direct attack . . .'

217

'Let's get away from here, for goodness sake . . .' Aoife cried, 'how much more of this obscenity do they expect us to take?'

'What we need . . .' Lizzie was proclaiming, ignoring both the First Aid antics and Aoife's distress, 'is one last great effort. A universal action. Resistance on a scale never seen before. A truly world-wide campaign – every city on the globe, every town, every street – blocked by demonstrators. Everything shut down – the schools, the factories, the supermarkets, the kitchens – just imagine – every housewife out on the street, mothers and children, sitting down wherever they happen to be – in the fields, the churches, the playgrounds, everyone sitting still – nothing moving, not a sound, and then from all over the planet, out of this almighty silence – the chant rising from a million voices, united: "We demand the right to live – we demand the right to live!" '

'How about some of that tea,' Juno asked, stretching her arms and yawning, 'should I try to get a few cups?'

'Yes, better than nothing, I suppose,' Aoife said.

'The demonstration or the tea?' Lizzie asked.

'Both, they're both wonderful ideas when I think about them.'

'Well, you can forget the tea,' Lizzie told her, 'I was up there about an hour ago and they had run out completely. They only had enough for people with badges in the first place.'

'Badges?'

'Yes – proof of entitlement to refreshment – you were expected to purchase one on the way in, it seems.'

'Typical, bloody typical! Trapped all night in a bomb shelter and we have to remember to buy badges!'

'We would like to take this opportunity,' the voice blared out, **'to apologise to all those unable to obtain refreshment, provisions having run out sooner than anticipated as demand was greater than supply. Those requiring blankets, however, may still acquire**

them from the duty desk on platform five. We would appeal to you all to remain calm until the all clear sounds and then to evacuate the premises in an orderly manner. Thank you.'

'The all clear – did you hear him?' Aoife's voice was shrill with excitement, 'maybe we'll get out tonight after all.'

'Can't get people to stand together, that's the problem,' Lizzie was continuing, 'they don't see the need for organisation and solidarity, do they? Even on the street tonight, there was one lot wanting to go up the high street and the other lot wanting to charge down – it was as much as we could do to keep them together. Tell you who was terrific though – absolutely fearless – pigs grabbed her at one stage; nearly broke her arm, but she pulled herself free and got down the line rallying the rest . . . shouting her guts out . . .'

'Who?' Juno asked.

'What's her name . . . do you remember her . . . long blonde hair and that terrific voice – you could hear it a mile off at every demo . . .'

'Oh yes, I remember her perfectly,' Juno said, 'the name would help of course.'

'Oh silly of me, of course, you should remember her – you two were together for a bit weren't you? Hard to keep track with all this changing about. Zoe! Terrific woman . . .'

'Zoe?' Juno stared in astonishment, her whole body alert.

'Yes, that's what I said, Zoe whatshername.'

'Do you mean to tell me she was out there with you tonight?'

'Isn't that what I've been saying? Superb she was – totally committed. Course she was with us in the camps – that's what toughened her. They arrested her twice, you know. She did two prison terms but it didn't break her.'

'My God – no wonder she didn't write from Paris!'

'Paris – who said anything about Paris?'

'Nothing – we're just a bit out of touch, the two of

219

us, lately. But how is she? How does she look? And where is she now?'

'Hard to say. Down here with the rest, I expect, somewhere about. The pigs tried to drag us off to the station but the officer in charge thought it would mess up official statistics so they shoved us in here instead. So I said . . .'

'Are you telling me,' Juno grabbed Lizzie's arm, 'that Zoe is *here* . . . *now*? Down here somewhere, tonight?'

'Calm down. What's the matter with you?' Lizzie asked, shaking free her arm. 'She's bound to be isn't she? How could she get out? You should have seen the street. The whole place sealed off. Thousands of them in full riot gear – not even Zoe would get past that lot . . .'

Juno sprang to her feet, stumbling over the placard Lizzie had propped against the bench and grabbed her jacket from Aoife's lap: 'I've got to find her,' she said, 'I've got to look for her. Will you two wait here until I get back?'

'Steady on – she could be anywhere,' Lizzie objected, 'you don't even know what platform she's on.'

'It doesn't matter. I'll find her. And when I do, I'll come straight back. you two just stay here, okay?' she said and began to push against the wall of shoulders in front of her.

'And where else, may I ask, could we go?' Aoife demanded.

'I don't know. But don't go *anywhere*. Whatever happens, stay here where I can find you.'

'Yes, yes, alright. For Heaven's sake go on if you're going.'

So Juno went. 'That's the last we'll see of her tonight,' Lizzie said to Aoife, as they watched her fight her way through the crowd, jumping over sleeping bodies, elbowing her way past those still upright until she disappeared: swallowed into the inchoate mass of human life at the far end of the platform.

Juno was still searching for Zoe an hour later, or was it more, when the all clear sounded. The forlorn, terrible wail, echoing through the vaulted tunnels, ricocheting from tiled walls and concrete floors; the siren to announce the return of safety, but its merciless rise shrill with the promise of death.

At first the crowd was frozen; too startled to think. Any change was frightening, lulled as they had become into a stagnant calm; resigned to helplessness, awful at the start but easier to accept as the night went on, easier than to resist or to understand. Now, at last, something was demanded of them: they were to be human again; individuals with personal needs and emotions. They were to act, to think. But what? How? For seconds together, as the siren howled over their heads, they stood silent, uneasy. Then, as the whine subsided slowly, a shout rose; a cry of relief, one voice speaking for them all. 'That's it – that's it – the bloody all clear! We can go up now!' And in one great surge they were moving forward, everyone pushing and heaving at once, almost trampling each other in their frenzy to reach the exits. Women grasped their children to their breast, men caught hold of their wives by the shoulder or waist, tugging them forward; now that all danger was past, resuming the role of guide and protector, leading them from darkness to light and home.

Juno had not found Zoe. She had searched everywhere. She had trudged the length and breadth of the Underground, fought her way past the stewards guarding the entrance from one corridor to the next. She had looked into every woman's face expecting to find Zoe's. At last, in desperation, she had cupped both hands to her mouth and shouted her name until people told her to be quiet – did she not know children were trying to sleep? Silent, despondent she went on, dragging her way from one lurid tunnel to the next. She went on until the all clear sounded, without having found her. Now, as she neared the place where she had left Lizzie and Aoife and saw the bench deserted, it seemed that she had lost them too. The crowd seethed about her like a tide in full flood, nearly sweeping her from her feet. She found refuge under an archway; her back pressed to the wall, her legs braced. She would wait it out. She remained there ten minutes or more until the river of people had

221

thinned to a stream: the last stragglers; the old, the homeless, the lonely; people who were in no hurry to relinquish a warm, dry shelter for the night and the company of others.

'Lost someone?' A woman in a British Rail uniform was sweeping beer cans and crisp packets from the floor.

'Yes,' Juno answered and described as best she could Lizzie and Aoife.

'No one like that down here, love. Your best chance is to go up to the main entrance and wait there. If they had placards they might be one of the ones arrested on the street. There was trouble earlier on, I know that.'

Juno ran to the stairs. The lift was working again now, but she preferred to make her own way up – besides, she might meet them along the way.

'You'd better hurry, dear, they'll be locking the gates soon,' the woman called after her. Juno shouted her thanks as she began the climb: a thousand three hundred steps, she had counted once. She did not count now, she just climbed steadily, head down, ignoring the grafitti scrawled on either side that had shortened other journeys: 'Is there a life before death?', 'I wanted to go out and change the world but I couldn't find a baby sitter.' 'Jesus Saves – His own Ass!' She began the steps at a run, taking them two at a time, but before she was half way up, she was panting and gripping the handrail.

At last she reached the top and turned into the main hall. The place was deserted or very nearly. Everyone had gone home, it seemed, but for a few staff members clearing up, sweeping the floors, locking the side gates and some Civil Defence people who were gathering their gear, face masks, stretchers and rolls of bandages.

Juno caught sight of a small, dark, coated figure sitting by the ticket office, head sunk on her breast, hands in her lap, as though sleeping. 'Aoife', she called out and hurried towards her. Aoife turned her head slowly and eyed Juno accusingly: 'What on earth kept you? I thought you were dead!'

'No – just looking for Zoe.' Juno threw her a half-smile, her most disarming, and held out her arms.

Then she saw Aoife's face: the red eyes, the swollen lips: 'What's the matter,' she asked anxiously, 'you look as though you've been crying. Have you?'

'Of course not,' Aoife wiped a hand roughly across her cheek, 'but whatever happened to *you* – don't you know it's almost dawn?'

'Well, I met this woman, you see, who knew . . .' Juno began a lengthy explanation and then quite suddenly she saw the dog! A small black and tan mongrel lying under the bench resting its muzzle on Aoife's shoe.

'Hey – who's This?' the dog's tail swayed slowly from side to side and it lifted sad, world weary eyes to Juno's.

'We rescued her from the pigs. If we hadn't been here she would probably be dead by now.'

'Dead?'

'Yes – or worse, the stupid bastards,' Aoife said furiously. A dark flush rose in her cheeks, 'Do you know that they intend to exterminate them all?'

'Who?'

'At the first red alert – the first bleep on one of their radars and they plan to round up every animal in the country and shoot it! Not content with wiping out the human race they have to murder animals too! And just for practice, to get us used to the idea – they're going round kicking them out of the shelters.'

'What is all this about, Aoife, for God's sake?' Juno was getting irritated. She knew she should not have been gone so long, but she was in no mood at this time of the morning, for one of Aoife's tirades.

'I told them they could keep their precious shelters,' Aoife rushed on, her voice shaking, her eyes unnaturally bright, 'I don't want to survive in their world – who needs it? If they want to ban stray dogs, then they can ban me too. But you don't have a choice of course – oh no – if they decide you're going to be saved then you are going to be saved! Meanwhile they're out on the streets with their army and their police force shooting helpless animals! *This*, is what they call crisis limitation and damage control! My God – the murdering, stupid fascists – I'd like to kill the lot of them!'

'Aoife!' Juno's patience gave abruptly, 'will you calm down for the love of God and tell me what you're talking about?'

'Calm down, you say – calm? Why should I be calm? You wouldn't be so bloody cool if you had heard what I did – if you'd seen the way they treated this dog. If it hadn't been for Zoe, I don't know what I would have done.'

'Zoe?' Juno leaped to attention, staring at Aoife: 'Did you see her? Were you talking to her? When?'

'Yes, yes. She came along five minutes after you left. If you hadn't been gone half the night, you would have seen her too.'

'But didn't you tell her I was looking for her? Where is she now? Why didn't she wait?'

'She didn't get much chance, did she? with those imbeciles dragging her off!'

'Dragging her off? Where? What do you mean?'

'I mean, arrested.'

'Arrested?'

'Yes, you know – lifted – taken off in a paddy wagon – sorry, police van . . . nabbed . . . detained at her majesty's pleasure – whatever you want to call it. The lunatic morons couldn't bear to end the night without arresting someone.'

'Oh Christ,' Juno swore, 'I'll go mad.' She rubbed a fist up and down her forehead, 'Do you think you could tell me, in plain English, what actually happened to her?'

'I'm telling you, aren't I? They arrested her because she punched one of the cops when he tried to get the dog away from me.'

'Oh, no,' Juno groaned, 'I should never have left you alone – I just knew something was going to happen. And where's Lizzie by the way? I'd almost forgotten her.'

'Gone down to the station with Zoe, to look after her. Try and talk them out of pressing charges.'

'Charges? What could they charge her with? Look, none of this is making any sense, do you think you could try it slowly, from the beginning?'

'There's nothing else to tell. It's all very simple really. The dog ran into the station just before the all clear. The cops came in after it, because it seems, it's against their little code book to allow: "any animal, domestic pet or stray, into an underground shelter classified for the purpose of this exercise and any subsequent exercise, as a public fallout shelter. And furthermore" – wait for it – (I know the bloody rubbish by heart, now) – "any member of the public who refuses to co-operate with the forces of law and order, or who knowingly conceals or attempts to conceal any animal in a thus designated area, will be liable to prosecution, imprisonment or fines." They recited their little speech; tried to arrest the dog, I grabbed it, they grabbed it back and Zoe punched one of them in the mouth and they lugged her off to the cop-shop. That's it . . .'

'Oh shite, Aoife – what a bloody mess – what a typical bloody mess! I knew something like this was bound to happen . . . you've been working yourself up to it all night. But did you *have* to start a row, five minutes before going home – and about a dog?'

'Did *I* have to start a row? About a *dog*?' Aoife's voice rose in outrage, 'do you hear yourself? Have you not listened to a word I've said? Would you have preferred me to just stand by and watch while they dragged off this unfortunate animal and God knows how many others to some bloody pound, in bloody Battersea or somewhere? Or perhaps I should just have shot it myself and got it over with . . . is that it?'

'Oh come on . . . you know I . . .'

'Oh yes – keep a clean nose – turn a blind eye – cause no trouble – Heil Hitler – so long as we all get a good night's sleep and you find Zoe!'

'*Aoife!*'

'Don't you know what this is all about? Can't you read between the lines, at all? Did you hear me saying they plan to exterminate them all? Domestic animals, farm livestock, strays, the lot – "To conserve essential supplies and living space." Living, they call it. The fucking Nazis! Do you realise that they expect us to destroy our own pets? One fine morning, when one of

225

their little sirens goes off we'll have to bring our animals down to a police station and watch them shot. Did you know this?'

'No, of course not, Aoife, but come on, – be reasonable . . . it's not the end of the world, is it? It was only an exercise, after all – a silly game. And it's not as if the dog was exactly in danger of radioactive fallout, if it *was* kicked into the street, was it?'

'She . . .' Aoife said furiously, 'he's a she. And it's not a silly game – and it's not only a dog. I wish it were. You're as bad as these mindless little fascists with their maniacal rules and regulations. Bloody Brits! Can't you see where it's leading? If you don't care about animals, can't you at least grasp the principle of the thing? If this is what they've planned for dogs – can't you imagine what they have in store for the rest of us? I mean who's next, for goodness sake – the sick – old people – queers? Who's going to decide who gets into a shelter and who doesn't? On what criterion? How can anyone decide who to save – and who to let die? Could you? . . . would you trust yourself? Could any of us – trust ourselves?' The tears were coursing down Aoife's face now and her thin, tensed body shook, as she stared fiercely into Juno's eyes.

'Alright . . . alright. I'm sorry, love . . . I know it's all crazy.' Juno dropped to her knees and threw her arm about Aoife's shoulders, 'I'm sorry, really . . . I know how you feel – it's awful. It's just that I'm tired. It's all such a bloody mess at this time of the morning, after a night like that – you crying your eyes out, Zoe and Lizzie arrested and now this dog to worry about . . . where are we going to take it?'

'Never mind . . . I'll worry about her, as usual,' Aoife said, with something like her normal tone.

'Okay, okay. But tell me what, exactly, is Zoe being charged with? Is it serious?'

'Hitting a police officer, I suppose . . . interfering in the course of his duties . . .'

'Doesn't sound like Zoe to get violent . . .'

'Well, she was provoked – my fault, probably. I said something like, should we expect them now to start rounding up Jews and homosexuals and refusing them entry into public tube stations? and one little creep said not a bad idea at that, and so Zoe let fly at him . . .'

'Oh, well . . . now I get it . . .' Juno burst out laughing and the dog, rearing up at the sound, lunged across Aoife's lap to swipe a bright pink tongue over Juno's face.

'See – what did I tell you?' Aoife declared, beaming, pleased as a mother whose child behaves well on its first day at school, 'you'd never have let them take her, either? Would you?'

'Hmm . . . that's what you think,' and Juno reached out a hand 'the great mutt,' to scratch it under its drooling jowls, 'I suppose we're stuck with you now, are we?' The dog's tail beat faster, it whimpered and rolled big eyes.

'Leave it to me,' Aoife said, smiling from one to the other, 'I'll find her owner or a new one. Until then . . . well . . .'

A cold wind blew in from the street. They sat side by side on the bench, looking out, too tired to speak. The dawn was visible now: a sullen yellow light seeping into the sky above the roof-tops. An empty beer can blown rattling along the footpath broke the silence. Aoife gazed at the dark, wet, leafless trees, the curtains drawn in the grimy windows of the terraced houses.

'Can you imagine this city – with nothing alive in it but human beings?' she asked, and her voice was hardly more than a murmur, as though she hadn't meant to speak.

'No,' Juno answered slowly, 'but it will never happen – they can't be serious.'

'They're serious alright. You should have seen them tonight – the look in their faces – just lusting to kill something.'

'Will Zoe be alright, do you think? Were they rough with you?'

'Oh not bad. They were keeping to the rule book for the occasion.'

'How did she look, by the way? You haven't said.'

Well? Same as always?'

'Yes . . . no. Different, somehow – thinner maybe. The same beautiful eyes, though. I'd forgotten.'

'We'd better be moving . . .'

'You know, one thing I'm sure of after tonight, Juno – I'd kill myself before I'd murder anything under government orders – human or animal.'

'We should kill some of them, before we start killing ourselves, don't you think?'

'Yes . . . that's what Lizzie said. She was saying we should be prepared. Armed if necessary. And she's right – if we had weapons we would have the power of decision.'

'Oh Lizzie! You know how she talks . . .'

'Yes, I know. But I'm serious. I don't want to survive on any terms. I don't want to fight for life. Are you listening?'

'Yes, I'm listening.'

'I don't want existence at any price. I want to be able to choose . . . to weigh the cost. Do you understand? And I want to have the means to choose . . . and the courage.'

'Yes.' Juno put her arm through Aoife's and pulled her close, 'I do know what you mean. We'll think of something.'

'What?'

'I don't know . . . but there has to be something . . .'

'Yes, something,' Aoife repeated, and after a moment she turned her face towards Juno, smiling. And Juno thought it looked natural again, for the first time that night; the haunted look gone from it, the mouth soft, her deep eyes glowing.

'What will we do now, then?' Juno asked.

'Go down and get Zoe, surely?'

'Yes . . .'

They stood up and walked out together into the bleak early morning light. The street was deserted, nothing moved. Blinds were down, doors locked, not a sound except the rustle of litter blowing in the unswept gutters. They might have been utterly alone in the city. As they turned down the hill, they saw the sun rising above the council tower blocks: a great scarlet globe; awesome, grotesquely incongruous, showing between the dirty sky and the yellowed brick.

'I suppose this is how it'll be the morning after.'

'You think so . . .?'

'The whole city emptied, this livid sky, the awful hush, the dead lying quietly in their houses . . . and then this great beautiful sun coming up, right on cue . . . just as always . . . rising over it all as though nothing had happened.'

'As a matter of fact,' Juno said regretfully, 'I read somewhere that if . . .'

'Don't tell me,' Aoife interrupted, 'I don't want to know. Let's imagine we can count on that much . . .'

They walked slowly on towards the corner where Juno said there was sure to be a bus of some kind or another before long, arm in arm, the mongrel trotting at their heels.

'By the way,' Aoife began, 'I remembered while you were gone . . .'

'What?'

'You were right about the night Kennedy was shot, after all. I *was* at the cinema – not with Craig . . .'

'I knew it!' Juno swung round gloating, her face lighting up. 'Didn't I tell you?' she cried, 'I knew you couldn't have been.'

'Yes, it was stupid of me . . . I got mixed up,' Aoife said, 'it was only afterwards, while you were off looking for Zoe, that I remembered . . . it was the other one . . .'

Juno, however, was not listening. She had rushed ahead, bounding down the street, the dog chasing madly behind her:

'Come on – or we'll be late!'

'It was the other one I was thinking of . . . years later . . .' Aoife called after her.

But Juno had begun to sing, at the top of her voice, the stray dancing about her feet, waving her arms in the air to conduct its fevered yelps: 'We'll meet again . . .'

'Oh not that, surely . . .' Aoife said as the mock soprano floated clear up the empty street, and she called into a last time:

229

'It was Bobby – you see – I was thinking of . . . it was the night Bobby Kennedy was shot that I . . .'

But Juno was swinging out from the bus, stop: 'don't know where . . . don't know when . . .' singing louder than ever, 'but I know . . . we'll meet again . . . some . . . sunny . . . day . . .'